Welcome Home

At the corner of the driveway to the house, there was a sign, hand-painted by Lindsay and decorated with ladybugs and a garden scene, that said, Welcome to Ladybug Farm. It never failed to make them smile. As they made the turn and started down the gravel drive, lined with tall oaks, the anticipation of some grand destination always made the heart beat a little faster. And then, coming out of the shadows and rounding the curve where the full, emerald lawn with its purple hydrangeas and brilliant pink peonies and carefully cultivated beds of hollyhocks and impatiens and showy, old-fashioned dahlias spread out like a ruffled quilt designed to show off all the colors of nature, there was always a catch of breath. In the background, the majestic blue mountains spilled their shadows onto a bright green meadow dotted with sheep. And in the foreground the big old house with its faded brick, painted columns, and tall, high windows seemed to reach out to them, and welcome them home. Bridget and Lindsay shared a glance as they pulled up in front of the wide front steps, each of them understanding what the other was thinking: *I can't believe we live here.*

Love Letters
from Ladybug
Farm

Donna Ball

BERKLEY BOOKS, NEW YORK

A BERKLEY BOOK
Published by the Penguin Group
Penguin Group (USA) Inc.
375 Hudson Street, New York, New York 10014, USA
Penguin Group (Canada), 90 Eglinton Avenue East, Suite 700, Toronto, Ontario M4P 2Y3, Canada
(a division of Pearson Penguin Canada Inc.)
Penguin Books Ltd., 80 Strand, London WC2R 0RL, England
Penguin Group Ireland, 25 St. Stephen's Green, Dublin 2, Ireland (a division of Penguin Books Ltd.)
Penguin Group (Australia), 250 Camberwell Road, Camberwell, Victoria 3124, Australia
(a division of Pearson Australia Group Pty. Ltd.)
Penguin Books India Pvt. Ltd., 11 Community Centre, Panchsheel Park, New Delhi—110 017, India
Penguin Group (NZ), 67 Apollo Drive, Rosedale, North Shore 0632, New Zealand
(a division of Pearson New Zealand Ltd.)
Penguin Books (South Africa) (Pty.) Ltd., 24 Sturdee Avenue, Rosebank, Johannesburg 2196,
South Africa
Penguin Books Ltd., Registered Offices: 80 Strand, London WC2R 0RL, England

This book is an original publication of the Berkley Publishing Group.

Copyright © 2010 by Donna Ball
Cover images: garden patio by Gardenpix/Masterfile; gerbera daisies by Peter Griffith; grassy field
by Jupiterimages/Photos.com/Getty
Cover design by Judith Lagerman
Text design by Tiffany Estreicher

First edition: October 2010

Library of Congress Cataloging-in-Publication Data

Ball, Donna.
Love letters from Ladybug Farm / Donna Ball.— 1st ed.
p.   cm.
ISBN 978-0-425-23717-5 (Berkley trade pbk.) 1. Female friendship—Fiction.
2. Farmhouses—Conservation and restoration—Fiction.   3. Weddings—Fiction.
4. Shenandoah River Valley (Va. and W. Va.)—Fiction.   I. Title.
PS3552.A4545L68 2010
813'.54—dc22   2010022328

PRINTED IN THE UNITED STATES OF AMERICA

10 9 8 7 6 5 4 3 2 1

Author's Note

The recipes in this book are included for entertainment purposes only and have not been tested. In fact, I would be very much surprised if any of them are at all edible!

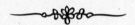

Dearly Beloved

1

A Day to Remember

There was a magical quality to the hours just before twilight at Ladybug Farm. The June air was balmy and scented with roses, and the golden light filtered across the lavender-shadowed lawn like something imagined by the brush strokes of a Renaissance master. Hummingbirds darted back and forth between mounds of ruffled pink peonies. A bluebird family chirped chattily over its evening meal, and a barn swallow dipped and soared in graceful, silhouetted arcs against the pale violet sky.

A wayward breeze stirred a set of wind chimes hung from the low branch of an apple tree and scattered a froth of white chicken feathers across the lawn. An apricot chiffon ribbon, limp and tattered now, tugged away from the porch column it decorated and floated across the grass. A bedraggled-looking border collie, dragging a length of mud-spattered lace that was caught on his back paw, pricked his ears forward as though he might give chase, then decided against it and plopped down onto the grass with an exhausted sigh.

Strands of wilted ivy were twined around the porch railings, each two-foot interval accented by a bouquet of drooping Apricot Delight roses and ribbon-wired bows in Hint of Spring green. Potted ferns, now slightly askew in identical white stands, flanked each of the windows and the door along the deep front porch, and baskets of what once had been freshly arranged Apricot Delight roses, augmented generously with live oak, poplar, and maple leaves, hung by ribbons from the rafters.

The floor was littered with apricot petals and paper cocktail napkins, monogrammed in Apricot Delight and Hint of Spring green. A banner of ivory silk hung drunkenly over the front door, and when Cici pushed open the screen door, it ripped. She did not even glance up.

She was a tall, slender woman with an athletic build, abundantly freckled skin, and sun-sparked blue eyes. She liked to describe herself as being in her midfifties, going on forty, but the truth was that she was closer to the end of that decade than the beginning. Today, despite her elegant suit, carefully coiffed hair, and perfectly applied makeup, she felt every year of her age, and then some.

Nudging aside an overturned champagne glass with the toe of her ivory brocade pump, she made her way across the debris-strewn porch to a rocking chair, and sank down heavily. Her honey-colored hair was beginning to come loose from its upsweep, and she had lost an earring. Her lipstick was long since gone. She undid the pearl button on the jacket of her ivory satin pantsuit, kicked off her shoes, and leaned her head back, pressing a pack of frozen peas to the side of her face.

The screen door gave another tentative squeak, the silk banner ripped further, and Lindsay came out, approaching Cici cautiously. "Did the aspirin help?" she asked.

Cici did not open her eyes. "A little."

Lindsay was four inches shorter and five years younger than Cici, and on a good day could easily pass for forty if she bleached the faint brownish splotch on her right hand. But today was not a good day. She was still wearing her apricot lace sheath with its flirty sweetheart neckline, but she was barefoot and bare-legged. She had complained all week that the dress was too young for her and that it clashed with her auburn hair, but she was too tired now to change into something else. As for the stockings—Nearly Nude Shimmer & Silk and specifically mandated by the bride—they had been the first to go.

She picked her way through the litter of spilled birdseed, scraps of apricot netting and spring green ribbons, torn napkins and white-and-silver wrapping paper, then removed an empty wine bottle from the chair next to Cici's and sat down. "Well," she said after a moment, "the good news is that everyone had a swell time."

Cici opened her one good eye and stared at her.

"I mean," Lindsay tried to explain, "not that everyone wasn't worried about you, but you saved the cake, and after the first little excitement, everyone forgot about it and moved on, and, if you think about it, at least you gave everyone a good story to tell. And no one was mad. Not really."

Cici looked at her for another moment, then closed her eyes again. Her tone was flat. "I'm so glad."

The screen door opened again, and the silk banner pulled

away from the wall and sagged down on Bridget as she came through the door. She wrestled with it for a moment, her petite stature and frothy chiffon dress making her look like an Easter egg doing battle with a marshmallow. Finally she simply jerked the fabric away from the remaining staples that held it to the wall and let it cascade to the floor like a fallen flag. She kicked it aside unceremoniously.

Bridget was the oldest of the three, with a sweet round face, a bouncy platinum bob, and an earnest innocence that made her look younger than either of her two friends. She was wearing Hint of Spring green in a delicate *peau de soie* with an empire waist and matching two-inch heels. The Nearly Nude Shimmer & Silk stockings actually did make her legs look longer, as promised by the manufacturer.

"Feeling any better?" she ventured hopefully to Cici.

Bridget winced as Cici removed the package of peas from her face to reveal the ugly red and purple bruise that had half closed her left eye and was beginning to discolor her cheek.

"Oh, yes," Cici said without expression. "I'm just fine. Thank you for asking."

Bridget hurried over to her. "It was an accident, you know. She's really sorry."

Cici returned the peas to her eye. "What did I say about goats?" she demanded simply.

Bridget wisely declined to answer that. "I found your earring," she said instead and offered up a mud-encrusted seed-pearl drop pendant.

Cici just stared at her for a moment, clearly debating whether maintaining her pique was worth the effort. Then a corner of her lips turned down ruefully, and she held out her hand. "Thanks."

Bridget smiled, dropped the earring into her hand, and took a chair, and the three of them sat in exhausted silence for a while, watching the birds and the changing patterns of muted light. In comparison to the chaos that had reigned only hours before, the muffled sounds of activity from the house sounded like a benediction.

"You know," Bridget observed after a time, "all things considered, it really was a lot of fun."

Cici tried to lift her head to look at her, winced in pain, and settled back again. "You did not just say that to me."

"Well, I mean, except for the storm."

"Tornado," corrected Lindsay.

"That hasn't been confirmed yet," Bridget objected.

"And the dog," Cici said without opening her eyes.

"And the groom's mother."

"And the groom."

"And the explosion."

"And the goat."

"Like I said," Bridget said uncomfortably. "All things considered."

No one spoke for a measure of time. No one had the energy.

"You know what the problem was, don't you?" Bridget said after a moment.

"Personally," replied Lindsay, a rather tired smile twitching at her lips, "I blame Michelle Obama."

Bridget smothered a giggle, and even Cici, without opening her eyes, managed a lopsided smile.

"Okay," Cici said, "Tell me what the problem was."

"Sex."

Cici opened her eyes and lifted her head to look at her two best friends. The three women thought about that for a while. Then Cici gave a slow, reflective nod of her head. "Do you know, Bridget," she said, "this time I think you've got it exactly right."

Lindsay agreed regretfully, "Sad but true."

"But it was a beautiful ceremony," Bridget said.

Cici glanced at one of the half-empty champagne glasses on the small table beside her chair. She had no idea to whom it belonged. She picked it up dubiously, sniffed the contents, gave the rim a cursory examination for lip marks, and drank it down.

"Yeah," she said, and smiled just a little. "It was."

To Love and to Cherish

2

What a Difference a Year Makes

Three Weeks Previously

Excerpt from Virginians at Home *magazine*

Cecile Burke, Bridget Tyndale, and Lindsay Wright are like the Three Musketeers—if the Three Musketeers wielded hammers and saws instead of swords, if they fought dry rot instead of highwaymen, and if they were ... well, girls.

The "girls" in question, just enough past middle age to consider it a compliment, each gave a considering tilt of her head, purse of her lips, or waggle of her eyebrows.

They were gathered around the oiled hickory table in the kitchen, a vase of fresh-picked daffodils between them. The raised fireplace at their backs smelled of last night's fire, and the breeze that came through the open back door tasted of snow not long melted, clean and clear, with the cool base notes of the winter that had barely passed. The ancient bricks that paved the floor beneath their feet and the walls around them gleamed in the sun that flooded through the freshly washed windows. The last of the asparagus and spring onions were on the cutting board, a chicken, aromatic with sage, rosemary, and garlic, was roasting in the oven, and a package of last year's peaches was thawing in the sink, waiting to be made into a pie. A ladybug landed on the magazine page, and Cici absently flicked it off as she read aloud.

The three ladies are part of a growing trend of young retirees who, having completed successful careers, seek a different kind of a success in the second half of their lives. Burke, an attractive blonde...

Cici lifted an eyebrow. "Attractive," she repeated, preening a little.

The other two ladies gave her an impatient wave. "Go on."

She started the sentence over.

Burke, an attractive blonde who knows her way around a power saw, owned her own real estate company in Baltimore. Tyndale spent most of her life as a homemaker, and Wright is a retired school teacher. They were best friends and neighbors in the same suburban cul-de-sac for over twenty years.

When the three of them came across an abandoned old mansion during a vacation trip through the Shenandoah Valley, it was love at first sight. Within the year, they sold their Maryland homes, combined their resources, and took on the challenge of their lives.

"Our dreams were a lot bigger than our abilities," confesses Burke, who likes to be called "Cici" by her friends. "We knew that none of us could have taken on a project this big alone. But together, we can do anything."

Bridget said, "Well, just about anything, anyway. I guess you didn't mention the chicken coop."

"What about it?" Cici challenged.

"It was a disaster!"

"We got it built, didn't we?"

"Will you go on?" Lindsay said. "Read."

Cici returned her attention to the magazine.

Blackwell Farms Estate—now called Ladybug Farm—was rich in history and even richer in challenges. The sprawling, hundred-year-old mansion came complete with an orchard, vineyard, barns, and livestock. Ida Mae Simpson, who has been keeping house at Blackwell Farms since the 1950s, recalls the heyday of the Blackwell Farms winery, and tells stories of the famous Blackwell Farms cheeses having been aged in the same caves that the Confederate army used to store munitions during the Civil War.

Cici smiled. "That was nice of them to mention Ida Mae. She'll get a kick out of it."

"If she doesn't sue the magazine for misquoting her," Bridget said.

"She has been crankier than usual lately . . ."

"Read?" prompted Lindsay.

But when the ladies took possession of the estate two years ago, the roofs were collapsing, the vineyard was so overgrown as to be practically unrecognizable, and the house was completely overrun by ladybugs—thus the name.

"The first few months were a little daunting," admits Bridget. "Well, okay, the whole first year. I don't think any of us really knew what we were getting ourselves into."

With determination and elbow grease, the ladies restored the beauty of the heart pine floors, the mahogany banisters, and the stained glass window overlooking the staircase landing. They uncovered two hand-painted murals flanking the fireplace in the first-floor sitting room, and reclaimed the six large, sun-flooded bedrooms on the second floor.

They trimmed berry bushes, pruned fruit trees, and brought back the rose gardens and fountains. They built chicken houses and saw a flock of sheep through a bitter winter. Room by room, they painstakingly restored the Blackwell mansion to the glory of a forgotten age.

"Financially, it's been a fiasco," Cici says frankly. "Old houses are expensive, and that's the bottom line. We never know where the money for the next project is coming from. But emotionally . . . this has been the time of my life. I wouldn't trade it for the world."

The next project for this ambitious crew is to restore the vineyard, with an eye toward eventually reopening the Blackwell Farm winery.

"We don't have the faintest idea what we're doing," says Lindsay with a laugh, "but that never stopped us before. The *great thing about wine is that it takes a long time to make, and we can learn on the job."*

Meanwhile, the vivacious redhead . . .

Lindsay grinned. "That's the part I was waiting for." Cici obligingly read it again.

Meanwhile the vivacious redhead is fulfilling her lifelong dream by opening an art studio in the old dairy barn of Ladybug Farm.

"It's something I've wanted to do all my life," Lindsay says. "It's why I became a teacher, really. I only have a handful of students right now, but I'm thrilled to be teaching them. And of course, my prize student is Noah."

Noah Clete, age sixteen, came to work at Ladybug Farm soon after the ladies purchased it, and almost immediately established himself as one of the family. Lindsay took his education in hand, nurturing his talent for art, and today Noah is an honor student at John Adams Academy in Staunton, as well as the holder of the prestigious "Young Artist of the Year" award from the Virginia Council for the Arts.

"Oh, my God!" exclaimed Cici excitedly. She flipped the magazine around to show them. "They included one of Noah's paintings! He'll die! Where is he, anyway?"

"I sent him to town to get more copies," Lindsay said, beaming as she snatched the magazine away from Cici to study it. "Oh, look, it's the oil painting he did of the crow in the apple tree. Hey, Bridget, look at you!"

Bridget peered over her shoulder to admire the photograph of her putting the finishing touches on a red velvet cake in the kitchen. "They printed my recipe," she noted happily. "The writer said she wasn't sure if there'd be room."

"Wait, there's a whole section on you." Lindsay continued to read out loud.

Bridget Tyndale is the driving force behind Ladybug Farm's newest enterprise, Ladybug Farm Fine Foods and Catering. Her exquisite homemade wine jams and delightful gift baskets can be purchased at many local shops and through the Ladybug Farm website.

Bridget wrinkled her nose. "One," she repeated. "One local shop. Which sold exactly a dozen jars of pinot noir jam."

"But the gift basket was a huge success at the church bazaar," Lindsay pointed out.

"Come on girls," Cici said, "the website has only been up a couple of months. What do you expect?"

Bridget sighed and Lindsay read on.

With the help of Cici's daughter, Lori Gregory, who graduates next year from the University of Virginia, Charlottesville, Bridget also runs a blog on which she shares her favorite recipes and observations about life on Ladybug Farm. You can enjoy this authentic taste of Virginia for yourself at www.ladybugfarmcharms.blogspot.com.

Bridget groaned. "I *hate* blogging."

"We know, we know," Lindsay and Cici replied in unison.

"How'd they get the address anyway? No one ever reads it."

"Your own personal PR agent, how else?" Cici gave a shake of her head that was half amazement, half amusement. "It's nice to know all those marketing courses Lori's been taking have paid off. She probably e-mailed the editor just to make sure no self-promotional stone was left unturned."

Lindsay lifted a hand for attention. "You close the article, Bridge. Listen."

After almost three years of hard work and sacrifice, the house is still not fully restored, and the farm is a work in progress. Every day is an adventure for the residents of Ladybug Farm, and not every adventure has a happy ending. If they had it all to do over again, would they have made the same choice? Do they have any regrets?

"When we bought this house," Bridget says, "we all had our ideas of how it was going to turn out, and big plans for what we wanted to do. Of course nothing turned out like we thought it would." And she gives a slow, shy smile that seems, in a way, to exemplify the charm of Ladybug Farm. "It turned out better."

Lindsay looked up, smiling, and the three women shared a moment of silent appreciation for the memories they had made together. But it was only a moment. The screen door squeaked and banged, and Noah exclaimed, "Hey, did y'all see this? They put one of my pictures in the magazine!"

He came in with a magazine upheld, page turned to the pictorial display, and Lindsay, grinning, held up her own copy to match.

"You're famous," Cici said, pulling one of the six copies of *Virginians at Home* out of his hand.

Noah hooked an ankle around the leg of a chair to pull it out from the table and plopped down, his head buried in his own copy. "Pretty cool," he admitted. "Of course, they didn't say much about me."

"A picture's worth a thousand words."

"I guess. I wonder how come they only used one."

Cici rolled up her magazine and rapped him lightly on the shoulder. "Because the article wasn't about you. It was about us."

"You're going to have lots of articles written about you," Bridget assured him soberly. "But we're old. This could be our last chance."

"Well," he agreed thoughtfully, "there is that." And then he laughed when all three of the ladies rolled up their magazines and pummeled him indignantly.

Noah Clete bore little resemblance to the sullen, gangly, greasy-haired teenager they had taken in a little over two years ago. He had lost his awkward angles and gained confidence. Two part-time jobs—one at Ladybug Farm and another at Family Hardware in town—had given him long muscles and sun-golden skin. His dark hair had remained neatly trimmed since a girl—now long forgotten—had mentioned she liked it that way, and was now worn short and spiked as much as the school dress code would allow. His voice had deepened, and he shaved regularly to keep the faint bristle of beard at bay.

When he had first shown up at Ladybug Farm, secretly sleeping in a shack in the woods and stealing from their garden to live, he had attended public school only sporadically but treasured a sketch pad on which he chronicled scenes from everyday life. Lindsay bribed him with art supplies and homeschooling, and discovered he was an excellent student, given the right motivation.

Last year he had won Young Artist of the Year in a competition of over three thousand students sponsored by the Virginia Council for the Arts. His charcoal drawing of a soldier at a train station was entitled "Homecoming." The award had included his choice of a cash award or a one-year scholarship to the college preparatory school of his choice. The women had brought all their persuasive powers to bear, but in the end all three were surprised by how easy it was to convince the once-mercenary young man of the advantages of spending his windfall on higher education.

Within weeks of applying, he had been accepted to the John Adams Academy for the Arts and Sciences, a privately funded college prep in Staunton, Virginia. The open-campus nature of the school, which was an hour away, made it possible for him to attend classes only three days a week and still keep up with his responsibilities on the farm, his part-time job, and his art. It was Lindsay's proudest accomplishment that, even though the majority of his education had been obtained at home, through her own rather inventive and sometimes bizarre curriculum, he was an honor student.

Before he had come to Ladybug Farm, it hadn't occurred to Noah that a boy with his background should even want to go to college. A year ago he had to be wrestled into a shirt and tie for church services once a week. Now he complained that the school uniform—khakis, blue shirt, and maroon tie—made him look like a used car salesman, but he got up early every school day morning to iron his shirt himself, and he had proudly paid for the uniforms out of his own earnings. He had spent most of his life trying to avoid school out of boredom, and downplayed his own intelligence in a misguided effort to escape notice. Winning the Young Artist award had changed what he believed was possible. But having the opportunity to attend a school like John Adams had changed everything else.

The phone rang. Lindsay looked exasperated as Bridget got up to answer it. "People have been calling all day," she said. "Does everyone in the county subscribe to that magazine?"

Noah grinned. "Hey, we're celebrities. Deal with it."

Bridget said into the telephone, "Wait, Lori. I'm going to put you on speaker."

She pushed a button on the wall phone and Lori's voice burst from the speaker in an excited squeal. "O! M! G! You guys are rock stars! Have you checked the traffic on the blog?"

Bridget said, "Well, I've been kind of busy. I harvested two rows of carrots and dug asparagus and gathered three dozen eggs and that crazy rooster tried to kill me—"

"Sixty-one comments!" exclaimed Lori.

Bridget's eyes widened. "Sixty-one?"

"Since this morning! I told you this would be a gold mine! I told you!"

Bridget said, "I'll be right back! This I've got to see. Talk to your mom." She rushed from the kitchen in search of her laptop.

Cici said, "How was the economics exam?"

"Aced it. Mom, listen. What we need to do now is get you on one of the local news segments—"

Cici choked on a laugh. "Doing *what*?"

"And Aunt Lindsay, if you're serious about getting your art school off the ground this is going to give you the boost you need."

"What I need," Lindsay pointed out, "is students."

"It's called synergistic marketing," Lori went on enthusiastically. "And this is just the beginning. Is that boy there?"

Noah said, "Hey, kid."

"Noah, listen. What I need you to do is . . . oh, wait. I have a text."

Cici demanded, "You're not texting and driving?"

"Walking, mom. I'm walking to class and talking on the phone and I really have to call you back. This could be important."

"Are you coming home this weekend?"

"I'll call you back."

"Don't text and drive!"

"I love you guys. Call you back."

"Good luck getting through," Lindsay said. "The phone has been—"

But she was talking to dead air.

Noah called toward the phone, "Glad I could help!" and turned back to the magazine.

Cici shrugged. "Ah well, the price of fame. She's probably fielding calls from Hollywood."

"Hey, there's a whole other page of photographs," Noah observed. "Nice one of the fountain and the patio."

Lindsay and Cici shared a smile as they returned to their

own copies of the magazine. The restoration of the fountain and the patio had been Noah and Lori's Mother's Day gift to them the year that Noah had decided to join the family permanently.

"Look at that vineyard," Lindsay observed. "It's as pretty as anything you could see in France."

"Prettier," Cici said. "They don't have mountains in France."

"Well, I think they have the Pyrenees."

"Not in wine country."

"Hey look," Noah pointed out, trying, and not entirely succeeding, to sound casual about it. "My grandma's paintings."

Cici read the caption out loud. "'The murals flanking the fireplace depict spring and winter views from the front porch of Ladybug Farm. They were painted in the 1960s by regional artist Emily Hodge, and uncovered during the restoration project.'"

"They could have mentioned that she was related to me." Noah frowned a little.

"There wasn't room to write everything, Noah. They had to save some room for advertising."

Until the murals were uncovered, and Ida Mae had related their history, Noah had known nothing of his family, or even that he had one. Discovering that his grandmother had been an artist, too—and that she had left her mark on the house where he now lived—had planted the first seeds of pride and purpose within him.

Bridget returned to the kitchen with her laptop open, tapping the keyboard with one hand. "Eighty-four!" She was practically chortling as she settled down at the table with her computer. "Eighty-four comments since this morning! That's more than I've gotten in the past month!"

Noah shrugged and turned another page. "Not much of an article, for all the time they spent out here."

"Well, they took a lot of pictures," Lindsay said, "and most of the exposition is in captions. That's the way they do it in magazines like this."

"'The eight-foot-wide chandelier,'" Cici read by way of example, indicating a color photograph of the chandelier that hung over the grand staircase, "'was imported from Belgium in the 1920s. It lowers on a chain and pulley system for cleaning.'"

"They should have used the soldier drawing," Noah said.

Lindsay glanced up. "What?"

"Instead of the oil painting. They should have used the picture that won the prize."

"It's not all about you, Noah. Look!" Grinning, Lindsay flipped the magazine around, proudly pointing to one of the pictures. "They used my room!"

"'Although the public areas of the house are restored to period, the sleeping quarters are decorated in individual styles. Artist Wright used a faux-plaster technique to create this mystical nature wall treatment in her bedroom.'"

Cici glanced up. "Say, Bridget. You should have Lindsay be a guest on your blog and write about how she did the plaster stencils."

Bridget, typing away, laughed out loud in delight. "Eighty-six! Eighty-six comments! And listen to this—ten of them want to know where they can buy the jam."

"Do we have ten jars left?" Cici inquired innocently, and

Bridget made a face at her. Every shelf in the pantry was lined with jam.

"Announcing . . ." Bridget read out loud as she typed. "Next week's special guest blogger, artist Lindsay Wright, on how to create the special painting technique featured in this month's issue of *Virginians At Home* magazine." She clicked Post and grinned at Lindsay. "Lori's going to love that."

"Synergistic marketing," observed Cici absently, still reading.

"It would've been even more *synergistic*," Noah added, placing slight, teasing emphasis on the word, "if you'd added a link to the magazine article." He tossed his copy of the magazine on the table and stood. "Here's the mail." He pulled a couple of envelopes from his jeans pocket. "I stopped by the PO when I was in town. Save the driver a trip out here."

"That was nice of you, Noah," Cici said, reaching for the envelopes. "Bills," she added as she glanced through them.

Noah said, "I've got to finish patching that fence before dark. I'll be gone all day tomorrow. Jonesie's got a big shipment coming in."

Cici said, "Do you want to borrow a car? We don't like you on that motorcycle at night."

"I'll be back before dark," he assured her. "Besides, I'm low on gas money."

Noah still owned and lovingly maintained the motorcycle he had purchased with the money he had earned his first summer at Ladybug Farm. None of the women was entirely comfortable with his using it to commute two hours round-trip to school, however, and even Noah had come to see the advantages of having alternate transportation in case of rain.

One of the three SUVs—four, when Lori was at home—was almost always available for his use.

Bridget looked in dismay at her post. "Rats," she said. "He's right about the link."

"Maybe Lori can fix it," Cici offered.

Lindsay frowned at Noah. "You're putting in an awful lot of hours at the store. Your scholarship depends on maintaining your grade point average, and you can't do that if you start working on the days you're supposed to be studying."

"It's cool," Noah assured her, although Lindsay thought she noticed a brief shifting of his gaze. "All I've got Friday is an art history essay and it's done. Do you want to read it?"

"I certainly do."

"I'll print it out tonight."

Cici said, still reading, "My car is gassed up if you change your mind."

"That's okay, I'm good."

Ida Mae was coming up the back steps as he reached the door, and he propped the door open for her with his hip. "I'll be leaving early in the morning," he added casually as the older woman edged her way past him, carrying a basket filled with cut dandelion greens. "And it might be after supper before I get back. So don't look for me."

He glanced into the basket Ida Mae was carrying and made a face. "We having greens for supper? Maybe you better not count on me tonight, either."

All three women braced themselves for the tirade they knew Ida Mae was about to unleash on him, and even Noah seemed surprised when she merely plopped the basket down on the soapstone counter next to the sink and started washing the greens, ignoring him.

Lindsay cast a quick startled look at Ida Mae's back. "Don't be a smart-mouth. And don't forget I want to read that essay before I go to bed."

"Yes'm." The screen door slammed and Noah bounded down the steps.

Ida Mae shouted after him, "Don't slam the—"

Noah reappeared before she could finish, an angelic smile on his face. "Farley's coming," he announced, and this time closed the door with barely a squeak.

"Hope he's got my pressure cooker fixed," Ida Mae grumbled as the sound of the sputtering pickup truck grew closer. "It's been two weeks he's been messin' with it."

"The safest two weeks I've ever spent in this house," Cici said, without looking up from the magazine. "That thing is scary."

"Even scarier now that Farley has worked on it," Lindsay added.

"Wimps." Bridget got up from the table. "Cooking is not for the faint of heart." She went to the kitchen drawer where they kept the household cash and withdrew a ten-dollar bill. "Ida Mae, let's pack up the rest of the breakfast muffins for Farley, okay?"

"You spoil that man." Ida Mae began piling the dandelion greens into the sink.

"Well, it seems the least we can do, after all he does for us."

Farley—none of them knew whether that was his first name or his last—was their closest neighbor, at three miles north, and their all-around handyman. Whether it was repairing a broken pipe, replacing a single roof tile, or plowing their driveway after a snowfall, he always charged ten dollars: no more, no less.

Ida Mae turned on the taps to rinse the greens and took the plate of leftover muffins from the cabinet. "Somebody needs to go get me a basket."

Lindsay got up and went to the pantry.

Cici said, "Ida Mae, the magazine article is out, did you see it?"

Ida Mae was a tall, rangy woman of indeterminate age with iron gray hair and a brusque manner that left most people completely intimidated. Today she wore cotton jeans and steel-toed work boots underneath a belted red flannel dress and a pilled blue sweater, all topped with a cotton apron printed with bright red roosters. Her weathered face showed absolutely no signs of interest as she glanced over her shoulder at Bridget. "You gonna help me pack up these muffins or not?"

Rebel, their antisocial border collie, charged forth with a murderous round of barking as Farley's truck pulled around the drive, and Bridget cast an anxious glance toward the back door before she hurried to take the basket that Lindsay had retrieved from the pantry. Rebel had been raised by Farley and had, in fact, been his gift to them when they discovered they had inherited a flock of sheep. But no one trusted the dog not to bite the hand that had fed him for the first three years of his life—particularly since he regularly tried to bite theirs.

Cici got up and came to help, the magazine in her hand. "Look, they even said something about you."

"I'll bet you never thought you'd see yourself in a magazine," Lindsay encouraged.

And Bridget added, tossing muffins into the basket, "It's a really nice article, Ida Mae."

Ida Mae turned off the faucet and shook out the greens, spreading them out to dry on paper towels.

"You worked so hard helping us get the house ready for the photographers," Cici said, urging the magazine on her. "Don't you even want to look?"

Ida Mae reached deliberately for a dish towel and took her time drying her hands. She looked at Bridget, sourly, then turned the look on Cici and Lindsay. She took the magazine.

The three women watched her closely as she slowly turned the pages, anticipating comments about "Dang fool Yankee trash tramping all over m'flower beds" and "fuss and bother just so a bunch o' rich biddies can look at how we live" and "working like yard hands for three damn weeks just for this?" Not to mention the inevitable derision over whatever mistakes had surely been made in the recipe, or the quotes. They waited, hardly aware of holding their breaths, until she flipped the magazine closed and returned it to Cici.

"Right nice," was all she said, and they stared at her as she placed the last of the muffins in the basket and turned back to the sink. "Thought these greens'd make a good salad with some nuts and cheese. How's that chicken coming?"

"Oh, um . . ." It was at that moment that Farley knocked politely on the screen door, and Bridget glanced anxiously toward the oven as she waved at him. "Hi, Farley."

"Afternoon, ladies."

Farley was a big man in faded overalls and a camo cap,

with a ginger-colored beard and a perpetual wad of chewing tobacco forming a small lump in one cheek. He carried a highly polished steel pressure cooker under one arm, and a soda can in the other hand. He spat a stream of brown juice into the can before adding, "Got your cooker."

Cici grabbed an oven mitt and opened the oven to check on the chicken. Bridget opened the screen door and stepped aside as Farley came in, leaving his soda can on the porch rail. He set the pressure cooker on the counter and Bridget handed him a ten-dollar bill. "Thank you so much for fixing this," she said. "Canning season is coming up and I don't know what we'd do without it."

Farley swept off his cap, mindful of being indoors, and tucked it into his back pocket as he somberly took out his wallet and placed the ten-dollar bill inside. "Weren't no problem," he replied. He added, without looking up, "Hear you ladies got your pictures in the paper."

Cici closed the oven door and smiled at him. "It was a magazine," she corrected. "Would you like to see it?"

"No thank you, ma'am," he replied, and returned his wallet securely to his back pocket. "Don't have much use for that kind of foolishness."

Lindsay raised an amused eyebrow but said nothing.

Ida Mae retrieved her pressure cooker and Bridget took the basket of muffins from the counter. "These are for you, Farley," she said. "They're fresh made this morning. Wild strawberry."

He looked surprised as he accepted the muffins, even though Bridget almost always had some kind of baked goods for him whenever he came by. "Why," he said, "that's right good of you, Miss Bridget."

Bridget smiled. "I hope you enjoy them." She smiled as she added, "See you in church Sunday?"

It was almost a running joke, since everyone knew the only time Farley went to church was on Easter and Christmas. But he looked back at her somberly and replied, "No, ma'am, I don't reckon you will. But I thank you for the thought just the same."

He removed his cap from his pocket, nodded at Cici and Lindsay, and left with his basket of muffins, settling the cap on his head as he reached the back steps.

"Strange bird," murmured Cici as she heard the truck engine start.

"Oh, he's a good soul," replied Bridget fondly, smiling after him. "Just lonely, I think."

"I hope he knows how to fix a pressure cooker, is all," Ida Mae said, and there was a certain amount of menace to her tone as she returned from placing the appliance on its shelf in the pantry.

"For ten dollars," Lindsay cautioned, "I wouldn't expect too much."

But the look Ida Mae gave her suggested consequences too dire for words should her prediction happen to be correct.

Cici started gathering up the magazines. "Well," she said. "It's been quite a day. But I guess it's back to scattering chicken feed and shoveling sheep manure."

"Damn," said Lindsay, "and I just had my nails done."

Bridget sighed. "Well, it was fun while it lasted."

But just then the phone rang, and the fun, such as it was, had just begun.

3

Opportunity Knocks

Bridget grinned as she reached for the telephone. "It's probably the *Today* show."

Cici held out her hand for the telephone with an air of resignation. "It's Lori," she said. "Doesn't that child ever attend classes?"

But the voice on the other end of the telephone was not Lori's.

"Paul!" she exclaimed. And to the others, "It's Paul! Wait, you're on speaker."

She pushed the button and Paul's voice, over a hundred miles away, declared, "Well? Now was it worth the trouble?"

Paul and his partner Derrick had been neighbors of the ladies when they all lived on Huntington Lane in Maryland, and had thrown themselves wholeheartedly into support of the Ladybug Farm project. It was Paul, the author of a popular syndicated style and fashion column, who had suggested an article on Ladybug Farm to his friend, an editor at *Virginians at Home*. The idea had been met with initial resistance from the members of the household who actually knew what it would take to prepare the old house for a photo session. But they had eventually been worn down, if not entirely overruled, by Lori. Eight months later, the fruits of their labors had seen print, but as to whether or not the herculean feat of preparing for the article was worth the effort . . .

"The verdict is still out," Cici told Paul.

"But it was a great article," Lindsay added.

Bridget closed the oven door. "Eighty-seven comments on the blog!" she announced happily. "No, wait—ninety!"

"Ninety-one," Paul said. "I just sent a comment."

Ida Mae harrumphed at the sink, wrapped the dandelion greens in paper towels, and stalked to the pantry.

"The phone has been ringing all day," Lindsay told him. "Everyone in town thinks we're celebrities."

"That's because for the past three months you've been telling everyone we know the exact day the magazine was going to hit the stands," Bridget said.

"Like you haven't?"

"The photos were great," Paul said. "You all looked beautiful."

"Lori is convinced this is the beginning of a whole new enterprise," Cici said, laughing a little.

"Well, you never know."

"I just got your comment," Bridget exclaimed. She paused to read it. "What do you mean, do we ever do special events?"

"Well . . ." The careful excitement in Paul's voice caused an escalation of alertness in his listeners. "As a matter of fact, something very interesting has come up. Do you remember my editor's sister's mother-in-law's best friend, the one who has the place in the Hamptons that Derrick and I visited last summer?"

"No," said Cici, "but if this is an invitation to join you this summer, we accept."

"It's better," Paul said.

Lindsay drew close to the phone. "You've got my attention."

"As it turns out," Paul went on, "she has a niece who's getting married in June and there's been some kind of disaster with the venue for the reception—flooding or mice or crabgrass or something."

"Crabgrass?" Bridget interrupted, eyebrows lifted.

"It was supposed to be a garden ceremony," Paul explained, "and of course trying to find a replacement at this late date is out of the question, and the whole family is half hysterical about it, naturally."

"Naturally," Cici murmured.

"So, Julie, my editor, happened to be in my office this morning when my copy of the magazine came in, and we were admiring the pictures of the house and garden, and Julie happened to mention what a perfect place for a wedding that would be, and I remember that you had actually talked about opening the place up for weddings at one time . . ."

"For a minute!" Cici corrected, alarmed. "We talked about it for a minute!"

"That was before we had a vineyard to take care of," Lindsay added quickly.

"And wine jams to make," Bridget said.

"And *long* before we knew how much trouble it was just

to get this place ready for a magazine reporter, much less a stranger's wedding."

Paul was silent for a moment. "What a shame." There was a note of exaggerated regret in his voice that immediately made the women suspicious. "But if you're not interested, you're not interested."

"We're not," Cici said firmly.

"Besides," Lindsay added, "we're way out here in the middle of Virginia. Why would anyone with a place in the Hamptons want to have her wedding here?"

"Well, for one thing, they live in Fairfax, not the Hamptons. And apparently, it's *exactly* what the bride's been looking for—the fountains, the gardens, the staircase . . ."

"You told her about it?" Lindsay's expression was both flattered and dismayed.

"She saw the magazine," Paul assured her.

Bridget said, "That staircase *would* make a spectacular entrance for a bride, wouldn't it?"

Cici smiled. "The minute we first saw the place, I pictured Lori walking down it in a white dress."

"And the bay window in the living room would be the perfect place for a bridal arch," Lindsay said. "We could open the pocket doors and seat a hundred people."

"Are we still talking about Lori's wedding?" Cici ventured uncertainly.

Bridget said curiously to the telephone, "How many guests are we talking about, anyway? And how would they get here?"

"That," replied Paul airily, "is not my problem. I'm just the messenger. All I know is that the bride was quite impressed with the magazine photographs and my description of the place—not to mention the cachet of having her wedding in an historic house that's been featured in a magazine. And Bridget, I wouldn't be a bit surprised if there wasn't some catering in it for you—a great opportunity to get your name out there."

A light came into Bridget's eyes. "That's right," she said. "They would have to have it catered locally."

"And you are the only local caterer," Lindsay pointed out. "The only one with a blog, anyway."

"I could do all the gift baskets," Bridget volunteered.

"Whoa, whoa, whoa." Cici held up a firm and staying hand. "You're talking about a society wedding here. Do you have any idea what's involved?"

"Not so society," Paul pointed out quickly. "From what I hear they are really trying to keep it simple. A garden wedding, family members and close friends. All they want is a nice spot for their wedding photographs."

"Well, I'm sure they'll have no problem finding a simple garden in someone's backyard in Fairfax," Cici said.

"With a vineyard and a mountain view in the background?" Paul interjected. "And a grand staircase and an antique rose garden with fountains and reflecting pools?"

"Good heavens," Lindsay said, looking pleased. "You make us sound like the Taj Mahal."

"Which we're not," Cici pointed out.

"Well, it's up to you," Paul said. "I just hate to think of that poor girl's heart being broken again. She was so excited when I spoke to her on the phone."

"This really *is* the perfect spot for a wedding," Bridget said, a little wistfully.

Paul asked, "Did I mention the budget?"

Cici was immediately alert. "What budget?"

"Well, the father of the bride was hoping not to exceed twenty thousand for the reception."

"Dollars?" exclaimed Lindsay. "For one *day?*"

"They call that simple?" Bridget gasped.

Cici simply stared at the telephone speaker.

"Washington dollars," Paul pointed out. "And that's about average. If you can quote anything under that, they'll consider it a steal."

Bridget looked at Cici. So did Lindsay. Cici cleared her throat. "Well, I guess it wouldn't hurt to meet with them. When can they drive out?"

"How about tomorrow?" Paul suggested quickly.

"Tomorrow!" Bridget jumped back to avoid the swinging door to the pantry as Ida Mae reentered the kitchen. "Couldn't you give us a little notice?"

Ida Mae scowled at the telephone. "We having company?"

"Hi, Ida Mae," Paul greeted her cheerfully. "And don't worry, you won't even know we're there."

Lindsay said, "This is not exactly a cottage, you know. This place takes a little while to get ready for inspection. Couldn't we do it next week?"

"We're on a short deadline here," Paul pointed out. "The wedding is in three weeks."

"Three weeks! Who plans a wedding in three weeks?"

"The invitations went out last month. They really only have a matter of days to get change-of-venue cards out, so they have to make a decision quickly."

Cici said, "I don't know . . ."

"It will just be the bride and her mother. All they need to do is walk around the property and talk to you about what they have in mind."

The three women glanced at each other. "That doesn't sound too hard," Bridget offered.

"I suppose it wouldn't hurt to talk," Lindsay agreed.

"Perfect!" They could practically see the sparkle in Paul's eyes over the telephone line. "I knew my favorite girls wouldn't let me down. And I have a feeling you're going to be *very* happy you did this. We'll be there about lunchtime."

Ida Mae muttered, "Good thing we won't know you're here."

Paul laughed. "Good-bye, my darlings! I'll see you tomorrow!"

The three women looked at each other for a moment. "Well," said Cici at last.

"Yeah," said Lindsay, and she grinned. "I guess we *are* famous. You know there's going to be no living with that daughter of yours now. It couldn't have been better if she had orchestrated it all herself."

"She practically did," Cici said.

Bridget thought out loud. "I should bake something. Maybe a seven-layer lemon-raspberry torte. We still have some raspberries in the freezer. And a shrimp and asparagus quiche."

Ida Mae opened the container of thawed peaches and dumped them into a mixing bowl. "Where're you gonna get the shrimp?"

"Ham and asparagus quiche," Bridget amended, her eyes glowing as the menu took shape in her mind. "And beaten biscuits with dill butter—no, I know! Scones with those stone cherries we dried last year. Ida Mae, let's save those dandelion greens for a salad tomorrow."

"Got a yard full of them." She poured sugar over the peaches. "You gonna make a cobbler or roll out a crust?"

"Crust. I wish the raspberries were in."

"You making a pie *and* a cake?"

"No, for the salad. Ida Mae!" Bridget's voice was alarmed as she snatched a bottle out of Ida Mae's hand just before she sprinkled the contents over the peaches. "What are you doing? That's red pepper!"

Ida Mae grabbed the bottle from her and slammed it down on the counter, her color flaring. "You don't like the way I cook, you can just do it yourself!"

She jerked off her apron, flung it on the counter, and stomped out of the kitchen.

The three women shared a cautious, questioning look.

"Definitely crankier than usual," Lindsay said after a moment, her voice subdued.

Cici cast a quick glance over her shoulder before agreeing, "Definitely."

Bridget picked up the pepper bottle, read the label, and returned it to the cabinet, her expression carefully neutral. "Guess I'd better get busy on that piecrust," she said.

❧

Every evening at twilight since they had moved into the house, they gathered on the front porch to say farewell to the day. A glass of wine, a sweater against the chill of a spring evening, a rocking chair for each of them ... and peace. For three seasons of the year, the routine never varied. In the summer, they watched the hummingbirds dart back and forth between the red feeders. In the fall, the cardinals and the blue jays scolded each other from the ancient boxwoods that flanked the porch. In the spring, barn swallows soared against the pale lavender sky.

The mountains grew black, and the low-hanging sun etched distant evergreens in brilliant gold. They settled into the taste and texture of the coming night and let go of the challenges of the day. It was as though, in that quiet hour, they reconnected with the place that had won their hearts, with their reasons for coming here, and with each other.

Bridget said, sighing a little, "What a difference a year makes, huh?"

"I don't know." Cici sipped her wine, her voice lazy and content. "This time of day, it seems that nothing has changed for thousands of years. Or ever will."

"Which is why I love this time of day," Lindsay put in with a sigh. She lifted her glass to Cici. "To things that never change."

"I'll drink to that," agreed Bridget. She tried, not very successfully, to hide her grin of pleasure in her glass as she added, "One hundred two comments on the blog. I guess that means I'll actually have to start posting to it more often than once a month now."

"Good heavens, what are they saying?"

"Nice things. How much they loved the article, and how beautiful our place looks, and how they wish they could live like this ..."

Cici choked on a laugh.

"And," insisted Bridget a little defensively, "twelve requests for information on gift baskets!"

"Say, that's great!" Lindsay lifted her glass to her.

And Cici added, impressed, "You go, girl. At thirty-six dollars a pop, that's not exactly chicken feed, you know. "

Bridget frowned a little, disconcerted. "Actually it is. Just about enough to keep the chickens in that organic feed they like through the summer."

"Ah, well. Easy come, easy go."

They were quiet for a while, listening to the distant muffled clucking of the chickens as they settled into their roosts in the coop behind the house, a single ferocious volley of barking from the border collie, Rebel, the soft baaing of the sheep in the meadow as they, too, settled down for the night. The sky was streaked with bruised red clouds and slashes of gold.

As they watched, a long-legged deer picked his way across the lawn, nibbling at grasses and budding flowers, accompanied by the soft clanging of the miniature cowbell that hung around his neck. Bambi had followed Lindsay home from a walk as a fawn, been adopted as a pet by Noah—who, as a country boy, should have known better—and made Ladybug Farm his home. They had tried building pens and fences for him to keep him safe from eager hunters, but as he reached maturity he simply leapt over them. It was Noah who had come up with the idea of the cowbell, to alert hunters to the fact that the deer was not ordinary prey. Now they fenced their flowers and their crops, and the deer roamed free.

Lindsay asked, "Are we really going to do this wedding thing?"

"I think it could be fun," Bridget said.

"You think everything is fun."

Cici was more thoughtful. "It's a lot of money. I don't see how we can turn it down."

"I know." Lindsay's enthusiasm, if it existed at all, was muted. "I just don't know how I feel about all those Washington society types roaming around all over the place."

Bridget stifled a laugh. "Some of those 'Washington society types' are our best friends! Not to mention my own son."

"You know what I mean." Lindsay was unmoved. "And just because Kevin works in DC doesn't make him one of them. Not yet, anyway."

"Good to know. You used to date one or two of those Washington society types, if I recall," Bridget reminded her.

"Which is why I can speak with authority on how smarmy they can be."

"Smarmy," Bridget repeated thoughtfully. "There's a word I haven't heard in a while."

Cici lowered her voice a fraction so as not to be overheard from the rooms inside. "You know Noah's scholarship is only for one year. And tuition at John Adams is not exactly cheap."

"Not to mention college," Lindsay added unhappily. She sipped her wine. "Believe me, I haven't overlooked that. Whoever thought I'd be worrying about college tuition at my age?"

Bridget said, "We promised his mother we'd take care of him."

Lindsay said firmly, "I'd make sure Noah went to college with or without that promise. He has too much potential to waste."

Cici said, "And if you didn't, Bridget and I would."

Bridget added simply, "He's one of the family now." And Lindsay smiled gratefully at both of them.

Cici asked Lindsay, "Have you heard from her since Christmas?"

There was no need to specify to whom she was referring. Noah's mother, Mandy Cormier, had come into their lives only last year, but hardly a day passed that they did not think of her. She had given up her son when he was only a toddler, believing him to be safe in the care of his grandmother. But the grandmother died unexpectedly, and Noah had never known his mother was alive. By the time Mandy found her son again, he was well on his way to becoming a full-time member of the Ladybug Farm household, and Mandy herself was suffering from a terminal illness. She had granted Lindsay legal guardianship of Noah on the condition that she, Mandy, be allowed to tell Noah about her illness herself. Unfortunately, she had also insisted that Noah be allowed to choose when—or whether—he wanted to be in contact with her, and so far Noah's choice had been silence.

Lindsay shook her head. "I sent her some photographs of Noah, and his first semester report card from John Adams." She hesitated. "I thought Noah might want to send her a card, after I gave him her mailing address. But I guess not."

"It's easier for him this way, I think," Bridget said softly. "He's had so much to adjust to the last couple of years. He'll deal with it when he's ready."

The two women glanced at her briefly, but no one had to state the obvious. By the time Noah was ready, it could very likely be too late.

The cowbell clanged softly. Squirrels chittered. Rebel, a black and white shadow in the deepening twilight, slithered across the lawn toward his bed in the barn.

Lindsay said, "We can apply for another scholarship. He'll probably get it."

"Probably," agreed Cici. "But a traditional scholarship only pays for tuition. There are still books and lab fees and uniforms and, well, what am I telling you for? He was lucky to win the money this year that covers everything."

"And there's still college."

"Right," said Cici.

"So, I guess we have to give the smarmy Washington society types a chance."

"Right."

"They might not even want us to do their wedding," Lindsay suggested.

"Don't be ridiculous," said Bridget, rocking contentedly. "Why wouldn't they? This place is perfect. We're perfect. And I'm going to blow them away with my food."

Cici said, "Well, then, I guess we've got the job."

Lindsay sighed. "Are we ever going to be able to retire?"

Cici rolled a glance her way. "Um, no."

Bridget said, very quietly, "We should talk about Ida Mae."

No one answered for a while. When Lindsay spoke, it was with her gaze fixed with solemn absorption on the deep purple pits of shadow that crept across the lawn. "She's really old, Bridget."

Cici said, "Maybe she's just going through a downswing. You know, like people do. It could be nothing."

"It could be something," Bridget countered, reluctantly.

"Old people have it tough," Lindsay said. "Their knees start to go, their hearing, they get arthritis and atherosclerosis, and with all that bothering them, it's no wonder they get confused now and then. It doesn't necessarily mean anything."

"Maybe," Bridget agreed, after a time. She did not sound convinced. "But what if it does mean something? She doesn't have any relatives. We're the ones responsible for her, have you thought about that? I mean, in case, you know, decisions have to be made."

"Why don't we just wait awhile before we leap to conclusions," Cici suggested.

Lindsay frowned into her wine. "We sure are responsible for a lot, aren't we?"

"Comes with the girl suit," Cici said. "Has there ever been a time in your life when you weren't responsible for a lot?"

From somewhere deep within the house, the telephone rang. But none of the women moved to get up.

"Noah will take a message."

"Or the answering machine will pick up."

Upstairs, a window slid open. "It's Lori," Noah called down.

"Tell her I'll call her back," Cici returned, tilting her head so her voice would carry.

The window closed.

Bridget said, leaning back in her chair, "Being a celebrity is exhausting."

Lindsay agreed, "Who knew?"

Cici considered that for a moment. "Good thing we're up to the task."

The three women allowed themselves a reflective moment, which slowly turned into a shared grin. They raised their glasses.

"Here's to us."

June 3, 2001

My darling—

There was a little blue bird in a bush outside my window today, and I thought of you. I had lunch in the park and watched some children trying to launch a toy boat in the pond, and I thought of you. I watched two young lovers holding hands on the street, and I thought about you.

I think about you all the time, and I love you. That's all I wanted to say. That I love you.

4

Dreams Coming True

Catherine North-Dere and her daughter Traci arrived with Paul at quarter to one.

Traci was a tall, model-thin girl with shoulder-length feathery blond hair and salon-tan legs that were displayed to perfection in khaki walking shorts and three-inch wedge sandals. An immaculately fitted rolled-cuff white shirt and a wool navy blazer casually tossed over her shoulders, along with a gold cuff bracelet, dangle earrings, and a messenger bag—Coach, naturally—completed her "afternoon in the country" look.

Yet it wasn't until she removed her designer sunglasses that Cici, Bridget, and Lindsay actually ventured a guess as to which was the daughter, and which was the mother.

Catherine's blond hair was a shade darker and a bit thicker than her daughter's. It was also more immaculately styled, curving perfectly toward the face at the shoulders to reveal realistic-looking honey-colored low lights. She wore custom-fitted boyfriend jeans, cuffed to display slim ankles and leopard-print heels, with a sand colored, form-fitting T-shirt and a black silk jacket with ruffled lapels. The diamond on her finger was three carats, minimum; her watch Piaget.

"Now *that*," murmured Lindsay in unabashed appreciation, "is some kick-ass Botox."

Cici shrugged, her arms folded. "I could look like that if I wanted to."

Lindsay stifled a guffaw. "You and what army?"

Cici elbowed her hard in the ribs, glaring.

"I'll bet she spends more on her hairstylist every month than I spent on my first car," Bridget observed, a little awed.

"This is what I'm saying," Cici replied. "All it takes is money."

"And a personal trainer," added Lindsay.

"And the ability to live on about three hundred calories a day," observed Bridget, and Cici scowled at her.

"But," added Bridget, "those shoes are to die for."

On that all three of them agreed.

The three women had been up since the rooster—the one Cici threatened to place in the stew pot at least once a day— let forth his first screeching crow, and they hadn't stopped moving since daybreak: sweeping the porch, polishing the windows, vacuuming, dusting, knocking cobwebs from under the stairs and out of the corners. Lindsay skimmed debris from the reflecting pool and swept the outdoor patios. Cici rubbed down the mahogany banister with lemon oil and built a cheery fire in the living room, which could hold a chill even this late in the season. Bridget made sure that Rebel, once he had finished arranging the sheep that made such a picturesque tableau in the distant meadow to his satisfaction, was securely locked in the barn.

They set the wicker table on the wraparound porch with an Irish linen tablecloth embroidered with pale pink roses, and used Bridget's Haviland china and Cici's sterling, and the antique napkins with hand-tatted edges that Lindsay had brought back from Germany. The centerpiece was a crystal vase of ruffled pink apple blossoms.

"So, we have a few less apples this fall," Bridget had said with a shrug as she arranged the stems. "The tree needed pruning anyway."

Ida Mae had grumbled about making such a fuss over a couple of no-account city folks they didn't even know, anyhow, and Lindsay countered tartly, "My mother always said that strangers are the only people worth making a fuss over, since you're not going to change anyone else's opinion of you. Besides, you're the one who always irons the dish towels when company is coming."

Now, as the elder Ms. North-Dere also removed her sunglasses and swept a slow, assessing gaze over everything within her view, the ladies found themselves wishing they had not only ironed the dish towels, but gotten manicures and maybe pedicures as well. Cici tried to look nonchalant as she ran a hand through her own honey-blond hair, Lindsay absently patted the pockets of her jeans for a lipstick, and Bridget looked down in dismay at her canvas print overalls and scuffed white sneakers.

"We should have dressed up," Bridget whispered.

Cici frowned uncomfortably. "It's not high tea with the queen you know. We're doing them a favor."

Paul lifted his hand to them as he got out of the driver's seat, and they waved back. He came around the car and offered an arm to each of the blondes. Paul, with his perfectly styled chestnut hair and blue eyes, always looked as though he had just stepped out of a high-priced magazine ad yet never looked out of place. He possessed the kind of effortless charm that few could resist, and these two were no exception. They wrapped their hands around his arms, laughing as he spoke to them, and he escorted them up the wide front steps onto the porch.

"Darlings," he said with a flourish, "may I present to you the legendary Cici Burke, Lindsay Wright, and Bridget Tyndale."

The ladies smiled and bobbed their heads in turn.

"Ladies, my pleasure to introduce Catherine North-Dere, mother of the bride, and her delightful daughter Traci."

"Cici, Bridget, dearest Lindsay . . ." Catherine swept forward and caught them each into an embrace as tepid as pool water, all boney shoulders and musky perfume. "I feel I know you already! You are so good to have us out, really. Paul has told us so much about you."

Her voice was smoky and warm and her smile seemed genuine, and the ladies relaxed a little. Cici said, "It's our pleasure, really. We love to show off our house."

"Well, I can certainly see why." With a breath of pure pleasure, she surveyed the view—the tranquil sheep in the emerald meadow, blue-shadowed mountains beyond, frothy apple trees in bloom, daffodil-lined paths, pink weigela and deep blush azaleas swaying in the breeze. "This is just magnificent. Isn't it, darling?"

"Heaven," replied Traci absently, snapping photographs with her cell phone. "Where's the chapel?"

Catherine's hand closed about her daughter's arm, tightly.

Her smile was frozen. "No chapel, sweetie. This is a *private home*, remember?"

Traci stopped taking pictures. "Oh. Right."

Catherine smiled apologetically. "This has been such a nightmare. We must have seen two dozen places in the past week, and the stress . . . well, you just can't imagine."

Bridget said quickly, "You've had a long drive. You'll want to freshen up. Let me show you inside."

Paul held his smile until the two blondes had followed Bridget inside, and then he came forward to kiss Cici, then Lindsay. "If this works out," he said, "you are going to owe me so big."

"Or maybe," Cici replied dryly, casting an uneasy eye toward the house, "you'll owe us."

Catherine was effusive about the staircase, the chandelier, the stained glass over the landing, the bay window in the living room. Traci whipped out her cell phone for pictures of the garden, the stone patio with the view of the mountains, the bubbling fountain, and the statue of the girl with the flower basket. She wanted to know what color the roses were and when they bloomed. Other than that, she didn't speak.

Bridget served minted asparagus soup with a smoked bacon and rosemary-infused olive oil garnish, and glowed beneath Catherine's praise. "Darling, you can't mean you have no formal training! This is indescribable. I'm telling you the truth, if you were to open a restaurant in Washington, you couldn't keep the crowds away. Paul, am I right?"

The four-cheese soufflé with a roasted pepper puree was as light as air, and elicited nothing but superlatives from their guests, and the mini scones stuffed with cherries and cream cheese were a sensation. In a very European move that caused both Cici's and Lindsay's eyebrows to shoot skyward, Bridget served the wild dandelion salad with raspberry vinaigrette after the main course, accompanied by miniature cheese biscuits and an exotic touch of pinot noir jam.

"It's absolutely transcendental," Catherine rhapsodized. "The difference fresh ingredients make—why, it's just miraculous, isn't it, Traci? I assume everything is organic?"

"Not officially," Bridget tried to explain. "Although we don't use pesticides or chemicals, you have to meet certain standards..."

Traci gazed out toward the meadow. "Do the sheep come with?"

Lindsay looked confused. "I don't know where else they would go."

"Now, darling." Catherine placed her hand warmly over Bridget's. The giant diamond on her finger prismed a brief spark of sunlight across the table. "This is what I'm thinking. Simple canapés, quiches, these wonderful little biscuits with your homegrown jams, fruit medley, fresh vegetables... everything organic and fresh from your very own garden... Why it's *exactly* the kind of menu we were looking for!"

Bridget said uncertainly, "Well, we can't really call it organic. And there's not an awful lot in the garden in June..."

"You could do that for fifty, couldn't you?" Catherine persisted hopefully. "With some of these lovely sauces?" She gasped with sudden delight and clapped her hands together. "Traci, I have it! The theme will be everything Virginian! We'll serve local wines and all the food will be homegrown right here on this beautiful farm! Locally grown is *so* trendy right now and incredibly politically correct." She turned quickly to Bridget. "You can get locally milled flour, can't you? And milk from your own cows?"

"We don't actually have cows," Bridget said.

Cici added, "And we really don't grow that much of our own food."

Catherine whirled on Paul, blond hair rippling. "Darling, what is the state flower of Virginia? Does anyone know?"

"Virginia creeper?" suggested Paul with a perfectly straight face, and Lindsay kicked him under the table.

"I know that," Bridget said helpfully. "It was in that movie, *The American President*, remember? Dogwood, I think. Yes, that's got to be it. Dogwood."

"Dogwood is a tree," Paul pointed out.

Bridget grinned. "That's exactly what they said in the movie!"

"God, Mother," Traci groaned, her thumbs working the keyboard of her phone. "I am *not* walking down the aisle with an armful of tree branches."

Catherine looked disappointed. "Well, that's too bad, isn't it? Dogwood. Is there a runner-up state flower?"

Cici said carefully, "Most people have the wedding theme in mind long before they start planning the wedding. I mean, isn't three weeks out a little late to be starting from scratch?"

"Darling," confided Catherine dramatically, "I can't *tell* you how many themes we've been through! Every time we get a new wedding planner we get a new theme! Everything from Cinderella's Ball to Winter Wonderland—in the middle of June, mind you! It's positively *outrageous*."

"Every time?" Cici kept her tone neutral, but she couldn't

prevent a single, meaningful gaze in Paul's direction. "How many wedding planners have there been?"

Catherine gave a limp-wristed wave. "Too many. But the last one was really the pits. I mean, really, when he booked us into a *swamp* . . ."

"I'm sure it wasn't a swamp when he booked it," Paul offered consolingly, and refilled her glass. "And you are getting your money back."

Bridget turned to Traci. "What kind of theme did you have in mind, dear?" she asked pleasantly.

The young woman looked up from her phone with an expression that suggested she had only then realized that an actual person was sitting on her right. "Are you a wedding planner?" she asked.

"Well, no, but . . ."

Traci turned back to her telephone.

"When will you start bottling wine?" Catherine asked suddenly. "Maybe we can do a vineyard theme! That first woman had that whole Tuscan thing going, do you remember, Traci? With the crumbling walls and the grapevine arbor and the girls all in purple? Can you do crumbling walls?" She turned to Cici, growing more excited as she spoke. "And if we could serve the actual wine from your vineyard . . ."

Paul laughed, holding up a staying hand. "I think you might be getting a little carried away, Catherine. You can't make wine on demand, particularly when the grapes aren't even on the vine yet."

"We don't have any crumbling walls," Lindsay added, looking offended.

"But we'll be happy to serve wine from our own vineyard," Cici said sweetly, "if you don't mind waiting three years until it's ready."

Bridget cast a warning look from one to the other of them. "There are some wonderful local wines," she assured Catherine. "And I'm sure we can find something you'll love once we settle on a menu."

Traci said suddenly, "I like it."

Everyone stared at her.

Catherine prompted, "The vineyard theme?"

Traci spared her a glance that was surely reserved for only the most imbecilic of her acquaintances, pushed a final button on her telephone, and pocketed it. "The *farm*," she explained with exaggerated patience. "The grass, the mountains, the sheep." She made a vague gesture with her hand. "Very now. Local, organic, outdoors, simple, back to basics, very Obama." She gave a firm, decisive nod of her head, and for the first time she smiled. "Let's do it." She stood. "Give them a deposit. I'm going to get a close-up of the sheep."

Catherine's eyes widened with delight even as her shoulders slumped with relief. "Why it is, isn't it?" she declared. "*Very* Obama! Perfect!" And suddenly she sat up straight, turning to Paul. "Are you thinking what I'm thinking?"

"The rose garden!" The two of them spoke in unison, and Paul held up his palm for a high five.

"There really isn't a lot of room for guests in the rose garden," Lindsay pointed out worriedly. "It's mostly paths."

"How many guests are we talking about anyway?" Cici said.

"Fifty," Bridget reminded her. "Fifty."

"Do you know what would make it perfect?" exclaimed Catherine excitedly. "One of those marvelous twig arbors!"

"It has an arbor," Lindsay reminded her. "A gorgeous white arbor with gingerbread details."

"But it's on the wrong side of the garden, isn't it? We want it to frame the mountains. I wonder how difficult a twig arbor would be to build? Surely there's some local craftsperson."

"White would be better," Paul pointed out, "for the photographs."

Catherine looked reluctant, and then asked Cici, "How difficult would it be to move the arbor to the other side of the garden?"

Cici's eyebrows lifted into her bangs. "It's anchored in two feet of concrete."

Bridget pointed out, "A garden wedding can be risky around here in June. What if it rains?"

"Well, that's the beauty, isn't it?" exclaimed Catherine happily, waving an arm at her surroundings. "We won't even have to rent tents—we have a built-in rain plan. The house is plenty big enough, and that barn looks brand-new! It could probably hold four or five hundred people, and how much fun would that be to decorate?"

"Well, I'm not sure . . ." Cici began.

Catherine reached across the table to squeeze Paul's hand. "You are a genius, darling, and I'll owe you for this for the rest of my life. I knew when I saw the photographs this was exactly what Traci wanted, but you're the man who made it happen! How can I thank you?"

Paul preened under her praise. "Call it an early wedding

present," he said. "And, of course, a chance to visit with three of my favorite people in one of my favorite places in the world." He winked at Cici. "Now I suppose there are a few details to work out..."

"Nonsense," declared Catherine, "whatever is easiest for these lovely people is fine with us." She unsnapped her purse and took out her checkbook. "The children," she confided to Bridget as she uncapped her pen, "are *so* counterculture chic I was afraid we'd end up having the ceremony atop some mountain in Tibet. Can you imagine the logistical nightmare? I mean, the Sherpas alone would cost a fortune. So believe me when I tell you, we will do whatever it takes to work with you!"

Cici glanced quickly at Paul and then at the other two. "We're not really professionals, you know," she began. "I'm not sure—"

Catherine gave a dismissive wave. "Don't worry a thing about it. Our wedding planner will take care of everything from setting up the chairs to ordering the flowers. Of course..." She paused thoughtfully. "It *would* be better to work with a local florist. I don't suppose you could recommend someone?"

She tore a check out of her checkbook and presented it to Bridget. "Will this serve as a deposit? We'll negotiate the catering separately, of course. Oh, and I do want to talk to you about providing gift baskets for the guests, and of course we'll want to order much more elaborate, custom gift baskets for the bridal party."

Cici saw the excitement building in Bridget's face and she struggled to catch her eye. "We'll certainly have to talk about it," Cici said, deliberately pleasant. "It sounds like a big project."

Bridget took the check and stared at it for a moment. She looked at Cici, her eyes big and her smile bright. "Not really," she said. She passed it to Lindsay, who looked at it, struggling to keep her expression neutral, and passed it on to Cici. Cici drew a breath to reply to Bridget, glanced down at the check, and stopped.

She smiled, folded the check into her pocket, and lifted her glass of iced tea. "Of course," she said, her smile growing expansive, "we love big projects."

And Lindsay added, "I might know someone who can help you with the flowers."

Suddenly the balmy afternoon quiet was shattered by the raucous screech of a rooster, followed almost immediately by the shrill scream of a human and the clatter and squawk of two dozen chickens. Bridget's face lost color.

"Rodrigo!" she gasped.

Catherine cast an alarmed look over her shoulder. "Traci?"

The rooster brayed furiously. The girl screamed. Catherine cried, "Traci!"

The three women knew immediately what had happened and shared a horrified look. They lurched from the table and raced down the steps, crying "Stay there!" when Catherine and Paul tried to follow. Cici, with her long legs and no-nonsense sneakers, quickly took the lead. She rounded the corner in time to see a terrified Traci stumbling away from the open door of the chicken yard, pursued by an enraged red rooster by the name of Rodrigo. His wings were spread, his feathers puffed, his chest thrust forward, and his beak parted to issue forth the most blood-chilling sound it was possible for a rooster to make. Traci, gasping out cries, ran backward, tripping in her high sandals, her hand extended behind her for balance. Every few steps Rodrigo would launch himself into the air with a triumphant crow, and Traci would scream and cover her face with her arms. Hens spilled out from the chicken yard and over the lawn. Catherine, leaning over the porch rail, shrieked, "Oh, my God, Traci, Traci!"

"Motherrrr!"

Bridget launched herself toward the escaping hens, trying to shoo them back with her hands, calling, "Chick-chick-chick-chick!" Traci fell backward against the barn door with Rodrigo flapping and flying and screaming at her only three feet away. Traci fumbled with the latch. Lindsay and Cici skidded to a stop, transfixed with horror.

"Traci!" Cici called. "Don't open—"

"The door!" screamed Lindsay.

Traci opened the door.

A black and white globe of fury launched himself through the air, snarling and barking. He flew over Traci's head as she collapsed into a ball on the ground. Rebel ignored her, bent on his real target, Rodrigo the rooster. Rodrigo immediately lost all his bravado when he saw the dog coming toward him. Tail whirling, nimble feet cutting and banking, Rebel chased the rooster back into the chicken yard, then circled back for the chickens. Feathers flew in a cacophony of squawking, but before Cici and Lindsay could pull Traci to her feet, Bridget was swinging closed the gate on the chicken yard—with all chickens and one indignant rooster safely enclosed—and Rebel was sailing over the fence toward the sheep meadow.

"Are you okay?" Bridget inquired of Traci as she jogged toward them. "I'm so sorry! Rodrigo is very protective of his hens."

Lindsay tried to brush the grass stains off of Traci's walking shorts, and Cici retrieved her sunglasses and her cell phone from the ground. "This is a working farm," Lindsay explained apologetically. "The animals are real."

Cici tried bravely to smile as she handed over the sunglasses and the phone. "I guess your mom will want her check back."

They walked back to the porch, where Catherine and Paul were waiting anxiously at the rail. But as soon as they mounted the steps Paul smiled, stepped back gracefully, and gestured them all back to the table with a welcoming sweep of his arm. "Well, then," he said, "is there any dessert?"

❧

Not only did Catherine not ask for her check back, by the time Paul's charm and Bridget's lemon torte had worked their magic on her she was apologizing to them. Traci seemed more embarrassed than annoyed, and made it clear that, once having decided on a farm wedding, she was not going to retract, no matter what the inconvenience—to herself, her mother, her guests, her fiancé, or anyone else who got in the way.

"Of course I'll have to have my dress redesigned," she warned her mother. "The train will have to go."

Cici smothered a smile as she tried to imagine the bride dragging a cathedral train across the barnyard, and Lindsay was taken by a fit of coughing. Apparently she had the same vision.

"And I'm thinking a hat instead of a veil," Paul volunteered.

"Excellent idea," agreed Catherine, scribbling notes in her day planner.

Paul winked at the three women seated opposite him.

Catherine and Traci began to talk about decorations, and Lindsay brought a sketch pad and some colored pencils from the house and began to sketch out some ideas. Catherine exclaimed, "You're a designer!" She turned to Traci, beaming. "Can you believe it, darling? A designer right here on the premises!"

Lindsay protested, pretending modesty, "I'm not really . . ."

"But these sketches are marvelous! Wait." Catherine caught her breath and lifted a finger, her expression a model of suspended hope. "I don't suppose—oh, please say you will!—you'd be willing to be in charge of the flowers and decorations, would you?"

"Actually," Lindsay admitted, smiling, "that's what I had in mind. Now, let's talk about budget."

Ida Mae, as grumpily stoic as ever, served coffee in rose-patterned cups, and Cici and Catherine negotiated a price— with the help of Paul, who kept kicking her ankle every time he sensed she was about to offer a bid that was too low. And when Catherine had happily agreed on an amount that was twice what Cici had originally thought would be fair, Paul added, "And just so we're clear, that price is just to reserve the property. You'll be responsible for all the supplies and the setup and teardown, and the catering and decor, including flowers, are separate."

"Darling, you should be in business," Catherine laughed. She slipped a card from her purse and passed it to Cici. "You draw up the contract, dear, and fax it to me in the morning." She turned to Bridget. "I'll call you next week about the menu, and we'll make an appointment for a tasting."

"And if you'll have the wedding planner give me a call, I can start putting together some sketches for you," Lindsay said.

"First thing in the morning, dear," Catherine assured her. She placed her hands down flat and cast a thousand-watt smile around the table. "Well, my dears, this has been just delightful. I know this is going to work out beautifully. We couldn't have asked for more, could we, Traci darling?"

The women stood as she did, and offered their hands all around. "We don't have any cards," Bridget apologized.

Catherine laughed. "Don't worry. I'll get all the information I need from the man of the hour, here. Traci, darling, let's walk down to the garden one more time. Good-bye, ladies. Thank you again for everything."

She gazed meaningfully at her daughter, who repeated, "Yes. Thank you for everything."

Catherine looped her arm through her daughter's, then hesitated before descending the steps. "The dog?" she ventured.

"Don't worry," Lindsay assured her. "He's with the sheep. We won't see him again till sundown."

"Perhaps," Catherine suggested, "on the day of the wedding, you might consider a boarding kennel?"

Cici said, "Actually, we don't—"

"We'll take care of it," Bridget assured Catherine brightly, and both mother and daughter looked relieved.

Paul said, "I'll meet you at the car." And when the two of them reached the path that led to the rose garden and the pools, he turned back to Cici, Bridget, and Lindsay, grinning. "Well, then. Eight thousand dollars for one day's work?"

"Not to mention the catering," Bridget said, barely able to contain her excitement.

"And the flowers are separate!" added Lindsay.

Cici shook her head in disbelief. "And to think of all those years I wasted having an actual job."

Lindsay added uncertainly, "Of course I've never really designed a wedding before. I don't know how to begin to charge her."

"You begin at a hundred dollars an hour plus fifty percent over the cost of the supplies and flowers," Paul told her, and when she stared at him, he assured her blithely, "It's standard."

"Boy, am I in the wrong business," Lindsay murmured.

Paul agreed. "Aren't we all?"

Bridget's eyes were shining. "Do you know how long I've dreamed about doing this? Planning menus, creating dishes, being *paid* for my food?" She threw her arms around Paul in an embrace. "Thank you!"

He laughed as he hugged her back. "If anyone deserves to have their dreams come true, it's you three."

"I wish you could stay," Lindsay said, as she gave and received her hug.

"So do I." He sighed. "The only thing I dread more than the three-hour drive is getting back to the city at the end of it."

Cici embraced him with one arm and kissed his cheek. "Give Derrick our love. How is he, anyway? Why didn't he come with you?"

Paul gave a small frustrated shake of his head. "Who knows? I never see him anymore. He works fifteen hours a day, and when he's home he's at the computer with the online art auctions. I couldn't even get him away for a weekend in Vermont, never mind a real vacation this year."

"This recession has been tough on the arts," Lindsay said sympathetically.

"He had to let most of his staff go," Paul confided, "so he's doing almost everything himself now. He's afraid if he hangs the Closed sign on the door for even one minute before normal operating hours it will mean the end of the gallery. I say, so what? It's not like he hasn't made a bloody fortune with the thing. Let it go, retire, buy a sailboat . . ." He grinned, and chucked Lindsay under the chin. "Spend more time in the country."

"You could take your own advice," Cici reminded him.

"You never know," he replied. Shoving his hands into the pockets of his perfectly pressed khakis, he gazed over the sun-strewn landscape with its colorful blossoms and majestic old trees, the sweeping meadow and misty mountains beyond. In the distance, the muffled sound of clucking chickens, trilling birds, splashing fountains, and nothing else. His expression was tranquil and wistful. "Every time I come here . . . you just never know."

There came a distant "Yoo-hoo!" from the vicinity of the front of the house, where the car was parked, and Paul roused himself from his reverie with a dry smile and a tilt of his head. "Meantime, the princesses await. Thank you for the incredible lunch and the exceptional company, as always." He blew them a kiss as he left. "I'll be in touch!"

The three of them followed him to the front and stood on the steps, waving, as he drove away.

"Wow," said Lindsay when they were gone. "How about that, huh?"

"The bride is a little strange," Cici said, "but she really seems to like the place. And the mother is nice."

"They met Rodrigo and Rebel," Lindsay agreed, "and they still want to go through with it. They must be really desperate."

"A wedding, right here at Ladybug Farm," Bridget said happily. "I mean, we talked about it, but did you ever think we'd actually do it?"

Cici laughed a little, shaking her head. "Wait until I tell Lori. Remember how she had this all planned out before she went away to UVA? The jams, the vineyard, and now the special events. Just like she imagined it."

Lindsay stuffed her hands into the pockets of her jeans, grinning. "We might be slow to catch on, but we *do* catch on."

"You know," Cici said thoughtfully, "at eight thousand a pop—and I'm not saying we should, mind you—but if we did two weddings a month, May through September, not even counting the catering or the decorating..."

"We could plant the rest of the vineyard," Lindsay said.

"Not to mention pay off the small business loan," Bridget added.

"And Noah's college."

"We could be solvent."

"Well, eventually, maybe," Cici said, and she smiled. "All in all, not bad for doing nothing, though, is it?"

"It couldn't be easier," Lindsay agreed. "All we really have to do is mow the lawn."

"And I'll touch up the paint on the arbor."

"We should put padlocks on the chicken yard gate."

"And do something with Rebel."

Cici looked at Bridget sternly. "We are not putting that dog in a boarding kennel. Even if we could find one to take him, we don't have enough insurance to cover the damage he'd do."

Bridget just smiled. "Do you know, we've been through an awful lot since we moved in here. The roof, the plumbing, the heating, the sheep . . . There were times when I thought we'd never catch a break."

"Most of the time," clarified Cici.

"But now . . ." She linked one arm through Cici's and the other through Lindsay's. "Just look at us. Our house is in a magazine! Lindsay has a real art studio with people paying her to give them lessons, and I get to cater an entire wedding, and people are coming all the way from Washington, DC, and begging us to host their party."

"Lori's doing great in college," Cici put in.

"And Noah got that scholarship," Lindsay said.

Bridget took a deep breath of the warm late afternoon air and declared, "Paul was right. Our dreams are actually coming true."

"And it's about damn time," Cici pronounced, and they all laughed.

"The best part is," Lindsay said as they turned to go into the house, "right now, for the first time in a long time, I can't think of a single thing to worry about."

But of course she spoke too soon.

September 10, 2000

My darling—

It's raining. I see your face in the droplets that form on my window. It's a face I can only imagine, and I dream about it every night. Sometimes I ache for you so much I can hardly breathe. It hurts. I never thought there could be a hurt so big.

It was raining the day I left you, do you remember? I hope not. I hope you don't think of me, and hurt like I do, every time it rains. I'd rather you not think of me at all.

Still, today I saw your face in the rain. I just wanted you to know that.

5

The Wonders of Modern Technology

SMarcello319: Buongiorno, mi amore! How does the world regard the most beautiful of all Americans of my acquaintance today?

LadiLori27: How many Americans do you know, anyway?

SMarcello319: Only the beautiful ones, mi amore.

LadiLori27: Maybe I'm not beautiful. Maybe that's not even my photograph.

SMarcello319: You would lie to Facebook?

LadiLori27: Maybe that's not your photograph either. Maybe you're not even Italian.

SMarcello319: Could anyone who is not Italian make the English this bad?

LadiLori27: You have a point. You couldn't do this much damage to the English language if you were translating it from Sanskrit.

SMarcello319: I am slain!

LadiLori27: LOL LOL

SMarcello319: I have for you the answer from my papa. But I think I will tell it to you in Italian if you cannot laugh no more at my English.

LadiLori27: I'm sorry. No Italian please! I hate looking things up!

SMarcello319: I know. This is why you make me to look up them for you.

LadiLori27: What did he say?

SMarcello319: He say you are very beautiful, too. And for beautiful American girl he will make introduction.

LadiLori27: Sergio, you are the best! Thank you, thank you! This could make all the difference!

SMarcello319: Yes, I am the best. I am happy you also see it.

LadiLori27: You're funny.

SMarcello319: And handsome.

LadiLori27: Maybe. But I don't believe everything I see on the Internet.

SMarcello319: Do you have a lover?

LadiLori27: Do you mean boyfriend? No.

SMarcello319: Would you like to have one?

LadiLori27: Thank you. But I'd rather have an internship.

SMarcello319: You have very much mistaken priorities.

LadiLori27: I also have a class.

SMarcello319: You are funny to talk to Lori. Will you be online later?

LadiLori27: I'll e-mail you.

SMarcello319: My breath is caught as I await your every word. Ciao!

Lori's smile was tender, secret, and deeply happy, and it lingered long after she had logged off. "Ciao," she said softly.

TO: HarborHomeone@Steingroup.com
FROM: Deerstalker@midmail.net
SUBJECT: Where were you?

I waited three and a half hours. You didn't even answer your freaking cell phone, if that even WAS your cell phone. Was this supposed to be some kind of joke???

Noah

TO: HarborHomeone@Steingroup.com
FROM: Deerstalker@midmail.net
SUBJECT: Liar

So I guess now you can't even be bothered to answer an e-mail. You must think I'm stupid. Well, I'm not. I thought you were a liar before and now I know you're a liar. I don't even know why I expected anything different.

Noah

TO: HarborHomeone@Steingroup.com
FROM: Deerstalker@midmail.net
SUBJECT: One More Thing

By the way, don't ever try to talk to me again, or e-mail me or even look at me if we happen to pass each other on the street someday. Nobody can say I didn't give you a chance. And if you tell anybody—and you know who I mean—that I ever even thought about making things up with you, I'll say you're a liar. Because you are.

And I'm closing this e-mail account. So don't even bother trying to answer. Not that you would.

Noah

But he did not close the account. And he did check for an answer, every single day, for the next two weeks.

🦢

The first call came half an hour after Catherine and Traci left the house—or, apparently, as soon as they could get cell phone reception. "Darling," cooed Catherine, "we were just looking at these photographs, and we noticed this huge tree branch protruding right out in the center of the view. It really ruins the mountain backdrop we'd planned for the wedding album. It wouldn't be any trouble to cut it down, would it?"

Cici, whose misfortune it had been to answer the telephone, was incredulous. "The tree?"

"Well, maybe just the branch."

"I'm afraid I really don't know which tree you're talking about . . ."

"Wait, I'm e-mailing you the photograph."

Cici cursed the day they had gotten high-speed Internet.

"Well, you know it's possible that if you just stood at a different angle the tree wouldn't be blocking the view at all."

"But that would mean moving the entire wedding party."

"Maybe only a few feet."

Dead silence. Cici hoped the cell phone had lost the connection.

Catherine said, "Just look into having the tree trimmed, will you, dear?"

The next call was from Traci. "I was just wondering about the chickens," she said. "They won't be clucking like that on the video, will they? I mean, sheep are pastoral, but chickens are just . . . rustic."

The phone calls continued into the next day. Catherine wanted to know the exact species of roses that would be in bloom on June 6 so that she could make sure the colors didn't clash with the bridesmaids' dresses. Then she wanted to know if it would be possible to screen in the wraparound porch in case of bugs, or, failing that, to build a cabana in the garden.

Traci wanted to know where the musicians would set up, and since cellos and violins really didn't go with the outdoor ambience, could they be screened with potted plants—or even better, a trellis with ivy and climbing roses?

And they mustn't forget about the dance floor. It would need to be at least twenty by thirty feet.

At six o'clock, they stopped answering the phone. At eight thirty, the answering machine picked up a call from Paul. "I hardly know these people," he said. "Really."

Lindsay observed worriedly, "I think I'm starting to understand why he kept wanting us to charge more."

Cici was frowning. "Maybe we should have thought this through."

"Don't be silly," Bridget insisted briskly. "You just have to be firm, that's all. We're not cutting down any trees and we're not getting rid of our chickens, and if they want a dance floor they're going to have to pay someone to build it. Are we businesswomen or not?"

Cici was impressed. "You really want this catering job, don't you?"

"It could be the beginning of great things."

"We just have to spell everything out in the contract," Lindsay said. "No tree cutting. No screening of the porch. No major construction of any kind. And anything extra, they have to pay for."

When the phone started to ring again, Cici glanced at her watch.

"No phone calls after nine," she said.

"Seven," countered Bridget.

"Six," bid Lindsay.

"Business hours are from nine to five," decided Cici, and turned off the ringer on the telephone.

With this, all three women gave a satisfied nod.

"We just have to set boundaries."

"We can do this in our sleep," Bridget assured them. "After all, look what we've already done." She gestured expansively to include the house, the yard, the outbuildings.

"Yeah," agreed Lindsay, cheering. "We can do this in our sleep."

"Good thing," observed Cici as the answering machine counter went up to thirteen, "because I have a feeling that's going to be the only time we have left."

TO: SMarcello319@mico.net
FROM: LadiLori27@locomail.net
SUBJECT: RE: Photographs from Home

Hi Sergio—

I loved your last e-mail. You paint such beautiful pictures with your words I hardly needed the photographs. I can't wait until I can see the stars in your sky, either!

Your mother is gorgeous! I guess that's how her son got to be so cute. :) I can't imagine living in a house that was built when Leonardo da Vinci was alive. But I know what you mean about stones crumbling and cellars flooding. The house my mother bought with her friends is only a hundred years old, but it has 'pieces falling off of it,' as you put it, too! Here are some pictures I took when I was home last month. The tall one with her arm around me is my mom, Cici (I made Aunt Lindsay take it so I could send it to you but I told her it was for my Facebook page. So I had to put it up in case she checked). You can see the grape vines in the background. Our vigneron (is that what you call it in Italian?), Dominic, says we can start harvesting the first grapes this fall if nothing disastrous happens. That means we can toast my graduation with our very first Beaujolais!

But long before then (fingers crossed and IF I get the internship) I'll be on my way to Italy. I don't know how I can hold out for six more weeks!

My roommate says I spend too much time on e-mail and not enough time studying (she's SUCH an egghead; don't you hate that?) and she's probably right. How was your philosophy exam? I'll have to cram all night if I'm going to squeak by on Business Admin in the morning.

I live for your e-mails. I really do.

Ciao—
Lori

P.S. Is that really your house? Is that really your mother? Is that really your picture? JUST KIDDING!

TO: Bridget@LadybugFarmLadies.net
FROM: Catdere63151@gsamil.com
SUBJECT: Menu

Bridget,

Yes, I think we are on the same page—heavy hors d'oeuvres and finger foods, or what some might call a "grazing" menu. :) (Sheep, farm, grazing, get it?) I'm picturing "stations" set up all over that gorgeous lawn of yours, maybe with little canopies over each table, and filmy curtains tied back with big bows . . . very *Lawrence of Arabia*, can you see it? I think we should have a protein from each group—fowl, beef, fish. You can get free-range turkeys, can't you? And I really don't understand the issue with shrimp. After all, Virginia does have the Chesapeake Bay! That's local, isn't it?

But I'm sure whatever you come up with will be fine.

XO
Catherine

TO: Bridget@LadybugFarmLadies.net
FROM: Teddydere@gsamil.com
SUBJECT: No Shrimp!

Bridget,

I told you, I am a vegetarian and that means NO shrimp. Besides, they are tacky and COMPLETELY overdone. Why can't we have lobster?

Traci

TO: Bridget@LadybugFarmLadies.com
FROM: Catdere63151@gsamil.com
SUBJECT: RE: Menu #3

Bridget,

Another thought—Mediterranean is terribly in right now. Maybe we could do something Mediterranean with a farmhouse flair?

Shrimp are very Mediterranean. And I checked with the Department of Agriculture—shrimp are definitely a local product.

XO
Catherine

P.S. Bringing the whole crew out Saturday for a tasting; I know you'll come up with a fabulous array of dishes!

TO: Bridget@LadybugFarmLadies.net
FROM: TeddyDere@gsamil.com
SUBJECT: Menu

Bridget—

Yes, I can eat eggs. I CAN eat anything I want. I just don't CARE for shrimp. So take them off the menu, OKAY?

Traci

TO: Catdere63151@gsamil.com
CC: Teddydere@gsamil.com
FROM: Bridget@LadybugFarmLadies.net
SUBJECT: Menu #5

How about this?
   Crispy asparagus with pecorino
   Mini beef Wellington
   Caramelized onion and black olive tart
   Local-caught Cajun catfish with remoulade dipping sauce
   Of course we'll have a fruit and cheese station and a selection of fresh-baked breads and muffins, along with a dessert bar, as we agreed. Let me know your thoughts.

Bridget

TO: Bridget@LadybugFarmLadies.net
FROM: Catdere63151@gsamil.com
SUBJECT: RE: Menu # 5

I don't know, dear. Catfish? Seems a bit pedestrian, don't you think? And the entire menu looks somewhat lean to me. Could we have more variety? And what about the vegetarians?

XOXOXO
Cat

TO: Bridget@LadybugFarmLadies.net
FROM: Teddydere@gsamil.com
SUBJECT: RE: Menu #5

I want an ice cream bar.

TO: Teddydere@gsamil.com
FROM: Bridget@LadybugFarmLadies.net
SUBJECT: Ice Cream

In June? Outdoors?

TO: LadiLori27@locomail.net
FROM: SMarcello319@mico.net
SUBJECT: RE: RE: Photographs from Home

Dearest Lori,

Your photographs make my day wonderfully! How beautiful you are! Every time I look at a picture of you I think, This woman, how can she be so perfect? Your hair is like painted by Titian, your face a Raphael masterpiece. But this you know already. And your mama, clearly she is an angel to have given you to the world.

Lori, you will come to my village and you will see the sun that rises over the hills and how it spills its gold over the ground so thick you think you can pick it up in your hands. We will lie on the ground together, you and I, and we will lose ourselves in the stars that cover my sky. You will know why poets and artists for centuries have found their muse in Italia, because here is where love lives.

It required me some time to determine what is "egghead" and so I asked my American friend in history of literature class who tells me I should know because I am one. This is because I am perfect in the philosophy exam. I hope this will not make you love me less? I am very happy to be perfect! Being perfect means I will acquire my degree in only six months and then I will leave Milano and return to the hills I love. You will know this feeling, Lori, this aching of the heart, this sickness of the spirit, this longing to be home. Being perfect is also wearying.

I will tell my mama to find the number of your telephone in the States, and ring up you to say I am her son and this is our home and I am yes, as you say, very cute. I also have four aunts and a grandmother and fourteen cousins, although three of them are too young to write, should you require further references.

I, also, spend too much time on the e-mail since I have come to know you.

Un bacion, mi amore—
Sergio

TO: SMarcello319@mico.net
FROM: LadiLori27@locomail.net
SUBJECT: RE: RE: Photographs from Home

Dear Sergio,

You make my day wonderfully, too. I've read your e-mail like twenty times. I still can't believe you're real.

Love,
Lori

TO: Cici@LadybugFarmLadies.net
FROM: Catdere63151@gsamil.com
SUBJECT: Contract

Cici,

Darling, just one more little change to the contract and I think we'll be fine. Instead of "not to exceed" 50 guests I wrote in "a minimum of"—just in case someone brings a date and takes us over the number. I know it's just a technicality, but better safe than sorry. Also, that part about "no material changes to real property," I just replaced the "no" with "Client agrees to reimburse provider for," which is much more fair to you. Faxing it off right now, if you'll just initial and get it back to me I'll put copies in the mail for you tomorrow.

Sorry for all the fuss, especially when we have so much to do! Don't you just hate lawyers? And my husband is one!

XO
Catherine

SMarcello319: Lori, do you Skype?
LadiLori27: Skype!!!

TO: RGregory@HRG.com
FROM: LadiLori27@locomail.net
SUBJECT: webcam

Hi Daddy—

Is it ok if I use the Am-Ex for a webcam for my laptop? The one I have is WAY too low-res for international transmission. Mom said No Major Purchases without prior approval but it's only $249.95 online plus S&H.

I promise I won't use it to upload porn. :)

XOXOXO
Lori

TO: LadiLori27@locomail.net
FROM: RGregory@HRG.com
SUBJECT: RE: webcam

LadiLori27 wrote: <I promise I won't use it to upload porn>

I should say No just for that.

Have a $249.95 webcam on me. And BTW forget what your mother says; it's my card.

Love you more—
Dad

TO: Lindsay@LadybugFarmLadies.net
FROM: Teddydere@gsamil.com
SUBJECT: RE: Flowers

Daisies?? Are you effing kidding me???? DO YOU KNOW WHAT WE'RE PAYING YOU?

TO: TeddyDere@ gsamil.com
FROM: Lindsay@LadybugFarmLadies.net
SUBJECT: RE: RE: Flowers

Deleted

TO: Lindsay@LadybugFarmLadies.net
FROM: Catdere63151@gsamil.com
SUBJECT: Decorations

Darling,

White bunting? Out of doors? Are you sure?

As for the color scheme, I must say I really don't know what it is just now. Yesterday it was navy and black. Perhaps you should check with Traci?

Yours,
Cat

From "Ladybug Farm Charms," a blog by Bridget Tyndale

Thanks to everyone who has been so nice about the magazine article in Virginians at Home. *If you haven't read it yet, you can see it online by clicking <u>here</u>. Guess what? Ladybug Farm has gone into the wedding hosting business! We're starting with a small affair for a darling young couple in June, and I'm trying to use as many fresh local ingredients as possible. We have a huge fig bush that gets lots of sun and usually has ripe figs by early June, so I thought of this recipe for a finger food. Try it at home and see what you think!*

Does anyone know where I can get fresh local goat cheese?

Three-Cheese Stuffed Figs

1 cup chèvre/goat cheese

¼ cup blue cheese or Gorgonzola

1 cup Neuchâtel

2 tablespoons honey

¼ cup very finely ground walnuts

2 dozen pitted, split figs

Blend the cheeses together in a food processor or by hand with the honey and finely ground nuts. Stuff each fig with 1 tablespoon of the mixture and refrigerate until firm.

For an exotic variation, add 1 tablespoon of chopped, fresh rosemary to the cheese mixture, or 6–8 sprigs of spearmint. I've also added 1–2 tablespoons of bourbon for an unexpected punch.

27 Comments

AHarding said:

Be careful when you're picking the figs. They attract wasps like crazy!

Bridget said:

I know! I got stung last year!

DK21 said:

I tried this recipe with the rosemary and served it as a starter for my special roasted vegetables and couscous. Very Mediterranean!

Bridget said:
I'll have to try it with couscous. Sounds fabulous.

Terrytown said:
I can't believe you don't have dairy goats on your farm! Then you could have goat cheese whenever you wanted.

Bridget said:
I'd LOVE to have a goat!

Secret Admirer said:
Dear Bridget,

I liked what you said the other day about the way the fog sits on the meadow in the early morning. I think about it sometime when I'm stuck in traffic on my way to work, and fantasize I'm there. The life you have sounds like paradise, and I hope you know how much we all envy you. It brings such light to my day to read what you write, and for an old fuss-pot bachelor like me the recipes are a treasure. I loved the recipe you posted for One Pot Stew. It was delicious, and—the best part—easy. When I cook for myself, I like things that don't take a lot of cleaning up afterward. Besides, sometimes I can't find more than one pot.

Bridget smiled and read the comment again. "Secret admirer, hmm?" she murmured, and typed a reply.

Bridget said:
I wish you could see our meadow today—it's covered with red clover! So glad you liked the stew. I'll try to post some more

one-dish recipes. I know it's not much fun to cook fancy meals
when you live alone.

"Secret admirer," she repeated aloud. She was grinning as
she clicked Post Comment. "What do you know about that?"

∂❧

Cici sat in her rocking chair, a glass of white wine in her
hand, and watched the mountains turn from gold to purple.
Bambi the deer wandered across the lawn, cowbell clinking
and head lowered to nibble the freshest sprigs of spring grass,
and Rebel darted out from behind the corner of the house,
barking furiously. When the deer raised his head and looked
at him, Rebel lowered his tail and slunk back around the corner of the house, almost as though embarrassed to have been
caught barking at a deer he knew.

The screen door closed with a familiar, friendly squeak as
Lindsay came out and, with a sound that was half sigh, half
moan, sank into her own chair. "I've done some calculations,"
she announced. "The time-saving devices of modern life are
actually *costing* me about three and a half hours a day."

Cici sighed heavily. "Boy, isn't *that* the truth? Do you know
it takes four or five times as long to type an e-mail or send
a text as it would to convey the same information over the
telephone? Why do people keep doing it?"

"To avoid conversation," replied Lindsay succinctly. "If you
talk to someone on the telephone, you actually have to listen
to the other person's opinion."

"Which is a total waste of time."

"Precisely."

Cici sipped her wine. "Do you hate them yet?"

"Oh, dear God. Don't get me started."

"At least we know what happened to the previous wedding planners."

Lindsay frowned. "Speaking of which, why isn't she the one sending me e-mails telling me what a rotten designer I am?"

Cici slid a glance toward her. "I have a bad feeling."

"Say it isn't so." Lindsay groaned. "Because if the wedding planner has quit, and I have to have one more interaction with that spoiled, pretentious, preadolescent, self-aggrandizing, social misanthrope—"

"Ah, come on," Cici protested, though without much vigor. "Traci's not that bad."

"I was talking about her mother!"

Cici choked on laughter and spilled her wine. "And you, a teacher," she accused, brushing drops of wine from her jeans. "I thought you were supposed to have patience."

"Listen," Lindsay said, "when you're the last line of defense in a classroom filled with thirty-five little people plotting to kill you, the last thing you're interested in learning is patience." She tossed back a healthy portion of her own wine. "Especially for idiots," she added.

Bridget came out with a plate of cookies, let the door slam unceremoniously behind her, and flopped down into her chair. "That blog is consuming my life," she declared. "Who in the name of heaven ever went to bed and dreamed up such a ridiculous, pointless, self-serving way to waste time?" She offered a cookie to Lindsay.

"Here's a hint. He was twelve years old." Before Lindsay could select her cookie, Bridget jerked the plate away, agitated. "I mean, when people don't read it, it's pointless, and when people do, it's pointless. And it takes up half my day!"

"Then stop doing it." Lindsay held out her hand for the cookie plate.

"Are you crazy? It's my business!"

Before she could snatch the plate away again, Lindsay seized it with both hands, took two cookies, and passed the plate to Cici.

"Besides," Bridget added, and the smile that played around her lips was secretly satisfied, "I've got a secret admirer."

Cici paused in the act of reaching for a cookie. "A secret admirer? Who?"

"Well, if I knew that, it wouldn't be a secret, would it?"

Lindsay grinned at her. "Well, you be careful. That Internet dating business is risky stuff."

Bridget gave her an impatient look and held out her hand for the cookie platter.

Rebel raised the alarm as Noah, returning from feeding the chickens, crossed the lawn. Noah dodged the lunging border collie absently, and Bambi didn't even raise his head.

Cici said, "Not really, you know. Did you know that last year alone, more people met their significant others online than any other way?"

"Oh, yeah? Where did you read that?"

"Online."

Noah mounted the steps, head down, hands in pockets. Bridget held out the platter to him. "Cookie?"

"Homework," he muttered, without looking up, and the screen door banged behind him.

Cici watched him go. "I wonder what's wrong with him."

"He hardly said a word at dinner."

"Teenage boys," observed Bridget sagely. "Believe me, you don't want to know what's going on in their heads. But you can't afford not to."

Lindsay sighed. "Some girl at school, I guess."

"It usually is."

Bridget reached into her back pocket and took out a folded sheet of paper, passing it to Lindsay. "Here's the menu."

"The final menu," queried Cici, "or the latest menu?"

"Final," Bridget said firmly.

Lindsay unfolded the paper and held it at arm's length, squinting in the dim light. "Wow. I didn't know they made print this small."

Cici snatched the paper from her and flipped down her glasses, which were nestled in her hair. She read out loud, "Brie en croute with Midori crème fraiche, chèvre and roasted pepper tarts, fried green tomatoes with bacon and bleu cheese crumbles, herbed-roasted pork with peppered peach chutney, fresh mozzarella with sliced vine-ripened tomatoes and olive oil, charred beef tenderloin with horseradish mayonnaise, honey-glazed fried chicken bites . . ." She looked up, leaning forward to stare at Bridget. "Are you serious? This sounds like the entire à la carte menu from the Waldorf Astoria."

"It's just for the tasting," Bridget said wearily. "They'll pick two meats and six accompaniments for the buffet."

"It sounds incredible. But not exactly something you can whip up in your spare time. How many are coming to the tasting?"

"Just the bride, the wedding planner, and the mothers. It'll be fine."

"I don't know, Bridge." Cici looked worried. "Are you sure you still want to do this? That's a pretty complicated menu and . . ." She cast a quick glance toward the house and lowered her voice. "It's not exactly as though you have a lot of help. Is it worth it?"

Bridget grimly stuffed the menu back into her pocket. "For thirty-five dollars a head it is."

"You go, girl," said Lindsay, sipping her wine. "And Paul would say add a fifty percent premium for fresh, local, and prepared on-site."

"Forty-five dollars a head," replied Bridget determinedly. "Besides, Ida Mae can follow a recipe, and Lori will be here to help with the actual wedding."

"Things must be desperate, if you're actually looking forward to having Lori in the kitchen."

"Let's hope it doesn't come to that," Bridget said uncomfortably. "But there are plenty of things she can do outside the kitchen."

Lindsay said sourly, "They want me to design escort cards."

Cici said, "Escort cards? But I thought this was a buffet."

"It is," Bridget assured her.

"That's what I told them," Lindsay said. "Escort cards are for sit-down dinners."

"And?"

"And Traci's matron of honor had escort cards with diamond chips in the corner. Traci has to have something better."

They watched red streaks appear across the sky, and the

apple blossoms soaked up the bright pink color. A bluebird visited the feeder that was hung under the eaves, gave the women a quick, bright look, and darted away.

Bridget smiled a little into the twilight. "Do you remember your own wedding?"

Lindsay nodded reminiscently. "The Fellowship Hall of El Camino Baptist Church in El Paso, Texas. We were just out of college, didn't have two cents to rub together. Our parents flew in, and Mama bought me a wedding cake at the local bakery. It was awful." She smiled. "I wore a white lace dress I bought in Mexico for twenty-five dollars, and twined baby's breath in my hair. He wore a blue suit. They wouldn't let us have champagne in the Fellowship Hall, so we had the reception in the park across the street, and danced to Cajun music until we were all too drunk to dance anymore." She sighed. "The wedding was the highlight of the whole marriage. And lasted longer, come to think of it."

Cici said, "I had the works. Six bridesmaids, all in buttercup yellow. A big puffy dress with a train halfway down the aisle. Freesia and candles and white satin bows on every pew. The groomsmen wore cutaways with gray satin cummerbunds."

"Sounds like a fairy tale," Lindsay said.

Cici shrugged. "I guess. I don't remember much about it. I was too stressed to enjoy it, and Richard and I had a big fight at the reception. I dumped a glass of champagne over his head."

Bridget and Lindsay chuckled. "Signs of things to come," Lindsay said.

Bridget's voice softened with fond remembrance as she said, "Jim and I were married at City Hall. Jim had just gotten a job teaching at Columbia and he had to be there the next day. I wore a pink suit with a corsage of sweetheart roses. My best friend Martha stood up with me, and afterward she threw rice at us on the steps and a policeman yelled at her for littering." She grinned. "We were brushing rice out of each other's hair all the way to New York."

Cici smiled. "And you were married how long?"

"Thirty-four years."

"Well, then," said Lindsay, leaning back in her rocking chair. "There you go."

"Right," said Cici. "It's not the wedding; it's the marriage that counts."

"Try telling that to Bridezilla."

"Or Bridezilla's mom."

Bridget said softly, "I miss him every single day."

Lindsay reached across and squeezed Bridget's hand. "You were lucky, Bridge. You got one of the good guys."

"There aren't many of them left," Cici said.

Bridget smiled. "I know."

They were quiet for a time. The mountains began to fade to black in the distance, and the warmth of the day leeched into the twilight, leaving a mild and not entirely unpleasant chill on bare arms and ankles. A light came on in Noah's room overhead. Lindsay finished her wine. Cici ate another cookie.

Bridget said reluctantly, "Well, I guess I'd better go fax this menu to the blushing bride." But she made no move to rise.

"And I've got to e-mail Catherine about the contract," Cici said. "Again."

"A lot of good our policy of not answering the phone after five did us," observed Lindsay.

"That's the price you pay for life in the modern world."

"If you ask me, life was a lot easier before we got so modernized."

No one argued with that.

They sat there for only a moment longer. Then one by one they got up, went inside, and went back to work.

August 12, 2003

My darling,

Sometimes during the day I think of things I want to tell you, or I see something that makes me smile, and I think how it would be if you could see it, too. Here are some of the things I wish I could have shared with you today:

   A vanilla-caramel swirl ice cream cone

   A fat rabbit that darted right out in front of me when I went to get the paper this morning

   A brown and white puppy with a red collar

   Are you eating ice cream where you are? Is someone making you smile?

   Please be happy. Because the truth is that I can never be until you are.

6

A Few Complications

The phone on the desk beside her began to ring, and Cici shouted up the stairs, "Fax!" Until the North-Deres had blown their way into their lives, the trusty old fax machine that Cici had kept for home use back in Maryland had been boxed up in the cellar behind Lindsay's rowing machine, a garment rack, and three boxes of unused glassware. Now it was plugged into an extension line of the house phone, and when the telephone rang the women never knew whether they were going to hear the frustrating *beeeep* of the fax machine or the sound of an actual human voice.

Until slightly more than a year ago, they had not even had cable television and had to drive to the library in town for high-speed Internet. But when Lori had finally convinced them of the practicality of bringing twenty-first-century conveniences to the nineteenth-century-house, they hadn't counted on how much space—and time—those amenities would consume.

There was a small anteroom off the main entry that,

according to Ida Mae, had once been a sewing room, and before that, a smoking lounge where men had enjoyed big smelly cigars. It had two sunny windows and a small coal heater which no longer worked, and the floor was covered with worn beige carpeting. The women had closed it off when they moved in, for it wasn't as though they were in need of extra rooms. When technology came to Ladybug Farm, however, they found a purpose for the little room.

Cici pulled up the carpet to expose the same heart pine floors that were in the living room. Lindsay painted the room pale yellow and Cici built shelves that she painted gloss white. They brought in a pretty Oriental rug and a comfy wing chair that Lindsay and Bridget upholstered in ivory silk with white brocade birds embossed into the pattern. Bridget hung a green birdcage in the corner, and sheers over the windows. An electrician brought in extra outlets and the Internet cable.

They found a nice big desk in unfinished pine at a yard sale, and whitewashed and sealed it to match the rest of the decor. They hung photographs in an attractive wall grouping of the three of them on shared vacations, and on the opposite wall, for a punch of color, Lindsay had framed one of her paintings, of a giant red poppy. Then they proudly brought in and set up their home computer.

Cici had spent most of her life in offices—her real estate office, her home office, other people's offices—and she wasn't that wild about having an office at Ladybug Farm. But even she had to admit the room was welcoming and attractive, as well as practical. And the best part was that, since it was sure to be the least used room in the house, the door could remain closed most of the time.

But of course, that was before Lori set up the website, which required constant monitoring, and Bridget's blog, which Bridget preferred to work on from her laptop, which required a wireless router. Soon all of their bookkeeping was transferred to the computer, as well as their correspondence. An extension telephone line had been brought in, because they couldn't hear the kitchen phone ring from the office. And now there was the fax.

The machine began to buzz and roll out paper, and Cici clicked Reply on the e-mail she had barely finished reading. *Just received the fax; returning it to you ASAP*, she typed. *Hopefully the eighth time will be the charm!*

Lindsay stood at the door behind her. "What do you think about this?"

Cici pushed Send and said gloomily, "Her husband is a *lawyer*. I'm telling you, we should have thought this through. Why am I doing this, anyway?"

"Eight thousand dollars," Lindsay reminded her. "Look at this."

Cici turned. Lindsay stood at the doorway with several lengths of pale printed calico draped over her arm—one pink, one blue on white, one yellow. Spread atop them she had arranged a square of Battenberg lace.

"What is that?" Cici asked.

"Remember all that fabric we found packed away in the attic?"

"Oh, right," Cici recalled. "You and Bridget were going to make curtains for the guest rooms."

"Right. But there wasn't enough of one color. There is, however," she pronounced triumphantly, "enough to make tablecloths. And look, with a white Battenberg topper to tie it all together . . . what do you think?"

Cici said uncertainly, "It's pretty. But how many table-cloths do we need, anyway?"

"I'm thinking ten."

Cici's eyebrows shot up. "Ten!"

"Four at each table, with one large one to accommodate the wedding party, which would of course be decorated differently."

"Oh. The wedding." Cici leaned back in her chair. "Of course." And then her gaze sharpened. "Wait. This started out as heavy hors d'oeuvres only. Then it was a buffet."

"With escort cards," Lindsay reminded her.

"So, now it's official? We're doing a sit-down dinner?"

Lindsay shrugged. "People have to have some place to sit, even if they're only eating hors d'oeuvres. Anyway, it's up to Bridget what kind of dinner they have. I've got enough trouble keeping up with what I'm responsible for. So." She held up her arm with the fabric draping over it, her expression hopeful. "What do you think? Simple, organic, *very* farmhouse. I'm picturing mismatched china bowls filled with Floribunda roses as the centerpiece at each table, Battenberg lace napkins with beaded napkin rings, and carrying out the whole country inn–tearoom theme, mismatched china and antique silver place settings."

Cici hesitated. "Don't you think that's a little . . . informal?"

Lindsay's face fell—first into disappointment, then into resignation. "Well, of course I do." She sank into the ivory silk chair and balled up the fabric. "I mean, it's not like I didn't *try* to sell her on dusky rose satin table covers with white gardenia votives floating in crystal bowls at each place setting, or ivory satin and champagne glasses filled with sweetheart roses—I mean, that's simple, isn't it? That's understated. But the girl is obsessed with a theme wedding. 'Country chic,' she says. 'Farm natural,' she says."

"Ceramic cows and burlap?" suggested Cici.

Lindsay returned a brief scowl. "Very helpful."

"So, where are you going to put these ten tables seating four people each—which by the way is only forty people, you know. We're in it for fifty."

Lindsay waved that away. "So, ten people sit at the head table with the bride and groom. And I measured—if we use the entire porch, we can get ten tables with four chairs around each one. So." Now her expression became hopeful again. "A tiny favor?"

Cici let her head fall back against the back of the desk chair. "Just as long as I don't have to put my initials on anything."

"Could you build two or three mock-ups—they don't have to be sturdy enough to hold food, just something that won't tip over when you touch it—so that I can stage the porch for the weekend?"

The phone rang. Bridget shouted from downstairs, "Got it!"

And in a moment, her voice muffled and her warmth sounding forced, they heard her say, "Oh, hi, Traci."

Cici sighed, as her gaze wandered to the view from the window. "Remember when all we had to do before lunch was weed the carrot patch and pick strawberries?"

Lindsay's gaze followed hers briefly, wistfully, but did not linger. "It will be worth it," she said firmly. Then, with a beseeching smile, "So, what do you say? A little scrap lumber, an hour or two?"

Cici looked at the fabric, at the contract that lay waiting in the fax machine tray, and at the view of the pear tree, dappled with spring green and ruffled white blossoms, outside the window. She stood, tucked in the trailing hem of her shirt, and declared, "If it will get me out of this office and away from the wonders of modern technology, I'll build you a blessed gazebo. I'm going into town for a jigsaw blade and some quarter-inch plywood. Just have the measurements for me when I get back. I guess I might as well order the materials for the dance floor while I'm there. And," she added, "I'm keeping the receipt for the bride."

"Plus ten percent labor!" Lindsay called after her, and Cici gave her a grinning thumbs-up as she left.

❧

Bridget sat at the kitchen table, intently studying the yellowing pages of Emily Blackwell's cookbook. "There's got to be something in here that's as elegant as shrimp Newburg but without the shrimp. And more folksy. And more local."

Ida Mae gave her a withering look as she carried a potted geranium to the sink for water. "I don't know what you're looking in that book for if you want wedding food for city folks. You need that French woman."

Bridget looked up, puzzled.

"You know, that movie star."

"Julia Child?"

"If that's the one that's all the time slopping wine all over everything."

Bridget sighed. "I don't know, Ida Mae, you might be right. French cooking with a Shenandoah Valley local Mediterranean country flair might be exactly what they're looking for."

The potted geranium dripped a trail of water across the floor as Ida Mae carried it, two handed, from the sink to return it to the plant stand in front of the window. Bridget quickly sprang up to help. "Here let me take that."

But as Bridget reached for the plant Ida Mae angrily snatched it away. "So, now I'm too feeble to carry a potted geranium, is that it?" she demanded.

"I didn't say you were feeble, I said . . ."

"I know what you said, Miss Priss. There ain't nothing wrong with my hearing, and I'll thank you to keep your opinions to yourself." Ida Mae set the pot down on the stand with a thud that splashed more water and dirt onto the floor. "There!" she declared in disgust as she surveyed the mess. "Look what you made me do!"

Bridget and Ida Mae had had their differences almost from the moment they met, as was only to be expected when two strong women ruled over the same kitchen. In time they had come to respect each other and even to work together as an efficient team. It had been a long time since Bridget had lost her temper with Ida Mae. And it had been almost as long since Ida Mae had made such a deliberate attempt to provoke her.

"What *I* made you do? That's what I was trying to stop you from doing!" Bridget quickly clamped down on further exclamations and turned away so that Ida Mae wouldn't see the flare of color in her cheeks. She jerked open the cabinet under the sink, looking for towels.

Ida Mae returned from the pantry with a mop in her hand just as Bridget straightened up from the cabinet with a towel. "Ida Mae," she said gently, "I know something's bothering you, but I can't help if you won't talk about it. None of us can. Don't you want to—?"

But before she could even finish the sentence, Ida Mae shoved the mop into Bridget's hands.

"And I've got too much to do to clean up your messes," she told Bridget. "So, you can just do it yourself."

With that, she turned on her heel and left the room, anger and contempt radiating from her with every step.

Bridget stood there for a moment, mouth agape. And just when she thought of something to shout after Ida Mae, the telephone rang.

It was, of course, Catherine.

❧

A typical day in late spring at Ladybug Farm began with a leisurely breakfast on the porch, watching the mist rise over the meadow and the iridescent hummingbirds run war maneuvers around the bright red feeders that were hung under the eaves. They drank coffee in their pajamas, munched muffins and fresh fruit, and planned their days. Cici usually had some project going around the house—matching a piece of hand-milled molding from the 1920s, patching the crumbling mortar in the stone floor of a patio, building a closet or a set of shelves. By eight o'clock, Ida Mae was usually busy polishing furniture and mopping floors, and Bridget was feeding the chickens, checking on the sheep, or working in the vegetable garden. On the days that Lindsay had students in for art classes, she was in her converted dairy barn studio by nine, preparing canvases and mixing paints. Otherwise she never lacked for occupation with the flower gardens, the trellises, the ponds and patios. As the summer progressed, the orchard, vineyard, and nut-bearing trees all needed attention, and when harvest began an entirely new flurry of activity consumed the household. There were very few moments of downtime at Ladybug Farm.

So far this day had included for Cici twelve phone calls, eight e-mails, four faxes, and a trip to the hardware store. She had finished framing out the dance floor and was waiting for the rest of the materials to be delivered so that she could start placing the floorboards. It was after noon, and she was feeding the chickens because no one else had had time to do it, and she still had the table rounds to make.

Every surface in the kitchen was filled with sample dishes, pots were steaming on the burners, and Bridget was madly whisking, slicing, and basting. Ida Mae was sulking about something and taking out her pique on the windows, which she was polishing to a dangerous sheen. Lindsay hadn't left the sewing machine all day, and Noah, it seemed, hadn't been heard from all week. Cici didn't blame him for staying out of the way. What worried her was that in only a matter of days, this kind of chaos had become the new normal.

When the telephone tucked into her back pocket rang yet again, she was tempted not to answer it. When she heard her daughter's voice, she almost sank with relief.

"Lori, please, please, *please* say you're coming home this weekend." Cici propped the cordless phone between her shoulder and ear and lifted the gallon bucket of water with one hand while she unlatched the gate to the chicken yard with the other. Chickens squawked and scattered as she entered, and she did an effective little dance to shoo them away from the gate with one foot while trying not to step in chicken waste with the other. "Remember that great idea you had to turn this place into a wedding venue? And how hard you worked to make sure the people at *Virginians at Home* knew about 'catering and special events'?"

"It worked, didn't it?" replied Lori chirpily.

"We're killing ourselves here! A little help?"

"I'm in Research and Development," Lori informed her. "You guys are in Manufacturing."

"Thanks a lot."

Cici splashed water into the trough and scuffed her shoe over a patch of grass to clean it. She picked up a rake.

"Mom, where are you? This connection is terrible!"

"I'm cleaning the chicken yard," Cici answered. "Do you see what I've been reduced to? Carrying a cordless telephone around the farm because someone has to be on office duty while Lindsay is sewing and Bridget is making wild peach blossom chutney or whatever it is she's experimenting with now." She raked the pile of chicken manure into a corner of the yard, to be collected later, and hung the rake back on its hook. "*Your* chickens, I might add, which *you* were so determined to have."

"Aunt Bridget liked them, too," Lori defended. "Besides, think how much you're saving on eggs."

"Not enough to pay for their feed. And we're all getting high cholesterol."

"That's a myth. Eggs do not give you high cholesterol."

"So, now you're premed?" Cici exited the chicken yard and latched the gate.

"Mom," Lori said, "I'm excited about the wedding and I can't wait to get back there and help, but I just don't see how I can do it this weekend. After all, this is just surveying the site and tasting the menu, right? The hard stuff hasn't even started yet."

"You wouldn't say that if you had to cut out three plywood table rounds, repaint the trellis, and pressure wash the porch by Friday." As she moved closer to the house, the reception became clearer and she asked, casually, "So, who is he?"

Lori's laugh was too light to be genuine. "Who is who?"

"You know who. The new fella."

"Really, Mom, I have this killer exam coming up and I have to stay on campus this weekend to study. Besides, I have some great news. That's what I called to tell you."

"Oh?" Cici had learned from experience to be wary of what Lori considered great news.

"It's a terrific opportunity, so perfect I really didn't even think I had a chance, which is why I didn't want to mention it to you before now." Lori's voice was practically breathless with excitement—or perhaps she was jogging to class, as she often was when she remembered to call her mother. "There's this internship program that I found out about online, where agriculture students can actually get hands-on experience at a real winery, with some of the top winemakers in the world!"

Already Cici had a bad feeling about this. "But you're not an agriculture student."

"That's why I didn't want to get my hopes up. But it turns out I can apply through the business department, with the approval of the agriculture head, and because I'm coordinating all my credits to transfer to the enology program at Cornell, he actually approved me!"

"Well," said Cici, having absolutely no difficulty restraining her enthusiasm. "That's really something."

"And you haven't even heard the best part! It's in Italy! *Italy!* And it starts in July, but don't worry, I'll be back for regular classes in September, and—the absolutely *best* part—five quarter hours credit, can you believe that? Of course, part of the credits are in language, so I guess I'd better learn Italian, but could you just *die*?"

Cici sat down slowly on the porch steps. "Internship?" she repeated. "In Italy?"

"Don't worry about the expenses," Lori assured her. "Dad's got it covered."

Cici pressed her lips together and tried to count to three. "You talked to your dad about this?"

"Oh, sure. But he's cool with it, don't worry."

Cici cleared her throat softly, and chose her words carefully. She had a sudden, disturbingly gratifying picture of serving up her ex-husband's head on a platter, lined with curly endive and surrounded by spiced apple rings, at the wedding buffet. "How did this, um, all come about?"

Lori hesitated, but she made no attempt to disguise the excitement in her voice as she confided, "Actually, there is this guy I met online . . ." And before her mother could smother her groan, she went on, "Don't worry, he's really nice. And he's awfully cute—at least the picture he posted is—and we've been having the best time, e-mailing back and forth. He's at the University of Milan, studying law. You have to be really smart to go to the University of Milan, but that's where he is. He was helping me to research a paper, and then I heard about this internship, and it turns out his father actually *knows* the owner of Cascino Giovani, which is—yes!—at the top of approved sponsors, and he's giving me a personal reference, which pretty much means I'm in. Well, as long as I keep my GPA up for another three weeks, anyway! He writes the most beautiful letters," she confided, with a touch of wistfulness in her tone. "Sergio, not his father. Are all Italians so . . . poetic?"

Cici ground her teeth together and drew in a slow breath. "I'm sure I wouldn't know."

The sun, slanting behind the neatly tied rows of just-budding grape vines, broke a sweat on her face. She heard the sound of a truck engine—too well-tuned to be Farley's—and tires crunching on the gravel driveway. She twisted around to see Dominic DuPoncier's white pickup rounding the far corner of the house, moving toward the vineyard. Dominic, in straw hat and plaid shirt, lifted his arm through the open window toward her. "Afternoon, Miss Cici!" he called. Cici waved back.

Dominic was the county extension agent, and his father, as it happened, had been responsible for developing the original Blackwell Farms vineyard and winery on this very site. He had spent his youth working with his father at what was now Ladybug Farm, and he was so excited when the women approached him with the plan of reestablishing the vineyard that he had volunteered his expertise, his labor, and practically every free hour he had for the past year helping them get started. He babied their vines as though they were his pets, and when he talked about wine making he left no doubt in anyone's mind why it was considered an art.

And thinking about him gave Cici an idea.

She said, "You know, Lori, I think an internship is probably a good idea. I'm just not sure Italy is the best choice."

"Well, maybe. But the positions at all the best wineries in France were already filled."

That was exactly what she had hoped Lori would say. "We have some excellent wineries in the U.S.," she said. "New York, Napa . . ."

"Oh, Mother, please. If you're talking wine, you're talking *Europe.*"

"Or European winemakers," she pointed out. "And I'm betting there's nothing you can learn at Casa Wherever—"

"Cascino Giovani," Lori supplied.

"—that you couldn't learn from Dominic DuPoncier. He not only worked at some of the best wineries in New York, he studied under one of the most accomplished winemakers in France: his own father."

Lori laughed. "Nice try, Mom. And don't worry, I intend to learn loads of stuff from Dominic. But not until you have an actual winery for me to intern at."

Cici worked hard to keep her tone neutral. "I thought your plan was to get a degree in wine making—

"Enology," supplied Lori helpfully.

"Right. A degree in wine making from Cornell after you get your business degree from UVA next year. Wouldn't it be more helpful to do your internship then?"

"Well, that's what I thought, too. But then I met Sergio in

this online forum and we got to chatting, and that's just not the way it's done in places where they make real wine."

"We're making real wine," Cici objected. And she frowned a little. "I guess."

"Practical experience is everything," Lori insisted. "And when I found out about this internship . . . well, how could I *not* go for it?"

Cici chose her next words carefully. "You know, Lori, before you moved out here, you were planning to spend the summer in Italy on an archaeological dig, remember? With that professor you had a crush on?"

"Oh, him." Her tone was dismissive. "He was a jerk. But Italy is my *destiny.*"

"I just don't understand why you didn't mention it to me. We could have talked more about this."

"Well, there was no point in mentioning it until it was certain, was there?"

"Is it? Certain?"

"Just about," Lori returned cheerfully. "I have one more exam, and if I pass it, I'm in! That's why I really have to stay and study this weekend. I'm really sorry," she added, and the contrition in her voice was genuine. "I promise I'll be more help as soon as finals are over."

Cici sighed. "Don't be silly, sweetie. You are being a help by staying in college and studying hard. Just keep your eye on the goal, okay?"

"Don't worry about that! Love you, Mom."

"I love you, too, sweetie. Good luck on the exam."

"Bye."

She pressed the Disconnect button and stood up, waiting

for the dial tone so that she could enter her ex-husband's number. But before she could punch the first digit, the telephone rang in her hand.

"Darling, it's Catherine." Cici closed her eyes at the sound of the familiar sultry voice, and was glad the other woman couldn't see through the telephone. "I just wondered if I could ask a teensy-weensy tiny favor."

Cici replied, as pleasantly as she possibly could, "Of course, Catherine. What is it?"

"We would just love to include a little information about the site with our change-of-venue cards, wouldn't that be darling? Nothing elaborate, you understand, just a paragraph or two about the history of the place, a description of the facilities, directions, of course, a list of nearby hotels and restaurants, that sort of thing."

Cici drew a breath to reply but Catherine went on. "And of course we'll need some pictures of the house and the garden, particularly of that lovely mountain view—without the tree branch, of course—a front view of the house from the drive, and, oh, I'd love a picture taken from the entry hall, looking up at the staircase, wouldn't that be marvelous? Or maybe a shot of the living room, and the stained glass window. Oh, what the heck, just send me both and I'll decide when I see them."

Cici mounted the front steps and crossed the cool, shady foyer. Ida Mae had used lemon oil on the banister and the citrusy aroma lingered. Her voice echoed a little in the high-ceilinged room, but she tried to keep her tone light. "With all of that, we could have a brochure."

"You have brochures? Well, that certainly makes it easier!"

"No," Cici corrected quickly, "no, we don't have a brochure. We're not a business, we're just a house."

"Well, now I'm confused. I thought—"

"What I mean to say," Cici explained patiently, as she reached the office, "is that all of this will take some time to put together. The photographs, the descriptions . . ."

"Oh, that's all right, dear. As long as you can e-mail it all to me tonight, the printer says he can have something ready to go out with the cards tomorrow."

Cici felt a small needle of desperation prick her skull as she sank into the desk chair and picked up a pen. "Don't you think it would be better to send out the information about the site in a separate packet? Maybe after you receive the RSVPs?"

"Well, I don't know." Catherine sounded just uncertain enough to give Cici the advantage.

"I think that's the way it's usually done with a destination wedding," Cici said confidently, making it up as she went along. "You give the destination address—Ladybug Farm, Blue Valley, Virginia—on the card, and in smaller print, after the RSVP, you add a line that says, 'further information to follow.' You should check with your wedding planner for the exact wording."

"Well, I don't know." However, Cici could tell that Catherine was taking notes. "We're on such a terribly short deadline. Two mailings. That seems a bit unorthodox to me."

"Well, this is an informal wedding."

"A *destination* wedding," added Catherine thoughtfully. "Why yes, I suppose it is, isn't it?" She became decisive. "I think you may be right. I'll mention it to Traci, and if you could just have all the information ready for me to pick up this weekend when I'm out there, that will be soon enough."

"Um, that's three days."

"That's not a problem, is it?"

"No. Of course not." Cici was doodling a long-haired female stick figure on the notepad, with spears sticking out of it at all angles.

"And we can finalize whatever little details we need to take care of then, too."

"Sure. That will be fine."

"Wonderful! So I'll see you then. And when you make the list of hotels, do include all price ranges, will you? And see what you can find out about group rates. Thank you, darling! Bye-bye."

"I'm not a travel agent," Cici muttered when the line was dead.

Cici's ex-husband, Richard, was an entertainment lawyer in Los Angeles who made his living catering to the whims of the rich and famous. Getting through to him at his office was never an easy task, and Cici was not in a very good mood by the time she managed it. Richard, as usual, did not waste charm on her.

"Do you know what would make you happy?" he demanded, after giving less than an adequate opportunity to state her case. "I've finally figured it out, after all these years. What would make you happy is if Lori could have been hatched, like a turtle, and a father didn't have to be involved at all."

Cici said, "For God's sake, Richard, I'm not asking you to abdicate your parental responsibilities, I'm just asking you to use them with a little more *discretion*."

Richard's voice sounded as though it were traveling the three thousand miles across country through a rock-lined tunnel to reach her. "Look, babe, I don't know what you want from me. You won the war, okay? Lori is in Virginia, I'm in L.A. And now you want to bust my chops over a stupid webcam?" Then his tone changed. "Make these changes and print me out three copies, will you, sweetheart? And get MGM on the phone."

Cici blinked. "What? What are you talking about, webcam? Am I on speaker? Will you for heaven's sake *focus*? This is our daughter we're talking about! And take me off speaker!"

A click, a sigh, a decided improvement in the sound quality. "Okay, okay, but make it quick, will you? I've got a meeting."

Cici closed her eyes deliberately but didn't even bother trying to count to ten. By the time she reached three, he would have assumed a bad connection and hung up. "Listen to me," she said, very distinctly. "I want you to stop—and I mean right now—encouraging Lori with this trip to Italy thing."

"What are you talking about? It's an internship. It's part of her education. Besides, I promised her a summer in Italy long before she transferred to the boonies. I'm just following through."

"Exactly!" Cici pounced. "There was a man involved then, too, if you recall—a certain professor twice her age? I'm almost certain she's developed a thing for some boy over there and that's what this whole sudden passion for Italy is about. As far as the internship—it's an internship she hasn't even gotten yet, and even if she does get it ... Come on, Richard! A twenty-one-year-old girl in an Italian castle for three months? What kind of education do you really think she's going to get? So just stop making it easy for her, okay?"

There was a beat, just a beat, of silence. Then Richard said, in a voice heavy with disgust, "Will you just stop trying to control everyone for once, Ci? Can you do that, do you think? Let your daughter be a kid, let the university decide its curriculum, and let me get back to work. Can you just do that, Ci? Huh? Okay? Thank you."

And before Cici could draw her next breath, she was listening to a dial tone.

She slammed the telephone down into its cradle on the wall, and it made a satisfying *clack* in the empty stone kitchen. But not quite satisfying enough. She lifted the receiver again, and slammed it down again. And again. And again.

She did not quite get the receiver out of the cradle for the fifth slam when the telephone rang again.

It was Catherine, and given the last telephone conversation she had had, Cici was almost glad to talk to her.

~

"So, that's how *my* day went," Cici said glumly, stretching out her legs and slumping low in the rocking chair. "Another crappy day in paradise."

"Whatever you do," said Lindsay, "don't let her go to Italy. Italian men think that seducing a woman is just an elaborate way to pay her a compliment. And they love to pay compliments—to pretty much every woman they see."

"Peanut soup! What's more Virginian than peanut soup!" Bridget sat in her own rocking chair with one foot tucked beneath her, an open cookbook and legal pad on her lap, a glass of white wine balanced precariously on the arm of the chair as she scribbled notes on the pad. She did not notice the odd looks Cici and Lindsay gave her. She didn't, in fact, even glance up from the cookbook.

Cici said to Lindsay, "It sounds as though you speak from experience."

Lindsay shrugged. "Everyone knows about Italian men. Although . . ." And she smiled, secretly, as she lifted her glass to her lips. "An argument definitely could be made that a girl hasn't really lived until she's been loved by an Italian man."

"Terrific," Cici said. "Fine. I don't even want to know. And Lori can go to Italy after she graduates. I just don't think I can stand another interruption in her education. At this rate, she's going to be thirty before she gets her bachelor's degree."

"Thirty," replied Lindsay thoughtfully, "is a long time to wait for an Italian man."

Cici regarded her sourly for a moment, then spoke to Bridget. "How are you going to serve peanut soup at a buffet?"

"Chilled," she replied without looking up, "sprinkled with crushed peanuts, served with a single hand-rolled cheese straw, in martini glasses. Very signature, local, farmhouse chic."

Cici nodded approvingly. "It sounds to me as though you're going to be able to write your own cookbook before this thing is over. Which is a good thing, by the way. You're going to need something to do when the North-Deres fire us."

That made Bridget look up. Both Lindsay and Bridget stared at Cici. "They're going to fire us?" Lindsay asked.

Cici nodded, rocking. "I've got it figured out. This is what people like them do. They torture the help until they get bored, and then they fire them. Why? Because they can. It's all a big game to them."

Bridget frowned. "Well, I hope not. I think I've finally come up with a shrimpless, seasonal, local, quasi-Mediterranean–Virginian menu that just might work."

"And we've already cashed the check," Lindsay added, looking worried.

Cici just smiled. "Not a problem," she replied. "In the middle of all that faxing back and forth to get the perfect contract, I was able to add one little word in front of 'deposit': nonrefundable."

Lindsay grinned. "Good job."

After a moment, Bridget admitted reluctantly, "This is a little harder than I thought it would be. But you know, it takes a lot of hard work to make dreams come true."

"And a lot of energy to get married," Lindsay added.

"I never understood that," Cici said.

"Marriage?"

"Well, that, too. But mostly the whole wedding thing. The thousands upon thousands of dollars and hundreds of hours—the dress, the church, the flowers, the candles, the reception hall, the cake, the band, the banquet, the party favors, the place cards, the little chocolates with the bride and groom's initials monogrammed on them . . . and for what? So two people who are already sleeping together can do it legally." Cici shook her head. "It boggles the mind."

"Well, not just sleep together," Lindsay pointed out. "But have babies and a mortgage."

"And a divorce," Cici said.

"I think it's sweet." Bridget's tone was not so much serene as determined. "Hopeful."

Lindsay said flatly, "Ha."

Cici raised her glass to that.

Bridget closed the cookbook, rocked back, and rescued her glass just before it slid off the arm of the chair. "I had another note from my secret admirer," she said.

The other two looked at her with interest. "What does he say?" Lindsay wanted to know.

And Cici teased, "Does he tell you how cute you are?"

Bridget made a wry face. "Mostly he just wants recipes."

"Typical man."

"No," corrected Lindsay. "A typical man would want you to cook them for him."

Bridget rocked thoughtfully. "Do you ever think about getting married again?"

Cici laughed. "Who, me? Are you kidding?"

"I used to," Lindsay said. "But the older I get, the more . . ." She searched for the right word. "Pointless it seems." She glanced at Bridget. "How about you?"

Bridget smiled. "I adored Jim, and we had a wonderful marriage. I wouldn't trade those years for anything. But doing it again? I honestly can't imagine."

"The truth is," observed Cici, "if men ever figured out how superfluous they are, I think the human race would be in a lot of trouble."

"Well," Lindsay said, "*superfluous* might be a little strong. I mean, they're really good at opening jars."

"And killing bugs," added Bridget.

"And working a jackhammer," Cici said, thoughtfully, and the three of them chuckled.

"God, how did we get so cynical?" Cici sighed. "When did the wedding become the best part of a marriage?"

"If this wedding is the best part of Traci's marriage," said Bridget somberly, "I already feel sorry for the groom."

"I think," Lindsay said thoughtfully, after a time, "being married is all about being in balance. I know men are from Mars, and all that, and if you sit down and make a list of what they're good for, the list is pretty short . . ."

"Painfully short," said Cici.

"Excruciatingly short, for some," Bridget clarified, trying to look serious, and they all burst into giggles. Lindsay threw part of a cookie at her and Bridget ducked.

"I was trying to make a point," Lindsay declared archly, when they had sobered somewhat.

"I actually agree with you," Cici said, and the other two looked at her in surprise. "The truth is, even if he's perfectly useless there's something about having a man around that makes you feel safe. As though, whatever happens, someone's got your back. That's his job. And when someone's got your back, you're a lot more likely to put yourself out there, to reach higher, to accomplish more. That's why people get married. Because they're more together than they could be apart."

"I always feel as though you girls have got my back," Bridget said softly.

Lindsay nodded. "Me, too."

And Cici said, smiling, "Yeah."

For a time there was no sound but the muffled creak of

rockers, and the occasional trill of a cricket. Inside the house, evening settled its gentle yellow glow. Outside, the day was reluctant to depart.

Cici said, "Lori won't be home this weekend. So it looks like you're stuck with Lindsay and me as your sous chefs."

"Well, that's better than nothing I suppose," Bridget replied, and she glanced around uneasily before adding, "Now all we have to do is find a way to get Ida Mae out of the kitchen. Frankly, these days she's more of a hindrance than a help."

"I know what you mean," Lindsay agreed, sotto voce. "I have to go behind her and clean what she's already cleaned."

"I was up at four thirty this morning doing laundry." Cici leaned forward to make herself heard, speaking very softly. "After she ruined two pairs of jeans and a sweater with bleach last week, I have to stay ahead of her."

They were quiet for a time. Then Bridget said, "We're just spoiled, you know. Before Ida Mae came we took care of the house and the cooking by ourselves. We don't have any reason to complain now."

"I know," Cici agreed. "The problem is that I've gotten used to her in the background, making meals, doing the dishes, running the vacuum, doing the laundry. We all have. And all the time I used to spend doing those things I'm now spending building trellises for the vineyard, or painting the house, or—"

"Teaching art classes," Lindsay volunteered.

"Or making wine jams," Bridget added.

They were thoughtful for a moment. "We really have grown to depend on her," Bridget said, her voice sad. "It's hard to think of her . . . you know. Going downhill."

"There's got to be some way we can persuade her to take it easy."

Both Cici and Bridget shook their heads at Lindsay's suggestion.

"It's not like we haven't tried that before."

"She practically snapped my head off for trying to help her water a plant this afternoon," Bridget recalled.

"There's really only one thing we can do," Cici said.

"Keep doing her job," Lindsay agreed.

"And keep her from finding out," added Bridget.

They rocked in silence for a while. The color faded from the sky, leaving a bleached blue gray canvas against which mountain silhouettes were painted, and in one corner, the accent of a single star. The night air smelled of green things and spring earth.

Lindsay said, "We'll have to get the grass mowed by Thursday to give all the bugs a chance to go away before the crowd gets here Saturday."

Bridget said, "Noah only works till three on Thursdays. He could do it in a couple of hours."

Cici gazed into her glass. "So, I was at the hardware store today, talking to Jonesie. I was teasing him, you know, about keeping Noah such long hours working." She looked up at the other two. "He said Noah didn't work at all last weekend."

At first there was no reaction. Then Lindsay frowned. "But Noah was gone from dawn to dusk Saturday. He said he was helping Jonesie with a shipment." She glanced uncomfortably toward the house, where a faint square of light filtered from Noah's window. "I wonder why he would tell us he's working when he's not."

"He's seemed a little moody lately, have you noticed?" Bridget sounded worried.

Cici gave a heavy sigh and a shake of her head. "Has he? God, I've been so caught up in this wedding thing I haven't noticed."

"Me either," Lindsay admitted. "How do people do it? Have jobs, run a household, *and* be good parents?"

"I guess there's a reason that nature arranges for you to have children when you're young," Bridget said.

"He's such a good kid most of the time." Cici frowned. "I hate to think we're the kind of people who only notice when something goes wrong."

"I don't know about you," Lindsay said, "but it's all I can do to notice when things go right."

"There's good news," Bridget said after a time, although she didn't sound very excited about it. "Four more orders for gift baskets—two medium and two small." She stood. "Any volunteers to help put them together? I'll need some help if I'm going to get them to the post office in time for tomorrow's mail."

"I'm in," Lindsay said, getting to her feet.

Cici pushed up wearily. "Remind me again why we wanted to do this?"

But no one had an answer.

October 4, 2006

Happy birthday! I've been wishing all day that I could tell you that. I baked a chocolate cake, because I remembered it was your favorite. But there was no one to eat it with. Still, just knowing you're in the world makes me glad I was born, too. So happy, happy birthday.

7

Love Stories

On Wednesday afternoons from two to four o'clock, Lindsay taught an art class in the long, stone-floored, whitewashed building that had once been a dairy barn. She put up flyers in the bank, at the post office and library, and at Family Hardware, where they carried the selection of paints and canvases she recommended. Her first class consisted of three people who had never held a paintbrush before. Lindsay launched into the basics of complementary and tertiary colors, perspective, composition, primary, secondary, and reflective light sources, and the following week not a single student returned.

She was disconsolate until Cici pointed out that all of her students were well over the age of fifty, and that adults simply did not have the time or the patience to learn theory. They wanted results. It turned out she was right. Bridget volunteered Lindsay to do a watercolor demonstration at the next garden club meeting, and she signed up six new students on the spot. They did not want to be artists. They just wanted to paint something.

And so, with her expectations lowered, Lindsay found the classes to be one of the most enjoyable things she had ever done. Attendance varied from week to week, mostly house-wives and retirees. They did landscapes and florals and still lifes, with an occasional cute bunny, deer, or raccoon to keep things interesting. For the more complicated compositions, Lindsay sketched the figures on the canvases before the students arrived, and she often mixed their colors for them. It didn't matter. Most people came to art class for the social-ization, anyway, for the sense of accomplishment and the pleasure of having something to show for their time. They finished a painting in one or two classes, and everyone went home happy.

Today each of her four students was finishing up a nine-by-twelve oil painting of an old-fashioned red water pump on a garden path with a barn roof in the distance. Lindsay had taken her inspiration from a photograph she'd seen in *Country* magazine, and had carefully sketched the pump and the barn roof onto each primed canvas the night before. She had suspected—correctly—that the class would not have the attention span for anything more complex today.

The class consisted of three women and one man. The women, who all rode to class together, used art class as their once-a-week catch-up time. This week they wanted to talk about the magazine article, and about their memories of the old days of Blackwell Farms, and about what fun it was to have their corner of the world featured in a real magazine.

Susan had sent a copy of the article to her daughter in Minneapolis, with a note—*This is where I take art classes!* Miriam remembered when the very building in which they were painting used to have cows in it.

"There was a little store right up front, there," she said, "where you could buy fresh milk every morning if you got here between six and eight. It was still warm from the cow sometimes! Of course," she remembered, "then the government got all involved with that pasteurizing nonsense and nobody could buy raw milk anymore. You mark my word, that's why all the schoolchildren have allergies these days— no fresh milk."

Lindsay concentrated on her lesson. "Now, everyone, take your fan brush, dip it in your painting medium and a little bit of titanium white, and scumble it into your blue sky for clouds. Just like this." She demonstrated on her own canvas. "Be careful not to get your brush too wet, or your clouds will be raining."

She smiled as she turned to examine everyone's work. "Maybe a little less paint, Pauline," she suggested, moving around the table where the four easels were set up. "Very nice, Susan. Frank..." She paused behind the chair of her only male student, a white-haired man with a neatly trimmed beard who came to class each week in the gray uniform of a garage worker. She had learned that he had owned and operated Highway Car Care for forty-five years before retiring. He had the most delicate touch with a brush she had ever seen in an untrained artist. "That's just wonderful. May I?"

Frank seemed a little shy—as well he might be, stuck in the middle of a group of chattering women—so Lindsay liked to take every opportunity to highlight his work and make him feel welcome. Besides, as anyone could clearly see, he had a natural gift for painting.

Lindsay took his painting and displayed it on her easel at the front of the room. "Look how he has the shadows running parallel across the path," she said, pointing with the handle of her paintbrush. "And the clouds seem to melt into the sky, just as they should. He picked up a little alizarin here to give weight to the bottom of the clouds. Very nice. Oh, and look." She smiled as she pointed out the final detail. "There's even a little bird here, flying into the barn loft. I like that. Let me show you how to do that."

She showed the ladies how to double-load a fine-tipped brush and let them practice on a piece of canvas board for a minute. "You see, it's really nothing but a lopsided *W*," she said. "There you go. Not too much weight on the brush."

She left the ladies to practice making *W*-shaped birds, and returned Frank's canvas to him. "You might want to add a bit more shadow underneath the barn eaves," she suggested, "to give it depth."

He picked up his brush and dipped it in dark paint. "It's not just a bird," he said.

Because Frank hardly ever volunteered information, Lindsay was surprised—and interested. So were the other ladies, who looked up from their work to listen. "Oh?" she said, wanting to encourage him.

With infinite care, millimeter by millimeter, Frank traced a dark line beneath the roofline of his barn. "I met my wife in 1962," he said. "She was a singer—I mean a real one, traveled all around. She was even on the road with Patsy Cline for a while."

Lindsay sat on the edge of the table, fascinated. "Really? I didn't know that."

"No reason you should." Frank continued his meticulous work on the barn roof. "She was real talented, my wife. Who knows what she might have been if she hadn't met me?"

Frank took a sable brush and gently, ever so gently, blended the line he had drawn into a shadow. "There ain't much call for singers in a little place like this, outside of church and all, and I worried that she'd be sorry to trade the life she'd had for raising a family. She never let on to me if she did, and over the years I just kind of let it go by."

He wiped his brush with a paper towel, dipped it in turpentine, and wiped it again, carefully cleaning each bristle. "She was always doing something with her hands, beautiful things, you know, embroidery and rug hooking and crochet. Her quilts won prizes at every county fair. She made all the kids' clothes, and hers and mine, too, long after we could afford to buy them off the rack. Now and again one of the town women would come up to her and say wouldn't she make a dress for them and she'd say no, her sewing was just for her pleasure.

"Well, it shames me to say it, but as time went on, I started to wish maybe she'd spent a little less time making pretty work with a needle and a little more time with me, you know, doing the things I liked to do. I mean, I could see the value in making clothes, but all those little do-dads and framed pieces and fancy pillow slips and whatnot, I just didn't have much use for them, to tell you the truth. So by and by, I just up and asked her why she spent so much time on that foolishness, anyhow, and you know what she said to me? She said, 'Well, now, Frank, there's all kinds of art. Singing is one kind of art, and painting is another kind, and that carpentry you like to do so much, that's another. I guess I'm never going to be a famous singer like Patsy Cline,' she says to me, 'but sewing is how I keep my voice alive.'"

Not a paintbrush moved in the room. Frank inspected the brush he had just cleaned, found it satisfactory, and carefully placed it in the felt liner of his wooden paintbox.

"After she passed," he went on, "I spent a lot of time watching the TV, especially late at night, you know, when a body has trouble sleeping. There was this painter on one time, you probably know him. The one that does all those stone cottages with yellow lights?"

"Thomas Kinkade?" Lindsay supplied.

"That's the one. I heard him say he puts his wife's initial into every painting, like a secret code only she would know about. And I thought that was nice. And I thought about all the different kinds of art, and about then is when I decided I'd learn how to paint. So now I put Wilma's initial in everything I paint—sometimes in a tree trunk, or a blade of grass, or a shadow on the road—as kind of a secret code between her and me. To keep her voice alive."

"That's beautiful, Frank," Lindsay said softly. She touched his shoulder, smiled, and stood up.

When the class was brought to a close, Lindsay instructed everyone to sign his or her work, and supervised the cleanup. Frank meticulously cleaned each brush until no trace of pigment remained, just as he always did, rubbed down his wooden palette with linseed oil, just as he always did, and said, "A man is only as good as his tools," just as he always did. He did not say another word about birds or ladies.

"Still waters run deep," Miriam murmured to her at the door, watching Frank get into his pickup truck and crank the engine. "Whoever knew old Frank had anything to say?"

"We all have something to say," Lindsay replied. She smiled at the other woman. "That's why we're here, isn't it?"

She was straightening up the tables and putting away the supplies when she heard a light rapping against the frame of the open door. She turned and smiled to see Dominic standing there. "Hi, Dominic. What's up?"

"I hope I'm not bothering you. I couldn't tell if you had any students or not."

"They just left. Come on in."

He looked down at his boots. "I don't want to get the place dirty."

Lindsay laughed. "Take a look around. You can't do much more damage than I have already."

Dominic was a nice-looking man with golden tan skin and sun-weathered gray eyes. His salt-and-pepper hair was worn long, grazing his collar, his hairline just high enough to make his face interesting. He was only an inch or so taller than Lindsay, and slightly built, but when he rolled up his sleeves, as today, the ropy muscles of his arms told a story about a life of physical labor.

"I stopped by the house," he said, "but it looked like they were pretty busy up there."

Lindsay shrugged. "We're pretty busy everywhere." And she explained, "We're having a wedding here."

"Oh?" He looked surprised and, oddly, a little anxious. "One of you ladies getting married?"

Again Lindsay chuckled, dumping her paintbrushes into a cup of mineral spirits in the utility sink. "Hardly. We're thinking about going into the wedding business, and this is our first one."

He shook his head in slow admiration. "You ladies sure do keep yourselves busy."

"That's one way of putting it."

He gazed around the room, smiling at the four identical paintings of red water pumps—some more identical than others—but mostly interested in the larger canvases that were drying on the long walls. Noah's paintings hung intermixed with Lindsay's—studies of hands, which were difficult for any artist and which he clearly had not yet quite mastered, some wild impressionistic renderings of animal eyes in the dark, some architectural studies, and a whole series of monarch butterfly wings. Dominic studied them for a time.

"Are these Noah's?" Lindsay nodded. "He's a talented kid." He turned. "Did I hear someone say that his grandmother was Emmy Hodge? I knew her, you know." And he gave a slightly self-deprecating grin. "Had a huge crush on her when I was Noah's age, the whole glamorous older woman thing and all. She was only here for a summer, but that was long enough to set me to dreaming about going to Paris and becoming a famous artist so that she would fall madly in love with me."

Lindsay gave a wide, delighted smile. "Is that right?"

"Of course, by the next summer I was in love with Kathy

Willis and wouldn't have recognized Emmy Hodge on the street. Good thing, too, because I still can't paint the side of a barn."

Lindsay chuckled again. "Me either, to tell the truth. Which is why I don't teach barn-painting."

"I'm not clear how Noah ended up here. Did one of you know his folks?"

"Actually, no." Lindsay swished each brush back and forth in the mineral spirits, cleaned off the excess liquid with a paper towel, and set the brush, bristle side up, in a stand to dry. "We thought his parents were dead—so did he. His mother left him to be raised by his grandmother, and when she died his father took him and moved out of state, which is how she lost track of him. I had actually looked into adopting him last year, and that's how his mother finally found out where he was. Apparently she'd had a pretty rough time of it during the early years, but she's back on track now, working as a counselor for troubled teens in Richmond. The tragedy is that not long before she found Noah, she discovered she has terminal cancer. When she realized how well Noah was doing with us, she decided it wouldn't be fair to burden him with her last few months of life. She asked us, actually, not to even tell Noah she was alive, but Ida Mae knew his grandmother, too." She gave a small, resigned smile.

"But that's a good thing, isn't it? At least he got a chance to know his mother before she died."

Lindsay shook her head sadly. "She made us promise not to tell him she was sick. And once he found out she was alive . . . he didn't want to see her. We've done everything we could to encourage him, without breaking our word. And she still thinks the kindest thing she can do is to stay away from him. So our hands are really tied."

He shook his head sadly. "That's a difficult situation. I have to admire you all for taking it on."

She finished with the brushes and turned, wiping her hands. "He's one of the family," she replied simply.

She liked the way he smiled at her, and when he turned back to look at the paintings she was flattered, and a little nervous, to notice that it was her work he seemed to focus on. And he studied the canvases as though he were in a museum.

"This is great," he said, without turning from his appraisal of a large oil painting of a cardinal in the snow. "The way the bird takes up the whole canvas, and the trees are so small in the distance . . . it makes you think about perspective, doesn't it?"

Lindsay was pleased. "That's exactly what it's supposed to do! Well, that, and make you smile."

He turned, smiling. "It does that, too."

Lindsay began gathering up the plastic trash bags that were attached to each easel. Because the paint and turpentine-soaked paper towels that the students used in every class were highly odiferous—not to mention flammable—she knotted each bag before stuffing it into the larger one she carried. Dominic fell easily into step beside her, knotting and handing her the bags from each easel.

"These aren't bad," he said. "You must be a good teacher."

"You need to take a class," she invited him. "As it happens, I have an opening or two."

"I don't know about that. I've got a few talents, but, like I said, painting is not one of them."

She smiled. "You might be surprised. The things we do in class are more like paint by number than fine art, and, frankly, talent is far down the list of course requirements."

"It must be hard for you," he said, with unexpected perception, "to go from those"—he nodded to the painting of the cardinal—"to paint by number."

She chuckled and took her trash bag to the door. "Some people would say there's not that much difference."

"I wouldn't be one of them."

"That's nice of you to say." She smiled at him for a moment, then looked away, a little embarrassed.

She took an oversized bottle of baby oil from a shelf over the sink and poured a measure into her paint-smeared hands. "It breaks down the pigment," she explained to Dominic as she worked the oil into her hands, "and it's a lot easier on skin than mineral spirits. Smells better, too."

He smiled at her. "I'll have to remember that." Then, "What's first on the list?"

"Of what?"

"Class requirements."

Lindsay wiped her hands with a paper towel, cleaning the paint from around her nails as she thought about that. "Oh, I don't know. A willingness to try, I suppose. A sense of fun. Yes," she decided, "that's it. The people who come to my class don't want to be artists," she explained. "They already *are* whatever it is they want to be. For them, painting is a way to pass the time, to learn something new, and, maybe, to explore a different kind of self-expression. I promise them they'll go home with a painting and a sense of pride in what they've done, and all I ask from them is that they have fun."

"Well, in that case," he said, with a small considering tilt of his head, "maybe I will sign up."

Lindsay smiled and tossed the paper towel into the trash bag. "Well, you're welcome any time—although exactly when you have time to do anything other than eat and sleep I can't imagine. Between your full-time job and working over here for free every spare minute you have, when do you have time for a life?"

He gestured easily toward the vineyard beyond the open door. "This isn't work. This is like coming home. This *is* my life."

A breeze from the open door tugged a strand of hair across Lindsay's cheek and she brushed it away with the back of her hand. "That's right. I forget sometimes that you probably know more about this place than we do. I'd love to hear more about what it was like when you were a boy here."

He smiled. "I'd love to tell you."

And then he startled her by stepping close to her, and lifting his thumb to her cheek, wiping it gently. Surprise must have flared in her eyes, because he looked embarrassed as he explained with a small gesture, "You had a little paint . . ."

"Oh." Lindsay touched her cheek, and laughed. "Can't imagine how that happened." She turned to take a paper towel from the work counter and wiped her hands, then, for good measure, her face again. "We should have you over one night for dinner. I know everyone would love to hear your stories." And then she added, with a cautionary lift of her finger. "After the wedding, of course."

He smiled. "After the wedding," he assured her. He

hesitated, and then seemed to come to some decision. "Actually," he began, "I was thinking—"

"Lindsay, are you there?"

Cici caught the doorframe with her hand as she swung by. The look of disappointment on Dominic's face was gone in an instant, and his customary easy smile was back in place as he turned to greet Cici.

"Oh, hi, Dominic," Cici said. "I didn't know you were here."

"I stopped at the back door but you were on the phone," he said. "I just wanted to tell you the ground is dry enough to work so we should probably get the vines fertilized by the weekend."

"Not this weekend!" Cici and Lindsay said together, and Cici explained, "We've got some people coming out Saturday."

"The wedding thing," Lindsay added, tossing the paper towel into the trash.

He scratched his head thoughtfully. "We shouldn't put it off much longer. If you don't mind working Sunday, I could come out after church and help you out."

"That would be terrific," Lindsay said gratefully.

"Thanks, Dominic," Cici added. "And plan to stay for supper, okay?"

Dominic glanced at Lindsay. "That would be real nice. Thank you."

He lifted a friendly hand to Cici, and then paused to nod to Lindsay before resuming his stride toward his pickup.

Cici watched him go with an appreciative smile. "Now there," she declared, "is one of the good ones."

"No doubt about it," Lindsay agreed, but her expression was a little distracted. "Do you think he . . . ?"

She broke off, and Cici turned to her curiously. "What?"

Lindsay gave an impatient shake of her head. "Nothing. I probably imagined it, that's all. What do you need?"

"Oh." Cici straightened up, the customary harried and unhappy expression of the past week returning to her face. "Photographs," she said. "You know, for Catherine's brochure?"

Lindsay rolled her eyes.

"Now she's decided to hire a graphic designer, and she wants me to e-mail her pictures of the house and garden, along with a list of nearby hotels with prices and directions . . ."

Lindsay choked on a laugh. *"Hotels?"* she repeated. "Plural? And nearby?"

Cici shrugged, even as she tried not to grin. "I said I'd do my best," she said. "Anyway, she wants us to send the photos, the hotel info, and a brief history and description of the house and gardens . . ."

Lindsay gave a long-suffering sigh and hoisted the trash bag. "I don't suppose she gave you any idea of what, exactly, she wanted photographed."

"As a matter of fact I have a list." Cici dug into her back pocket.

And that was when they heard Bridget scream.

❧

What the Misses North-Dere did not understand was that Ladybug Farm was a working farm, with at least a hundred tasks that demanded the attention of its proprietresses every day. Those tasks were far more urgent than whether or not sugared almonds or monogrammed chocolates were served with the coffee. And furthermore, with every e-mail, every phone call, and every menu change, the "heavy hors d'oeuvres" that were initially discussed were morphing into something very closely resembling a sit-down dinner. Who *cared* what kind of candy was served with the coffee when all you were offering was hors d'oeuvres?

Those were the kind of fuming thoughts that were occupying Bridget's mind as she came down the back steps with a laundry basket filled with damp sheets and tablecloths to be hung on the line. One of the few points on which she had finally come to agree with Ida Mae was that the sun was far superior to electricity when it came to drying and freshening whites, and laundry was only one of those hundreds of things that, right now, were more important to Bridget than the menu crisis at someone else's wedding.

She eased the screen door closed with her hip, came down the brick steps with the plastic basket of laundry balanced before her, and noticed in dismay that something had made a shambles of the pretty little pansy bed at the bottom of the steps. Then she noticed the rest.

The white sheets and lace tablecloths that she had hung earlier were strewn on the ground or hanging by one pin on the line. Dirty paw prints and grass stains smeared the fabric, and one of the tablecloths was torn right down the middle. For a moment she was too shocked to do anything but stare, but her breath came back to her in a rush and she exclaimed furiously, "Rebel! You bad dog! You bad, bad dog!"

Rebel was, of course, nowhere to be seen.

She marched over to the scene of the disaster, plopped the basket of clean laundry onto the ground, and started snatching up the ruined linens.

It was then that she noticed that the dirty smears on the fabric weren't exactly paw prints. They were more like... hoofprints. Bambi? She started to straighten up, squinting in the sun, looking around for the deer, and then she felt something brush the back of her knees. She whirled around, full of invectives for the deer, and found herself staring, not into a pair of big brown eyes as she had expected, but into a pair of narrow yellow ones. She gasped and stumbled backward. The creature lunged at her. That was when she screamed.

Lindsay and Cici arrived just as Bridget, who had tripped over the laundry basket, was scrambling to her feet. Ida Mae came stiffly down the steps, flapping a towel and shouting. A brown and white goat stood a few feet away, bleating in confusion.

"Good heavens!" exclaimed Lindsay, staring. "Where did that come from?"

Cici helped Bridget to her feet. "Are you okay?"

"Nasty damn thing," Ida Mae swore, snapping the towel in the direction of the goat. "Look what it did to my laundry! Get on out of here! Shoo! Shoo!"

"Wait!" Bridget cried as the goat bounded a few feet away. "You're scaring him!"

"That's what I mean to do," returned Ida Mae, advancing menacingly on the goat. "Shoo! Get!"

"How did a goat get all the way out here?" Lindsay said. "I mean, they don't just wander around in the wild, do they?"

Cici said, "Look, it's got a rope around its neck."

Bridget held out a staying arm to Ida Mae. "Ida Mae, stop it. Just hold on for a minute." She took a couple of cautious steps toward the goat, who eyed her warily but didn't move. "Maybe he's got some kind of identification."

Ida Mae gave a snort of disdain, but she stopped waving the towel. "Goats don't wear collars."

Lindsay insisted, "He's got to belong to somebody."

"She," Ida Mae said shortly. "Ain't you got eyes? That's a milking goat."

Bridget, holding out her hand invitingly, murmured, "Nice goat. Good goat, don't be afraid, I won't hurt you. Good fellow, I mean girl ..."

The goat stayed its ground uneasily, watching her with wary yellow eyes. Bridget got within a hand's reach of the animal, and from out of nowhere Rebel lunged from his border collie crouch, lightning fast and without a sound. He charged the goat, which leapt into the air as though on springs, landed in a panicked run, and charged toward the house. Bridget screamed, "Rebel, no!" Ida Mae threw the towel at the goat, Cici ran to put herself between the older woman and the terrified goat, and Lindsay lunged to catch the rope that dangled from the animal's neck. But it was Rebel who, with a well-placed nip to the goat's back leg, turned it away from the house and out into the yard.

Bridget cried again, "Rebel!"

The dog, as usual, ignored her. Herding the goat as he would a sheep, cutting and turning, lunging and crouching, he pushed the terrified creature in an erratic pattern across the yard, heading toward the edge of the woods. Bridget shouted and chased after him.

Lindsay looked at Cici, "What is she *doing*?"

"Gone plumb crazy is what," Ida Mae replied. She raised her voice. "Let that critter go! Get it on out of here!"

Bridget cut to the east of Rebel, shouting and waving her arms at him. The goat swung suddenly toward her and she dodged out of the way just in time.

"She's going to get trampled," Cici worried, and ran after them.

Chickens squawked and feathers flew as Rebel chased the goat past the chicken yard, and Bridget, with big scooping motions of her arms, managed to turn it toward the barn. Cici raced ahead and swung open the barnyard gate. Rebel cut to the right, and then to the left, and the goat, bleating in agitation, trotted right through the gate. Cici slammed the gate shut and latched it, then leaned against it, breathing hard, as Bridget caught up to her.

"Thanks," Bridget gasped. Then to Rebel, who was sniffing curiously through the wire fence, "Good work. Good dog."

Cici stared at her. "Good dog? Are you kidding me?"

Bridget bent over with her hands on her knees, catching her breath.

Lindsay trotted up. "Did you catch him? Where is he?"

Bridget managed, "Her." She gestured to the barnyard.

Lindsay's gaze followed her hand. "What are you going to do with it?" she asked, ever practical.

Cici said, "Good question."

The three of them turned to watch the goat, which, having apparently forgotten the recent trauma, explored its new surroundings at a leisurely pace, occasionally plucking up a mouthful of scrubby grass. Rebel, bored with prey he could not reach and always quick to show his disdain for humans, streaked off in search of other adventures.

Bridget said, "It's kind of cute, isn't it?"

Lindsay said firmly, "Someone is missing a goat. I'll call the radio station."

"And the newspaper," Cici added.

Bridget said, "I'll get her some hay."

"What if no one claims it?" Lindsay worried, and Cici gave her a sharp warning look.

Bridget's expression glowed with delight. "Then we have a goat," she exclaimed, beaming. "A beautiful nanny goat!"

"You got yourselves a peck of trouble, that's what you got," Ida Mae declared, coming up behind them. "And you're gonna have some sour milk tonight, too, with all that running and jumping around. You better hope somebody claims it before milking time."

The three women stared at her. "Milk?" Cici said. "We have to milk it?"

Lindsay put both her hands in the air firmly. "Don't look at me."

"I am *not* milking a goat," Cici declared unequivocally. "I don't even like goats. Why are we talking about this? We're not keeping this goat!"

Bridget chewed her bottom lip. "Well, I suppose I could learn." She turned hopefully to Ida Mae. "Is it hard to milk a goat?"

Ida Mae threw up her hands and stalked away, muttering, "Worthless damn women . . ."

Bridget smiled and leaned on the fence, surveying the new resident. "A goat," she said. "Imagine that."

8

Rising to the Occasion

From "Ladybug Farm Charms," a blog by Bridget Tyndale

According to the American Dairy Goat Association, a dairy goat averages 3–4 quarts of milk per day during its ten months of lactation. More people drink goat's milk throughout the world than cow's milk and those who do should be much healthier. Goat's milk averages only 3.5% butterfat, and is much more easily digestible than cow's milk. Additionally, the natural homogenization process of goat's milk is much less likely to cause certain undesirable side effects, such as high cholesterol, that artificially processed cow's milk does in humans.

Goats thrive best when allowed to graze a half acre or more of pasture grasses and weeds. They are curious and naturally agile, and do not like to be confined. Strong fences are recommended for goat-keeping.

Apparently, someone overlooked that last bit of advice, because guess what wandered onto Ladybug Farm today? A nanny goat!

I've been browsing recipes all day and I'm amazed at how many great-sounding ways there are to use goat cheese. What are some of your favorites?

Of course, I have to learn to make goat cheese first.

Nannymom said:
Here's a <u>link</u> to one of my favorite recipes for Strawberry, Walnut & Goat Cheese Salad with Pomegranate Vinaigrette.

Bridget said:
That sounds wonderful! Thanks!

Corky said:
Be careful what you wish for!

Bridget said:
You're right! I DID say I wanted a goat!

Pam2Be said:
Goats make wonderful pets. My daughter-in-law just puts a diaper on hers and lets it wander around in the house like a dog.

Bridget said:
Oh, dear. I'm afraid my housemates would have a thing or two to say about that!

KTBird said:
There's a difference in taste between imported French chèvre and domestic. I make a wonderful tart using French chèvre, Swiss chard, and bacon. Make a piecrust with 2 tablespoons

chopped fresh rosemary worked in and line a 9-inch pie plate. Meantime, fry 6 slices of bacon; remove and crumble. Sauté 2 chopped scallions and one large bunch of Swiss chard (leaves only) until chard is wilted. Layer the chard mixture, crumbled bacon, and 8 ounces chèvre. End with crumbled bacon on top. Bake at 350 degrees for 30 minutes or until bubbly. Enjoy!

Bridget said:
Thank you, KTBird. That sounds fabulous. I wish we still had chard in our garden.

Illinoisgirl said:
We had goats growing up. They stink! And they eat everything in sight.

Bridget said:
Everything I've read says that nanny goats don't have any odor, and they're very particular about their diet. Does anyone else have more information?

SecretAdmirer said:
Hi, Bridget—
I'm glad you got the goat that you wanted. I love goat cheese, but it's not very practical for every day, is it? Sometimes the simple things are the best. Can you make macaroni and cheese with goat cheese?

Bridget said:
To tell the truth, I like simple things, too. Here's one of my favorite recipes for something simple—no goat cheese required!

Three-Cheese Macaroni

Prepare pasta according to package directions to measure two cups cooked. (Try using a mixture of pastas—angel hair, spinach noodle, penne—for different texture and taste.)

Melt 2 tablespoons butter in a 1-quart saucepan. Add ¼ cup flour and stir. Salt and pepper to taste, sprinkle with ¼ teaspoon nutmeg.

ADD:

1 cup milk

¼ cup shredded Asiago cheese

¼ cup sharp white Cheddar

¼ cup shredded Swiss cheese

Cook and stir over low heat until cheeses are melted and mixture starts to thicken. Remove from heat.

In a small buttered casserole dish layer half the pasta. Sprinkle with ¼ cup grated Cheddar. Pour half the cheese sauce over this. Top with remaining pasta, remaining cheese sauce, and a mixture of 2 cups Cheddar and ⅓ cup breadcrumbs. Dot with butter.

Bake at 350 degrees until bubbly and golden brown, approximately 20 minutes.

TO: Bridget@LadybugFarmLadies.net
FROM: LadiLori27@locomail.net

Aunt Bridget—

You REALLY don't have to answer every comment on your blog! The idea is to let other people write your content. Hey, congratulations on the goat! Can't wait to see it.

TO: LadiLori27@locomail.net
FROM: Bridget@LadybugFarmLadies.net

Well, it seems rude not to answer, although it does take an awful lot of time. When are you coming to see the goat? And us?

TO: Bridget@LadybugFarmLadies.net
FROM: LadiLori27@locomail.net

Hope to be home next weekend. I have a killer exam. Who's your Secret Admirer?

TO: LadiLori27@locomail.net
FROM: Bridget@LadybugFarmLadies.net

I have no idea. It's kind of fun to speculate though. Now get off the computer and start studying!

TO: Bridget@LadybugFarmLadies.net
FROM: LadiLori27@locomail.net

Can you e-mail me some macaroni and cheese? :)

Noah said, "Cool goat."

Cici frowned. "We're not keeping him."

"Her," corrected Lindsay.

Lindsay and Cici were struggling to carry a bale of hay from the barn into the barnyard; Noah leapt over the gate to take it from them. "Where'd it come from?" he asked.

Cici gladly relinquished the bale to him and stripped off her work gloves, wiping her forehead with the back of her hand. "God's endless supply of homeless animals, as far as I can tell. But we're not keeping him."

"Her," Lindsay said. She wiped her hands on her jeans, frowning a little over the marks the twine had left in her palms. "How was school?"

"Good." Noah stripped off the twine and shook out the hay. The goat trotted over and allowed him to scratch it behind the ears. "I learned about quadrangles and self-determining governments. How many bales do you want?"

"One," Bridget said importantly. She arrived on the scene a little out of breath, consulting a printout from the computer. "According to this, milking goats thrive on a diet of alfalfa, herbs, and wild grasses." She looked at the other two women quizzically. "Is there any alfalfa in that hay?"

Lindsay shrugged elaborately. "Hay is hay."

"This is fescue," Noah supplied. "Ya'll gonna milk this goat?"

"We are going to find its owner," Cici said firmly.

Bridget looked at Noah pointedly. "Do you know how to milk a goat?"

He shrugged and got to his feet as the goat abandoned his petting for the more enticing allure of hay. "Just like milking a cow."

"I think we should make cheese," Bridget announced, holding open the gate for them.

"I think you're out of your mind."

"And I found these plans on the Internet for building a goat house," Bridget added, waving the printout.

Cici stared at her. "It has to have its own *house*?"

"It's not a very fancy house. Easier than the chicken coop."

Cici stopped dead in her tracks. "Bridget, get serious. The last thing we have time for now is building a goat house. *Or* a goat!"

"I know," Bridget admitted. "But we'll rise to the occasion. We always do. When God gives us lemons, we make lemonade, and all that."

Cici's expression did not soften. "And what are we supposed to make when God sends us a goat?"

"Barbecue?" suggested Noah, grinning.

Bridget glared at him. "Chèvre," she corrected firmly.

When Cici drew in a sharp breath, Lindsay stepped between the two of them, linking her arm with Cici's. "Remember that yogurt we had in Greece?" she said wistfully as they started back toward the house.

"It was made from goat's milk," Bridget reminded them.

Cici agreed, somewhat reluctantly, "It just doesn't taste the same from the supermarket, even when it calls itself Greek yogurt."

"That's because it's not fresh." Bridget's tone was hopeful.

"That goat belongs to someone," Cici said firmly. "We are *not* keeping it."

"Speaking of goats," Noah said, "I'm hungry enough to eat one. What's for supper?"

"I think Ida Mae said something about a meat loaf," Bridget answered.

He shot her a suspicious look.

"You're not cooking?"

Bridget gestured expansively. "Been a little busy here, what with weddings to plan, goats showing up unannounced . . ."

Noah said, "Um, I think I have a date."

"With whom?" Lindsay asked.

He thought about that for a minute and then grinned. "With a pizza?"

"Nice try," Cici said. "But you know the rules. We have dinner at home during the week."

He groaned. "But the last time she cooked there was grit in the mashed potatoes!"

Bridget replied mildly, "Then maybe you could go in and help her wash the potatoes."

"I have homework."

"Then you'd better get started washing the vegetables," Lindsay said, "and set the table while you're at it. Then clean the chicken yard and get started mowing the grass. You should be able to get the back finished before dark. I can start on the front in the morning."

He stopped walking and stared at her. "All that because I said there was grit in the mashed potatoes?"

"No," replied Lindsay evenly, "all that because this is your house, too, and it needs to be done. And because," she added with absolutely no change in her tone or manner, "you seem to have plenty of time on your hands since you've cut back your hours at the store."

A quick belligerence flashed in his eyes, which was modified almost immediately by caution. "What are you talking about?"

"I was talking with Jonesie the other day," Cici supplied. "He mentioned you didn't work at all on Saturday."

"And that was after you told us you were helping him unload a big shipment all day long."

Noah's eyes slid from one to the other of them, shrewdly, as though searching for vulnerabilities. Finding an impenetrable fortress in their unity, he decided on another strategy. "I didn't actually *say* I was working. I said Jonesie was expecting a big shipment Saturday and I would be gone all day. Both of those were the truth."

None of the women looked impressed. "Where were you?" asked Lindsay.

He hesitated. His lips compressed, as though he were debating whether to answer. Finally he said, allowing his gaze to wander over the landscape beyond their heads, "I went to see somebody."

A quick glance between the women. Bridget said, "Why didn't you just tell us that?"

He shrugged, still not meeting their eyes. "I didn't think you'd understand."

"Understand," suggested Lindsay, a bit sharply, "or approve?"

He shoved his hands in his pockets. A stubborn insistence came into his eyes, which they all knew from experience was the first sign of a conversation that was about to stumble to a pointless end. "I was home before dark. I didn't lie. I told you I was going to be late for supper. I didn't break any rules."

Cici heard Lindsay's sharp intake of breath and she spoke above her, calmly. "Noah, you're the one who wanted to take a part-time job. We agreed you could work as many hours as you wanted as long as your schoolwork didn't suffer. But letting us think you're working when you're not is wrong and you know it. We need to know where you are. What if there had been an emergency?"

"I've got a phone," he replied, too easily. "That's what it's for."

"Which has nothing to do with the fact," Lindsay said firmly, "that you led us to believe you were working when you weren't. And we still don't know where you were all day."

"And that's the same as a lie," Bridget said.

He scowled. "It's not a lie."

They were silent.

"All right." He shoved his hands in his pockets, glaring at the ground. "I shouldn't have tricked you."

"Thank you," Lindsay said.

Cici softened a bit. "You know we want to meet your friends, Noah."

"She's not from around here."

Bridget said, "We still want to meet her, and let her parents know who we are, if you're going to be spending time with her. Why don't you invite her out here on Sunday?"

"We can't, Sunday," Lindsay pointed out. "Dominic's coming out to help us fertilize the vines."

Noah looked relieved.

"Next weekend then," Cici suggested. "And we'll need her parents' names and phone number before you see her again."

He muttered, "Maybe I won't see her again."

"That's up to you," Lindsay said mildly. "But those are the rules. And we'll let you know tonight what your punishment is for breaking the rules and deceiving us. Change out of your school clothes before you start on the chicken yard."

"And I hope you don't have any plans for the weekend," Cici added, "because we're going to need you to help us set up for the wedding menu tasting, and to help with fertilizing the vineyard on Sunday."

He scowled. "I thought you hadn't decided my punishment yet."

There was a warning edge behind Cici's pleasant smile. "I'm starting to get some ideas."

"This wedding business is for girls," he said sulkily, his hands thrust into his pockets. "I'd rather build the goat house."

Lindsay said, "The wedding business is for everyone. There's a lot of money involved, and it's money we need."

"You've got money," Noah countered reasonably, for the topic of finances—particularly his own—was one in which he always took an active interest. "You got the loan for the wine-making business, and you've got a brand-new barn to store it in. As soon as you start selling it to those fancy hotels in Washington you'll be rolling in dough."

Bridget said, "I'm afraid it's not exactly that easy, Noah.

And even if it were, there are a lot of major expenses coming up before we sell the first bottle."

"Like what?"

"Like college," Cici said.

"Lori told me her dad paid for her college."

"*Your* college," Lindsay said, with a touch of exasperation. "And let's not have that conversation again about whether or not you're going because obviously you are."

"And John Adams isn't exactly free," Cici added. "I know you've applied for another scholarship but that only covers seventy percent of the cost." She shrugged. "We have a lot of expenses coming up, Noah. And when you have expenses, you work. It's as simple as that."

The women had gone three or four steps before they realized they had left Noah behind. When they turned he was standing with his feet planted and his balled fists visible in his pockets, his face a tornado of emotions.

"What business is it of yours?" he exploded, completely without warning. "Why do you care? I'm not even your kid!"

And, as they watched in astonishment, he shoved past them and bounded up the back steps, banging the screen door hard behind himself.

"Well, that was fun," Cici said in a slightly lowered tone when he was gone.

Bridget looked troubled. "We shouldn't have mentioned the tuition. Children shouldn't worry about things like that."

"Don't be silly," Lindsay said, but she looked uneasy, too. "The latest thinking is that kids should be involved in family finances as much as is practical. That's how they learn responsibility."

"Where did you read that?"

"I'm a teacher. I keep up."

"But you know how seriously he takes things," Bridget said. "He would have rebuilt that barn all by himself if we had let him, every stick and nail."

Cici said, "Something is definitely going on with him."

"It's a girl," Bridget speculated.

Lindsay gave her a dry look. "Do you think?"

"Maybe we should have the Reverend Holland talk to him," Bridget suggested.

"Whatever he's done," Cici said adamantly, "he doesn't deserve that. Maybe we should make an appointment with the school counselor."

"Oh, great." This from Lindsay. "How special is he going to feel when his three mommies show up at school? Things are hard enough for him as it is."

"We have to ground him," Cici said.

"That seems redundant," Bridget argued. "All he has time for now is chores, school, and work."

Lindsay said unhappily, "Apparently not. And you know as well as I do this entire relationship is based on trust. If he can't be trusted to be where he's supposed to be, we have a big problem. "

"And if he can't be honest with us," Cici added, "we have a bigger one."

"A week?" suggested Bridget.

"Two," said Lindsay, grimly.

"That's practically the rest of the school year!"

Cici shrugged. "You do the crime, you do the time. We've got to be united on this, Bridget."

"Besides," Lindsay added practically, "we're going to need his help around here for the next couple of weeks."

Bridget gave a shake of her head. "You guys are tough. Remind me never to get on your bad side."

"Come on," Cici said to Lindsay. "I finished the table rounds you wanted. Help me carry them around front and we can set them up and see how they look."

From inside the house, the telephone began to ring. Bridget glanced at her watch and sighed. "It's not five yet. I guess we have to answer it."

"Maybe it's someone about the goat," Cici suggested hopefully as Bridget started up the stairs. "Hurry!"

Lindsay and Cici turned toward the workshop. "He probably hates us," Lindsay said unhappily.

"It can't be easy," Cici agreed somberly, "a teenage boy, living with three old women . . ."

"We are not old!" Lindsay exclaimed indignantly.

Cici grinned, and bumped her friend's shoulder with her own. "Come on," she said, "relax. Parenting would be no fun at all if you couldn't torture the kids once in a while. Besides, Noah should count himself lucky. He skated on a technicality. We would have been perfectly within our rights to take away that motorcycle. That's what the good Reverend Holland would have done."

"Maybe he would have been right." Lindsay sighed. "At least when Noah's without wheels we know where he is."

"Cici!" Bridget was at the back door, telephone in her hand. "It's for you."

Cici rolled her eyes. "I don't suppose she could take a message."

"It wouldn't matter. You'd have to deal with her sooner or later."

"Catherine?" Cici inquired of Bridget as she took the telephone.

Bridget shrugged. "Believe it or not, no."

She went to help Lindsay with the table rounds as Cici spoke into the phone. "This is Cici."

The table rounds were not heavy, but they were cumbersome, and it took the two of them to maneuver one around the house to the front porch. Bridget and Lindsay reached the steps just as the screen door slammed and Cici came out.

She was dressed as they had last seen her, in rolled-up jeans, sneakers, and an untucked T-shirt, her hair escaping from her attempt to pull it back with a clip, her face devoid of makeup. What was different was that she had her purse over her shoulder and her car keys in her hand. Every freckle on her face stood out in stark relief, and her eyes had a stunned, blank look to them.

"Um," she said, as though not quite sure where the next words were coming from, "I have to go."

"Go? Where?" They propped the table top against a hydrangea bush and started toward her.

"Charlottesville." Cici moved down the steps without looking at them, clutching the keys as though they had the power to unlock some magic door only she could find. "To Lori. That was the hospital. There's been an accident."

For Better or For Worse

April 13, 2005

Sweetheart,

It's funny how, as time goes on, the things you used to think were so important are hardly worth remembering anymore, and the things you barely noticed suddenly seem like the most important things in the world.

Important: The way the kitchen smelled on a winter morning and pancakes were cooking.

Not Important: A pair of red leather boots I worked six months of nights to pay for. I don't even know what happened to those boots now.

Important: Your smile

Not Important: My own laundry room

Important: Being safe

Not Important: Being rich

Important: Watching you sleep

Not important: A new car

I wish I hadn't made so many mistakes over things that weren't important. I wish I could take them all back.

Especially the one where I lost you.

9

Good in a Crisis

Later they would think about that moment, and how everything changed from light to dark in an instant. It was not the first time for any of them. A child runs into the street. A husband clutches his chest. A parent doesn't know you anymore. Light to dark. One moment they were talking about goats and weddings on a spring afternoon. And then everything changed.

They knew this place, where the throat seized and the heart started flooding adrenaline and the world suddenly shifted, unmistakably and irretrievably, on its axis. They had been here before. But that did not make the terrain any less terrifying. Or navigating it any easier.

But because they had been here before, they knew the choreography, almost without thinking. Lindsay took Cici's keys and got her friend settled in the passenger seat just as Bridget arrived with Lindsay's purse and cell phone. Bridget packed an overnight bag for Cici, told Noah and Ida Mae what had happened, phoned the Reverend Holland and asked him to look in on Noah, and was on the road little more than half an hour behind Lindsay.

Cici arrived just in time to drop a kiss onto her groggy daughter's forehead before they took her to surgery. "I warned you about texting and driving," she said shakily, trying to smile and fight back tears, and not succeeding very well at either one.

"Texting and walking, Mom," Lori assured her. Her speech was slurred, one eye blackened and swollen shut, the other slitted and unfocused. "You look pretty."

"So do you, sweetheart," Cici said, smoothing back her tangled copper hair, and then the orderlies came.

The emergency room doctor told them that, in addition to a few scrapes and bruises, the most serious injury was a fractured tibia, which would require surgery to set and stabilize. Cici was filling out the paperwork when Bridget arrived.

"They say it's routine," Lindsay explained to Bridget. "The surgery should only take an hour and a half. She might be able to go home in five or six days. But she'll be on crutches for the rest of the summer."

"Thank God," Bridget said, her shoulders sagging with relief, "that it wasn't more serious. Of course"—her gaze went to Cici, immersed in forms at the nurses' station—"nothing is routine when it's your baby going under the knife."

"They call it 'pedestrian versus scooter,'" Cici informed them when she returned. And although her face was still tight and her eyes anxious, her expression was wry as she sank down into a hard plastic chair. "Apparently she *was* texting and walking, and she walked right out in front of an oncoming motor scooter. Can you believe that?"

Both Bridget and Lindsay winced. "She is so lucky," Lindsay said.

"It could have been so much worse," Bridget agreed.

Cici nodded. "It happened on campus, where the speed limits are low. Still ..." She trailed off with a subdued shudder.

"Pedestrian versus moving vehicle," observed Lindsay, "never turns out well for the pedestrian."

Bridget called home with the report, and Cici called Lori's father in California. He did not answer, of course, so she left a message. Lindsay brought up the first round of coffee from the cafeteria, and they settled down to wait.

"Hospitals," Cici said, sliding down in her chair so that her head rested against the back. She cradled the coffee cup against her chest, warming her hands. "They all smell the same."

"You'd think someone would invent something for that," Bridget said.

"Like that hotel scent," offered Lindsay. "Hotels all smell the same, too—or at least the high-priced ones do. Why can't hospitals smell like that?"

Bridget wrinkled her nose. "Then no one would ever want to stay in a hotel, because it would smell like a hospital."

"Funny how that smell triggers such vivid memories," Cici said.

They were silent for a moment, each of them revisiting their own unhappy memories of hospital corridors, hospital beds, hospital smells.

Then Bridget smiled softly. "Not all the memories are bad. Sometimes being in a hospital reminds me of my babies."

"Yeah," Cici agreed. "When Lori was born, being in the

hospital for three days was the first vacation I'd had in five years. Lying in bed all day watching soap operas, twenty-four-hour room service, three thousand calories a day . . . I begged the doctor to let me stay over the weekend, but he wouldn't sign off on it."

"I don't know," Lindsay said. "I think there's something wrong with a society that makes women give birth in the middle of its most disease-infested population, like having a baby is such a high-risk behavior that mother and child have to be isolated from the healthy people."

"That's why they send women home the next day now," Bridget said.

"Unless of course it's more convenient for the doctor to slice the mother open to take the baby out."

Cici said uneasily, "Please, less said about slicing open?"

"Sorry, Cici." Lindsay reached across and squeezed her hand.

Bridget smiled and patted Cici's knee. "Routine surgery," she assured her.

Cici managed a faint, but grateful, smile.

Half an hour passed. They watched the minute hand on the clock.

Bridget said, "When I called home, Noah was mowing the grass. Ida Mae said he had already finished the back and had the front half done."

Lindsay smiled. "He is a good kid."

"I love the way the air smells right after the grass is mowed," Cici said. "Especially in the evening, when the dew starts to fall."

"I don't love the gnats though," Bridget said.

"They'll be gone by tomorrow afternoon."

"I hope Noah ate some supper," Cici said.

Bridget made a move to rise from her chair. "Do you want me to go down to the cafeteria and bring up some sandwiches?"

Cici shook her head, sipping her coffee. "I was just thinking about the way the kitchen smells at suppertime. I like Ida Mae's meatloaf."

"Especially when she makes apple pie with it," Lindsay said.

"And remembers to peel the apples," said Bridget.

"Either way, the kitchen smells wonderful."

Cici sighed wearily and closed her eyes, resting her head against the back of the chair. "I hate this place," she said.

Bridget and Lindsay sipped their coffee, and didn't say anything else at all.

❧

The surgeon came into the waiting room precisely on schedule and reported that all had gone well, just as he had expected. Lori was in Recovery, and would be taken to her room in an hour, at which time they could see her. While Cici bombarded the doctor with questions, Bridget stepped aside to make telephone calls, and Lindsay went to the nurses' desk to make certain that Lori's room included a cot for her mother, and two comfortable chairs for those who would be staying by her side. When the nurse informed her that visiting hours were over at eight p.m., Lindsay just smiled and thanked her for the information. She then reminded her, firmly but pleasantly, to make certain the cot and the chairs were set up by the time Lori was brought to her room.

Bridget persuaded Cici to have something to eat while they waited to see Lori, and the three of them went down to the cafeteria. The decor was orange and beige stripes, the tables and chairs were antimicrobial plastic, and the whole place smelled like cooked cabbage. Cici pushed around a salad and nibbled on crackers, and Bridget and Lindsay shared a tuna salad sandwich and a bag of potato chips. The tuna was oddly tasteless, no doubt due to fat-free mayonnaise and low-sodium seasoning, so they bought an extra bag of chips.

Bridget said, "We'll get you settled into a hotel first thing in the morning. I'll go down and talk to the auxiliary ladies about which ones they recommend as soon as we see Lori. I packed three changes of clothes for you, but it's no problem to go home and get more."

Cici said, "You guys don't have to stay over."

"Don't be ridiculous," Lindsay replied.

"I'm not driving back tonight," Bridget insisted. "You know I can hardly see in the dark. I brought our toothbrushes," she told Lindsay.

"But we've got Catherine and the crowd coming this weekend," Cici remembered suddenly. She sank back in her chair in despair. "I don't know if I can be there. How can I leave Lori? And that stupid brochure, and all the cleaning and painting and cooking..."

"We can handle it." Lindsay opened the second bag of chips and poured a measure onto Cici's plate. "I'll get Noah to help me with the brochuré. And you've already done the hard part. They'll just have to use their imaginations about the paint that needs to be freshened."

"Ida Mae can help me with the cooking," Bridget said. "I have the recipes; all she has to do is follow them."

Cici picked up a potato chip, looking uncertain. "Are you sure?"

"Ida Mae is a good cook," Bridget said firmly.

"Who sometimes forgets to wash the vegetables," Cici worried.

"She won't this time. She knows how important this is to us."

"Say!" Suddenly Lindsay beamed a smile. "I just realized— with a broken leg, Lori won't be going back to the dorm. And she's going to get awfully bored just sitting around at home with nothing to do . . ."

"So, blogging and researching local food sources will definitely help her pass the days," Bridget volunteered, with a smile in her voice.

"Not to mention cutting fabric and putting together centerpieces and about a thousand other things none of us knew where we were going to find the time to do," Lindsay said, pleased. "There, you see? Every cloud has a silver lining."

Cici suddenly pressed her hand to her mouth and burst into tears.

"Oh, honey! We're sorry!" Lindsay and Bridget swooped in on her, their arms around her shoulders, their hands petting, their voices comforting and contrite. "We didn't mean it. Sweetie, it's okay. We didn't mean to make light of this.

Lori is our princess, you know that, we'll wait on her hand and foot . . ."

"No, no . . ." Cici choked on a sound that was part sob, part laughter. "It's just that . . . I'm so lucky. When I think about how this might have ended—I'm so lucky." She extended her arms and drew them into her, heads on her shoulders, hands entwined. "And I love you guys so much!"

&

Lori was pale-faced and groggy when the three of them tip-toed into her room. The bruise that had closed her left eye was rainbow colored, and her right leg was elevated on several pillows and encased in plaster from ankle to knee. She murmured, "Hi, everybody. Where's the goat?"

Bridget smiled as she bent over her, smoothing back her hair. "We decided to leave her home this trip."

Lindsay added, "It's the drugs."

Cici pulled a chair close to the bed and took her daughter's hand. "How're you feeling, sweetie?"

"Like I'm going to throw up."

Lindsay discreetly placed a small blue basin on the pillow next to her. "Do you want some ginger ale?"

"Okay," Lori whispered, and closed her eyes. Within seconds she was asleep.

Cici smiled at Lindsay. "Maybe not."

The next time Lori woke she seemed a little more coherent. "How bad is it?" she croaked, as Cici fed her ice chips from a spoon and Bridget gently blotted her forehead with a damp cloth.

"You're going to be fine," Cici assured her. "Just a tiny broken bone in your leg. The doctors put a pin in—"

"So, be careful going through airport security." Lindsay smiled.

"No, no," Lori said miserably, and her hand fluttered to her bruised eye. "My face. How bad is my face?"

The three women shared a look that spoke volumes about the values of twenty-one-year-old women, and Cici assured her daughter that, with a little pancake makeup, she could still win the Miss America pageant if she chose to. And, safe in that knowledge, Lori fell once again into a deep and untroubled sleep.

Lindsay and Bridget retreated to their chairs with the magazines they had bought in the gift shop, and Cici fell asleep holding Lori's hand. At two in the morning, Lindsay gently extricated Cici's hand from Lori's and replaced it with her own while Bridget guided Cici to the cot on the other side of the room and covered her with a blanket. At six a.m. Bridget took Lindsay's place while Lindsay went down for coffee, and when she returned Bridget was spooning ice chips to a fretful Lori and Cici was demanding that the nurse give her daughter something for the pain now, not in twenty minutes as scheduled.

The following hours were spent proving that it requires at least three family members, two orderlies, a physical therapist, a nutritionist, an orthopedic resident, three interns, and the full-time attention of the entire nursing staff to properly see to the needs of one temporarily indisposed college student. Cici engaged in long question-and-answer sessions with the medical professionals while Bridget and Lindsay supervised Lori's interaction with the staff and made certain her personal needs were attended to.

They called Lori's roommate and asked her to pack a bag with some of the essentials—pajamas, toiletries, makeup, iPod—and left messages for her professors. They made a reservation for Cici at a nearby motel. When Lori only grimaced at her lunch tray, Bridget volunteered to go out and get her a hamburger. She only ate a bite or two of the hamburger, but finished all of the strawberry milkshake, which made Cici happy, and which they all agreed was proof positive that she was well on the road to recovery.

While Lori napped, the three of them made a quick trip to the orange-striped cafeteria for rubbery grilled cheese sandwiches and Cokes. "This place is exhausting," Bridget said, sinking down into her chair. Her makeup, like that of the other two ladies, had long since worn away, leaving her face colorless and puckered, with bruised spots under her eyes and wrinkled lips. Her hair, pulled back from her face in a short, flat ponytail, looked more gray than platinum. She peeled open a corner of her sandwich. "And I don't think there is a real food product in this entire building."

Lindsay gave her sandwich an unenthusiastic sniff. "I may have to go back upstairs and fight Lori for that hamburger."

"I don't know how anyone ever gets well here," Cici said, as she resolutely took a bite of her sandwich. "Lori's schedule isn't this hectic at college. Bath, X-rays, meds, vital signs, draw blood, change dressing, eat this, drink that, take this, push this button, squeeze this rubber ball, follow my finger..."

"And that's just the patient," Lindsay said. "The caretakers have it much harder."

"They should pay *us* for letting Lori stay here," Bridget said, and tossed her sandwich down in disgust. "And I've a great mind to go back in that kitchen and introduce that cook to butter and cheese."

"Both very useful ingredients in a grilled cheese sandwich," Lindsay agreed. She tore her sandwich in half, regarded the stringy contents without enthusiasm, and returned both halves to her plate.

"We're spoiled," Cici said. She took another bite of her sandwich, chewed without tasting, and swallowed resolutely. "We are probably the only three people in this building right now who actually know what real food tastes like."

"Tomatoes warm from the vine," Bridget said, and her voice was filled with abject yearning.

"Strawberries that taste like strawberries smell," said Lindsay.

"Bright yellow eggs."

"Blueberry muffins."

"Raspberries, when you pick them first thing in the morning."

"Stop it," Bridget warned. "I'm going to cry."

Cici stared at them, the half-eaten sandwich poised a few inches from her lips, her expression grim. "Both of you stop it," she said. "If I don't eat, I'll get grumpy. And if I get any grumpier, they're going to kick me out of this place. So let me eat."

"Raspberries," Bridget remembered suddenly, sitting up straight. "Where am I going to get local raspberries for the brandy sauce in June? Our raspberries aren't ready until the end of July!"

"There's got to be some variety that ripens in June," Lindsay suggested. "Check the Internet."

"*Local* is a relative term," Cici said. She tore off another bite of her sandwich and choked it down. "What you need to do is define *local*. Ten miles? Twenty? Two hundred?"

"Well," Bridget said uncertainly. "The crab comes from the Chesapeake Bay. How far away is that?"

Lindsay asked, "How are you getting crab from the Chesapeake Bay by this weekend?"

"Oh, no!" Bridget's eyes flew wide and she extended her hand across the table. "Give me your phone!"

Lindsay fumbled her cell phone out of her purse while Cici chewed another bite of rubbery cheese. "She's ordering it," Cici explained as Bridget walked quickly away, punching numbers on the keypad.

Lindsay said, "For the love of God, Cici, put down that sandwich. We're taking you out to dinner tonight for something greasy and salty, with chocolate mousse cake topped with fudge sauce served on a bed of dark chocolate puree for dessert. You can't live like this."

Cici shook her head and glanced at her watch. "You two need to get on the road. I'll be fine."

Bridget returned to the table, looking relieved. "Crisis averted. One pound of Chesapeake Bay crab will be delivered to Blue Valley Grocery by ten a.m. Friday morning."

"I mean it," Cici said. She gave up on the sandwich and placed the remains on her plate. Her blue eyes were faded, her hair mussed, and even her freckles seemed listless, but her expression was determined. "I can manage here. But we can't leave Noah another night, and we can't blow this wedding. We've already cashed the deposit check," she reminded them.

"Don't worry," Bridget assured her. "Don't you worry about a thing. We've got it all under control."

"Sure," Lindsay said. "Like I said, we've already done the hard parts. We'll be fine."

"Have you checked your e-mail lately?" Cici inquired darkly.

Lindsay and Bridget shared an uneasy glance. Bridget said, "Maybe we should just scoot home and check in."

Lindsay compressed her lips briefly, thinking. "We'll make a run to the drugstore," she decided, "and lay in a supply of candy for you and soft drinks for Lori. Promise me you'll go to the hotel tonight and take a shower."

"And wash your hair," Bridget suggested.

Cici glanced sideways at the lank strands falling toward her face. "I can take a hint."

"And for God's sake, get some decent fast food," Lindsay said. She gathered up their leavings on a tray as they stood.

Cici placed a hand lightly on each of their arms and smiled. "I'm going to be fine," she said. "Really. And so is Lori."

"Oh, we know that," Lindsay assured her with a sigh. "All the two of you have to worry about is a broken leg and an extended hospital stay. We're the ones who have to deal with the mother of the bride."

❧

Bridget and Lindsay made their final shopping trip while Cici returned to Lori's room. The doctor was in there when Cici pushed open the door, and Lori's expression was so stricken that Cici's heart went to her throat. "What?" she demanded, hurrying forward. "What's wrong?"

"Oh, Mom," Lori said, her eyes filling. "He says I'll be here another week. How can I stay here a week?"

"I said," the doctor corrected, scribbling on his clipboard, "that if you continue to do as well as you have done, you could be out of here by Wednesday. That's six days."

Cici pressed her hand to her thudding heart, weak with relief, and tried to find some words of comfort for her daughter. All she could manage was, "You're lucky your leg is in a cast or I'd wring your neck. You scared me to death."

"But I have an exam Monday! I can't stay until Wednesday!" Lori turned pleading, tear-filled eyes on her mother. "Tell him!"

Now that Cici's heartbeat was almost back to normal, she could take a breath. But before she could speak, the doctor shook his head. "Sorry, no chance. She's doing well otherwise, though," he told Cici, and Lori pressed her head back against the pillow, eyes closed in despair, as he briefed Cici on her progress.

"You don't understand," Lori insisted when he was gone. "I've *got* to take that exam. If I miss it I'll get an incomplete for the entire semester, and if I have an incomplete I'll be taken out of the running for the internship, and I can't miss out on this, Mom, I just can't!"

Cici nodded sympathetically and sat beside Lori, tucking a tissue into her hand. "I know how much you were looking forward to this."

"I had a personal recommendation!" She pressed the tissue to her eyes. "I was going to live in a real Italian *castillo*. I was going to learn wine making from the experts. Sergio and I had plans. Now it's all over. Everything I planned, everything I worked for . . ."

"I'm sure your friend will understand," Cici said. It was easy to be generous now that she knew Lori was not spending the summer in Italy.

Lori leaned her head back helplessly against the pillow. A lone tear escaped from her closed lashes and trickled down her battered cheek. "How?" she said tiredly. "I can't even contact him. I don't have a phone, or a computer . . . Anyway, it wouldn't make any difference. It's over. Just like everything else I try, I've totally screwed this up."

Not even the return of Lindsay and Bridget could lift Lori's spirits. "I can't do anything right," was her new anthem, and it was uttered in the most morose tone any of them had ever heard from the naturally ebullient Lori. "Every time I get a little bit ahead, something knocks me back down." She gestured resignedly to the cast on her leg. "Why does everything always happen to *me*?"

Lindsay smiled. "We know that feeling, sweetie. It's been the story of our lives since we moved here."

"Every challenge we face is a chance for personal growth," Bridget pronounced, and at the looks she received from the other three she quickly offered, "Look, honey. We brought chocolate."

Bridget spread out the contents of their shopping bags across Lori's bed—candy, hand lotion, a hairbrush, mirror, nail polish, paperback books. Cici gave her two friends a grateful look, but Lori barely noticed.

"I've worked so hard," she said. "This whole year, everything I've done—up in smoke."

"Not everything," Cici said, trying to inject patience into her tone. "It's just one course. You'll make it up."

"Maybe you could talk to the professor," Lindsay suggested to Cici. "He might let her take the exam later."

"I can do that," Cici said, but Lori was already shaking her head.

"He's going on sabbatical," she said. "Even if he wanted to give me a break—which, I'm telling you, this guy does not—he couldn't. It's now or never."

There was a timid knock on the half-open door. "Um, excuse me?"

A dark-haired young man with his arm in a sling hesitated in the doorway. "Lori Gregory?"

Cici stood with a questioning, welcoming smile. "Hi," she said. "Lori would be the one in the hospital bed. I'm her mother."

He hesitated, then came forward uncertainly, his right hand extended. "I'm Mark Clery," he said, shaking Cici's hand.

"Cici Burke," she said.

Lori studied him with a puzzled expression on her face. "Do I know you?"

He glanced uncomfortably from Cici to Lori and took another step closer to the bed. "I'm the one who, uh . . ." He gestured at her leg with his good arm. "Hit you."

Lori regarded him with absolutely no sympathy. "Thanks a lot," she said, flatly.

"Lori!" That was from Bridget.

Cici admonished her daughter. "You're the one who caused the accident, you know!"

And Lindsay apologized to Mark. "She's on a lot of pain medication," she explained. "She's usually much nicer than this."

"I know," Mark said. And he tried to smile at Lori. "I'm in your poli-sci class." He added earnestly, "I tried to miss you, I really did. I ran the scooter into a curb, but it was too late. I'm really sorry."

Lori drew a breath, and released it in a long-suffering sigh. "Thanks," she said, in a slightly more genuine tone than she had used before. And she added, "I guess it was my fault." She glanced at her mother. "And I guess my life isn't really over. It just feels like it is."

"She's upset because she's missing a final," Cici explained. She smiled at her daughter. "Her life is not over."

Bridget indicated his sling with a quick and sympathetic smile. "Is your arm broken?"

He looked from Lori to Bridget, the discomfort in his face apparent. "Oh. No, ma'am. I just dislocated my shoulder."

"Lucky you," Lori sighed, then, quickly, "I mean, I'm sorry. I hope you feel better."

Mark looked relieved. "You, too," he said. "And I'm sorry. You know, about the exam."

Lori sighed again. "Thanks."

An awkward silence fell.

"Well," Mark said. "I guess I better be going. I just wanted to make sure you were . . ." Once again he lifted an awkward hand toward the cast. "You know."

"It was awfully nice of you to stop by," Bridget said.

"Wasn't it, Lori?" Cici prompted.

Lori managed a quavering, pathetic smile. "Nice."

Mark started toward the door, then turned around. "Oh, I almost forgot." He reached into his pocket. "Your phone."

Lori's face lit up as though he had just presented her with a perfect score on her final *and* a winning lottery ticket. "My phone!" She sat up straighter against the pillows, extending both hands for it. "Does it work? Was it damaged?"

"It seems fine," he said, presenting it to her. "I found it in the grass, but they had already taken you away."

She didn't even look up. She was already texting.

"Thank you, Mark," Cici said, sincerely. "You may have just saved her life. Not to mention mine."

The young man had a nice smile. "That's okay," he said. His eyes lingered on Lori. "Tell her I hope she feels better."

"He seemed nice," Bridget said when he was gone.

Lindsay helped her gather up the candy and toiletries from Lori's bed. "Very nice manners."

"Unlike some people I could name," Cici said.

Lori said, "Mom, please. Texting, here."

Cici lunged for the phone, with a flash of impatience. Lindsay intercepted her, Bridget stepped between Cici and Lori, and Lori didn't notice anything at all. Then a male voice boomed from the doorway.

"Where is my princess?"

Cici froze. She didn't blink, she didn't breathe. Bridget and Lindsay stared at her and then, slowly, all three gazes moved to the door.

The doorway was filled with pink roses—not just one

dozen, nor even two, but three or four. Below the roses was a pair of legs clad in custom-tailored khaki slacks and Italian loafers. No socks. The roses moved away to reveal a face. Cici gasped.

"Richard," she said, a little hoarsely. "What are you doing here?"

January 13, 2006

Dearest,

I know you probably hate me. After all, this is all my fault. You didn't want this. You didn't ask for it. It's not your fault we're apart. I should be sitting with you right now, talking to you instead of trying to write my feelings down. It's not your fault. It never was.

There's so much I should say, I know, but the truth is I'm not very good at writing my feelings down. I think about you. Life is so hard without you. I miss so much about you. Sometimes I make lists in my head of things I wish I could tell you, but my head gets so full that when it comes time to write them down I've forgotten. But here are a few things I wanted to say to you today:

Don't stand around in wet socks. I know you get busy with other important things and it's too much bother to stop and find dry socks, but I'm not there to remind you, so do it anyway.

When someone is nice to you, say thank you. Men forget to do that, which is why women are always going along behind them writing thank-you notes. Write your own thank-you notes. Be a man.

Learn to cook, for heaven's sake. You can't live on fast food, and you can't depend on someone else to take care of you forever. Besides, it's sexy.

So is keeping a clean kitchen.

Laugh, darling. Laugh a lot.

And please don't let your feelings for me keep you closed away from love. Because the world is filled with people just aching to show you how much they love you, if only you will let them.

I am one of them.

10

The Trouble with Men

"Daddy!" Lori squealed, and flung open her arms. "Daddy, Daddy, Daddy, *Daddy*!"

Richard thrust the roses unceremoniously into Cici's arms and rushed to his daughter's side, wrapping her in his embrace. "Now then!" he declared. "What's all this I hear about you dropping out of the Olympics? The press has been all over me, but I assured them a little thing like a broken leg wouldn't keep *my* girl down."

Lori giggled, and he caught her face between both his hands and kissed her forehead, then both cheeks. "How're you feeling, sweet thing? Tell me all about it."

Lori proceeded to do so, with eyes shining and voice animated, and Lindsay watched with a slow cynical shake of her head. "What is it about a daddy that can turn a woman into a ten-year-old girl in a heartbeat?"

"Oh, I don't know," Cici said. "Maybe the fact that he only shows up when there's a crisis?"

Bridget, who was the only one who bothered to lower her

voice, offered, "It's not like we haven't been by her side for twenty-four hours straight or anything."

"Of course," Cici observed, "we didn't bring her six dozen roses. What am I going to do with all these? There aren't enough bedpans in this hospital to hold them."

She dumped the roses onto Lori's bed table, and interrupted her discourse to repeat, as pleasantly as possible, "What are you doing here, Richard?"

"And where else should I be when my little girl needs me?" He pinched Lori's cheek and rose to address Cici, barely missing the gagging gesture Lindsay made to Bridget behind her hand.

"Thanks, by the way," he added in a lower tone, "for leaving a message telling me my only child was in surgery, but *not* leaving a callback number."

"Oh." Cici looked blank for a moment. "Sorry."

Richard was the kind of man who not only aged well, but, thanks to the best cosmetic assistance money could buy, hardly aged at all. His teeth were impossibly white, his tan flawlessly golden, and his luxuriously thick, expensively styled hair was a gorgeous shade of silver. He jogged to stay fit, played racquetball to be seen being fit, and had one of those faces on which a few craggy lines only added character. Having presumably come straight from the airport, he was nonetheless impeccably groomed in razor-creased khakis, navy blazer, crisp white shirt. He turned to Bridget and Lindsay and smiled politely.

"Ladies," he said. "You're looking good."

Lindsay smiled thinly. "Nice to see you again, Richard. You've put on a little weight, haven't you?"

The comment caused Richard to immediately suck in his stomach, and Cici struggled to keep a straight face.

"Lori," she said, "Lindsay and Bridget have to get back to the house. They're leaving now."

Hugs and kisses followed, promises that everything was going to be fine, inquiries as to whether Lori needed anything from home. As she passed, Lindsay said to Cici, seriously, "Are you *sure* you're going to be okay?"

"Really," Cici said, "I'm good."

"Because we can stay," Bridget insisted, glancing at Richard.

Cici hugged her. "Thank you." She hugged Lindsay. "Thank you both."

"Call if you need anything." Lindsay held the embrace a moment longer than Cici did.

"Anything at all," Bridget added, looking anxious.

Cici smiled. "I'm good. Promise."

When they were gone, Richard observed, "Your friends certainly have aged, haven't they?"

Cici glared at him. "My friends," she responded deliberately, "were up all night with your daughter."

He returned her cold stare measure for measure. "Well, they could have saved themselves the trouble if someone had bothered to let *me* know what was going on."

"This is ridiculous," Cici said. "What are you doing here, anyway? Whoever would have thought you'd fly three thousand miles just because you couldn't get an answer on the telephone?"

"I've flown three thousand miles for dinner," he replied coolly. "And this is my little girl you're talking about. Who, might I point out, never broke anything when she lived with me."

Cici's smile was as convincing as a circus clown's and her voice dripping with saccharine as she said, "I really want to slap you right now."

"I can hear you," Lori said, but when they both turned, guiltily, to look at her, she was smiling at something that had just appeared on the screen of her telephone.

Richard took her arm and gestured, with a curt nod of his head, toward the door. Lori didn't even notice when they stepped outside.

Cici had already drawn a breath for rebuttal to whatever it was he was about to say, but he cut her off. "Listen," he said lowly, in that way he had of commanding attention without demanding it. "I can see you're in a mood, and I understand why. I know it's been a rough night for you. But whatever else you think of me, Lori is my kid and I'm crazy about her. You scared the hell out of me, okay? Leaving a message like that—accident, surgery—what was I supposed to think?"

Cici could see the remnants of raw emotion in his eyes and she felt a stab of remorse. "I'm sorry," she mumbled, dropping her gaze. "I guess I wasn't thinking straight."

He sighed and ran a hand through his thick wavy hair. "I guess I can understand that. But how about we call a truce for a while, huh? Just give me a break and let me enjoy the fact that I get to spend a little bonus time with my daughter and not . . ." There was actually a catch in his voice. "Attend a funeral. Okay?"

"Oh, Richard." Cici tried to imagine what the cross-country

plane trip must have been like for him, but her mind balked. She touched his arm, feeling miserable.

He looked down at her hand, and then at her eyes, and she was surprised by the tenderness she thought she saw there. She quickly withdrew her hand.

"I think," she said, shifting her gaze away, "I'll go to the hotel and wash my hair."

Richard regarded her appraisingly. "Good plan," he replied, and, just like that, the Richard she knew was back, and whatever sympathy she had begun to feel for him evaporated.

Cici scowled. "Tell Lori I'll be back in a couple of hours."

But Richard had already turned away, pushing through the door to Lori's room, and as she left she heard his voice booming cheerily, "So, sweet pea, killer motor scooters aside, how do you like the school?"

And, perhaps even more irritating, Lori actually looked up from texting long enough to reply. Neither one of them noticed when Cici left.

❧

At the corner of the driveway to the house, there was a sign, hand-painted by Lindsay and decorated with ladybugs and a garden scene, that said, Welcome to Ladybug Farm. It never failed to make them smile. As they made the turn and started down the gravel drive, lined with tall oaks, the anticipation of some grand destination always made the heart beat a little faster. And then, coming out of the shadows and rounding the curve where the full, emerald lawn with its purple hydrangeas and brilliant pink peonies and carefully

188 ~ Donna Ball

cultivated beds of hollyhocks and impatiens and showy, old-fashioned dahlias spread out like a ruffled quilt designed to show off all the colors of nature, there was always a catch of breath. In the background, the majestic blue mountains spilled their shadows onto a bright green meadow dotted with sheep. And in the foreground the big old house with its faded brick, painted columns, and tall, high windows seemed to reach out to them, and welcome them home. Bridget and Lindsay shared a glance as they pulled up in front of the wide front steps, each of them understanding what the other was thinking: *I can't believe we live here.*

Rebel charged up from his post underneath the porch in full voice, turf flying under his paws and saliva spraying from his snarling muzzle. He skidded to a stop before the SUV, focused a full ten seconds of furious, lunging barking at the right front tire, and then, tail wagging, casually walked away.

Bridget turned off the engine and sat there for a moment, taking it all in. "It is good to be home," she said fervently.

"So good," agreed Lindsay with a sigh. She hoisted her purse over her shoulder and opened the door. "And I am dying for a shower."

"I never understood how a hospital could make you feel so filthy. I don't think I'll ever get the smell of disinfectant out of my hair."

The two women got out of the car, slammed their doors closed, and then stood there, noses wrinkling, eyebrows drawing together, looking around.

"What *is* that smell?" Lindsay said at last.

"Did Noah forget to clean the chicken yard?"

"A commercial chicken plant wouldn't smell this bad." Lindsay looked at Bridget uneasily. "It couldn't be the goat?"

Bridget guarded her nose and mouth with her hand. "It would take more than a goat—or a herd of goats—to smell like that. Besides, nanny goats don't smell."

"Then what—?"

"It smells like . . . like fertilizer." Bridget's eyes widened slowly as she turned to Lindsay. "You don't suppose . . . ?"

"Surely not." Lindsay drew in a cautious breath and coughed, spreading her fingers over her own nose. "I told Dominic we were having company tomorrow."

"We can't serve lunch on the porch with this—this smell!" Alarm was rising in Bridget's eyes, and her voice. "We can't even have them *sit* on the porch!"

"I don't think that will be a problem." Lindsay's voice was muffled by her fingers. "Nobody's going to want to get out of the car."

They hurried up the front porch with their hands over their faces and closed the front door behind them quickly. They were met by the sight of Noah and Ida Mae lugging a mattress around the corner where the grand staircase spilled into the foyer, moving toward the sunroom.

"What are you doing?" Bridget gasped.

Ida Mae gave her an impatient look as she shuffled along with her shoulder to the mattress. "Stands to reason, don't it, that girl is going to need some place to sleep when she comes home? And she can't climb stairs with her leg in plaster. So we set her up a temporary little place in the sunroom. It don't get too terrible hot there this time of year, but just in case, I whipped up some curtains on that sewing machine of yours."

For a moment, Lindsay was too stunned to react. "Using the calico?"

"There was plenty of it."

Lindsay shook off her dismay and hurried forward to help. "I know you're as strong as an ox, Ida Mae, and you can leap tall buildings at a single bound, but let me do this, okay?"

Ida Mae relinquished her place to Lindsay, both hands pressed to the small of her back. "About time you got here," she said. "Next thing you know I'll be in traction, myself."

Bridget pressed a hand to her heart, her eyes misting— although how much of that was due to exhaustion, and how much to genuine emotion, was uncertain. "You made curtains? Ida Mae, thank you. Thank you so much."

The older woman looked uncomfortable. "Well, I ain't saying it's much. Not up to your usual, anyhow. But it'll get her through."

"I know Lori will love it," Bridget said sincerely. "We're hoping she'll be home on Wednesday."

"Well, at least we'll be shed of them city folks by then," Ida Mae said with a curt nod of satisfaction. "That woman called about fifty times. I finally just let that machine pick it up."

"Thanks, Ida Mae." The fatigue was starting to show in Bridget's voice as she contemplated wading through all those telephone calls, hoping against hope that none of them was a last-minute change in the menu. She let her purse slide off her shoulder and propped herself up wearily against the foyer table. "Listen, I'm really going to need your help if we're going to pull this thing off for tomorrow. Did you get a chance to look at the recipes I marked?"

"Already got the chicken thawing," replied Ida Mae, "and the boy picked up the crab this morning. We got it under control."

For a moment Bridget was so overwhelmed with gratitude that she couldn't speak. Finally she managed a "thank you" on a single, exhaled breath. Then, hesitantly, "I don't suppose you know why the yard smells like—"

"So, I spruced up the flower beds for you a little while I was at it," Noah was saying as he and Lindsay came out of the sunroom. "And I started building that goat house Bridget wanted. The goat already chewed through the rope on the gate twice, but I got her back. Meantime I had an idea about that brochure you were talking about. I thought, what if instead of pictures we used a sketch of the house, maybe with some flowery things and wedding birds—you know, doves—on the front fold, all in black and white, to give it kind of a classy look. Then inside we could just use a repeat of the sketch, in miniature, to separate the paragraphs. If you don't take up all that room with photographs you can use a single fold instead of a trifold brochure. Anyhow, I made a mock-up for you to look at."

Lindsay drew an astonished breath, but before she could even speak he went on, proudly, "And I got the grapes fertilized for you this morning. Farley came over and helped. Don't worry," he assured her, "I called up Dominic to ask him what to use and he said chicken sh—I mean, manure, mixed with that fish stuff he left in the barrels in the barn would do the trick. It sure does stink though, doesn't it? I figure ya'll'd be tired after your party," he explained generously, "and no need for you to have to get out there and work on Sunday."

Lindsay stopped and turned to look at him, and for a long moment she said nothing. Bridget straightened up slowly, holding her breath. Then Lindsay grasped Noah's face in both hands, looked him hard in the eye, and kissed him soundly on the forehead.

"Thank you, Noah," she said earnestly, "for taking the initiative. And you're grounded for two weeks. School and work only."

"Damn," he swore, scowling fiercely.

"Nice try though," Bridget told him, smiling. "Really nice. And the flower beds look terrific."

"Also," Lindsay added casually, "next time ask us before you take on a big job like the grape vines."

"Yeah, I know." Noah gave her a sly look. "Dominic said you asked him to supper Sunday after he finished with the grapes. But don't worry. I said he should come on anyway."

Bridget looked at Lindsay questioningly, and Lindsay patted Noah's shoulder, perhaps a bit too firmly. "You're a treasure, Noah. A real take-charge kind of guy. Now, how about taking a paintbrush and some white paint and touching up the arbor in the rose garden?"

He tossed her a salute and headed for the door. Ida Mae said, "I got cheese biscuits in the oven. I mixed in some chives like you said. I never heard of putting raspberry jam on cheese biscuits with ham, but I reckon you learn something new every day."

She left for the kitchen, and Bridget watched her go, her expression softened with affection. Lindsay came over to her, bumped her shoulder with her own, and smiled. "Family," she said, and Bridget returned a weary, contented smile.

"Yeah," she agreed. "Just when you think you've got them figured out, they go and do something nice."

For a moment they leaned together, reveling in the moment. Then Lindsay asked, "What are we going to do about the smell?"

Bridget hesitated. "Scented candles?"

Lindsay gave her a dour look." I don't think so."

"Maybe there's some kind of—I don't know—odor neutralizer for fertilizer. I'm going to call Farley."

Lindsay suppressed a groan. "Don't call Farley. Don't call anybody. He'll just try to fix it and make things worse. Noah tried to fix things. Dominic tried to fix things. That's the trouble with men—they're always doing something when there's absolutely nothing to be done."

"Well, what are we going to do? Even if we serve lunch inside, they're going to want to tour the gardens, and the wedding planner will have to do measurements and whatnot, and after all this work they're going to cancel everything because of the fertilizer, I just know it." There was genuine panic in her eyes as she confessed, "I spent over $250 on the food for the tasting. We can't lose this job!"

"Maybe that wouldn't be the worst thing that ever happened to us," Lindsay said, barely mustering the energy to get the words out. "Do you know how long it's been since I've slept?"

"At least as long as it has been since I have. And I have twelve hours to prepare a meal that should take two days to do right."

They looked at each other for a long, bleak moment. Then Lindsay said, "I guess we'd better get started, then."

৵

After her shower, Cici decided to close her eyes for just a minute, and when she woke up it was after five. By the time she made it back to the hospital, Lori was finishing her dinner, and she and her father were joking about the quality of the Jell-O while CNN played on the overhead television. Cici came forward and kissed her hair, and Lori said, "You smell good."

"I also come bearing gifts." Cici opened the bakery bag she carried and brought out two chocolate cupcakes.

Lori's eyes lit up. "I love you, Mom." She began peeling the paper cup off one.

Richard occupied the chair that had been pulled up close to the bed. He took out his phone and dialed in to check his messages. Cici gave him a hard look and after a moment he understood. "Right," he said. He stood and offered the chair to her.

"So," Cici said as she took her seat, "what have you been up to all day?"

"Well," Lori answered, swallowing a bite of cupcake, "first Prince William came to visit, then we took in an opera, and after that . . ."

"Very funny."

"That phone of hers hasn't stopped ringing all day," Richard said. Then he spoke into his own phone. "Hi, sweetheart, I thought I told you we're not taking any meetings with Caplin . . . no, let him stew in his own juices for a while . . . Yeah, that's fine, let me know."

Cici smiled mirthlessly. "What a nice visit the two of you must have had then," she said. "Of course"—she turned a meaningful look on Richard—"it might have been easier to do it by phone."

He ignored her and dialed another number.

Lori said, "Kelley came by with my stuff. And look." She pointed to an array of teddy bears that had joined the dozens of pink roses that were arranged in jars and vases around the room, along with a cluster of balloons. "People have been sending things all afternoon."

Cici smiled. "Now you're starting to get the hang of being sick."

The nurse pushed open the door. "I don't remember seeing cupcakes on the menu," she remarked with an admonishing smile as she took Lori's tray. "You know the rule is that no outside food can be brought in unless you share with the nursing staff."

"Talk to my mom," Lori said. "I have half a cupcake left," she added generously, holding it up.

The nurse laughed. "Thanks, but you look like you need it more than I do. You have some friends waiting outside," she added, "but we only allow three visitors at a time. Shall I send in one?"

"Oh," Lori said, and was unable to hide her disappointment. "I guess."

Richard flipped his phone closed and came forward. "Send them all in," he said. "Your mother and I were just going to go get a bite to eat."

"I just got here!" Cici protested as he took her arm and gently tugged her to her feet.

Richard kissed Lori's cheek. "No booze or loud music," he advised, and she laughed.

"I'll be back in an hour," Cici said as he ushered her toward the door. "And if you get tired, just tell your friends to leave."

But even as Richard opened the door three high-energy, cheery college students pushed inside, bearing more balloons and teddy bears and all of them talking at once. Lori squealed with delight and opened her arms to receive the gifts and the hugs, and Cici muttered, "You always have to be the cool dad."

"Seeing those kids will do her more good than anything you or I could do." He dropped her arm as they reached the elevator. "Besides, I'm starved."

"What a pity," she replied. "Because the one thing you won't find in this hospital is food."

"Good thing I called ahead for reservations at Bon Homme, then," he said. "Continental cuisine, wine cellar, and just around the corner. Also . . ." The elevator pinged and he touched her shoulder to escort her inside. "Brick oven pizza."

Cici lifted an eyebrow. "Now I remember why I married you."

He smiled at her as the elevator doors closed.

❧

Bridget didn't have to call Farley. He was waiting at the back door when she came down from her shower, somewhat refreshed and dying for a cup of coffee. When she smelled the aroma of fresh brew intermingled with that of sautéed onions and warm cheese biscuits and sweet caramel sauce, she blessed Ida Mae with every fiber of her being and made a private vow never to think another mean thought about her—for at least the rest of the week.

The woman of the hour was saying, "I'll tell her you was here," as she closed the screen door. She had a quart-sized jar of clear golden honey in her hand.

"Farley brought you some honey," Ida Mae said as Bridget came in. She set the jar on the counter and went back to the stove.

"Red clover," Farley called through the screen door.

"Oh, hi, Farley," Bridget said. She detoured, a little reluctantly, from the coffeepot to the back door. She stepped out onto the porch and quickly closed the kitchen door behind her, trying not to make a face at the smell that was even stronger on this side of the house.

"I'm glad you're here," she said. "I want to ask you something."

He took his cap off quickly, and Bridget noticed the absence of his customary chewing tobacco and soda can. "It's from the bees that live on the far side of your meadow," he explained. "You know, where it's all covered with red clover of a season? I thought you might like it."

"Why, thank you, Farley," Bridget said, smiling. "That was really thoughtful. And thank you for helping Noah fertilize the vineyard this morning, but what I wanted to ask you was—"

"Weren't no problem," he replied. "Sorry about the smell, but you just keep your windows closed for a day or two and it'll be fine."

"Well, that's the problem. You see—"

"Miss Bridget," Farley said somberly. He held his cap

against his heart and the expression in his clear hazel eyes was grave. "I heard about the tragedy that struck your house. Now, you know I'm not much of a churchgoing man, but if it would help your feelings any, I'd be proud to sit by you at preaching on Sunday and pray for the good Lord to lay his hand on that precious girl."

Bridget's astonishment was so great that her jaw actually dropped. "Why—why, I . . . that's so sweet of you. I don't know what to say. But Lori's fine, really, she'll be coming home next week."

He looked disappointed. "Glad to hear it." He started to put his hat back on, then turned back, an expression close to hopeful in his eyes. "But about Sunday . . ."

"Sunday," Bridget repeated slowly as her beleaguered thought processes gradually began to catch up with the conversation. "Farley, did you say the smell would be gone in a couple of days?"

"Yes'm," he allowed. He cleared his throat and straightened his shoulders. "But what I wanted to say was—"

"That's it!" exclaimed Bridget. "That's exactly what we have to do!" She stretched to her tiptoes, caught the big man's face between her hands, and kissed his cheek. "Farley, you are a lifesaver! Thank you!"

She hurried back inside, calling for Lindsay, leaving Farley to touch a wondering finger to the place her lips had been.

❧

Lindsay was on the telephone in the office, and a big grin was spread over her face. "Dominic," she declared, "we are going to make you the best dinner you ever had! Just not on Sunday," she added quickly. She hesitated, and laughed in response to something he said. "You bet. Thank you! You saved our lives."

She turned to Bridget as she hung up the phone. "Dominic says—"

"The smell will be gone by Sunday," Bridget supplied.

"Which means we just have to move the tasting to Sunday afternoon."

"Which means we actually have time to get ready for it!"

Lindsay sank back into the chair and Bridget leaned against the doorframe with folded arms, each of them taking a moment to enjoy their victory. Then Bridget tilted her head toward the telephone. "You called Dominic."

Lindsay shrugged. "Was that Farley's truck I heard pulling up?"

"Hmm. He brought some honey." Bridget was thoughtful for a moment. "You know, if this whole thing with the fertilizer hadn't happened, we would have killed ourselves getting ready for tomorrow."

"I didn't want to worry Cici," agreed Lindsay, "but with just the two of us and Ida Mae—even if Noah could have been drafted to polish the silver and peel potatoes—we would have been up all night."

"Literally. And it still would have been a disaster, because my brain is fried."

"Mine, too."

Bridget grinned. "So, I guess the moral of the story is that sometimes men are worth the trouble."

"Even if only by accident."

Bridget turned for the door, suddenly energized. "I'll tell Ida Mae to put the food back in the refrigerator."

"And I'll call Catherine." Lindsay turned back to the phone.

"And then," Bridget began.

"Bed!" they finished in chorus.

When Richard walked into a restaurant, he got the best table, the head waiter, the reserve wine. Part of it was the Hollywood cachet that clung to him like cheap cologne; part of it was just being—well, Richard. He expected the best, and he always got it.

Cici forgot how much that used to annoy her. Now she remembered only how much she missed living like that.

"So," Richard said, slicing into his porterhouse, "tell me about this farm of yours."

"You wouldn't like it. Not a supermodel in sight. And no home gym."

Cici had ordered a smoked chicken and fire-roasted pepper thick-crust pizza with sun-dried tomatoes and, yes, shaved truffles, because Richard was paying. She took a bite and barely repressed a moan of ecstasy as Richard said, "Very funny. You have horses, I suppose. Isn't this part of the country known for its jumpers?"

Cici held up a staying finger. "Please," she murmured. "This is a sacred moment." She took another bite of the pizza. "Oh, my God. Ida Mae never made anything like this."

He smiled at her across the candlelit table. "Well, whatever it is about that farm, it must agree with you. You look great."

Cici was so surprised she almost forgot about the pizza. "Thank you."

He cut and speared another bite of his steak. "I mean it. Ten years younger, at least. And I like your hair."

"Oh." Self-consciously she touched her freshly blow-dried locks. "Miss Clairol Honey-Blond."

"It's longer, isn't it?"

"Since the last time you saw me, five years ago?"

"Lori sends pictures," he pointed out with a small frown. "And you're in most of them."

She didn't know what to say to that, so she turned back to her pizza.

"No horses," she said after a moment.

"What?"

"We don't have horses," she explained. "We have sheep. And chickens, and a deer, and a crazy dog. And a goat," she remembered.

"Good God." He paused with a forkful of baked potato poised in midair. "It sounds very . . . *Beverly Hillbillies*."

She laughed. "Not a bad comparison, actually."

"And somehow this . . . paradise . . . managed to seduce my daughter from her future as president of a Fortune 500 company to a major in—what does she call it? Agronomy?"

Cici looked at him levelly. "Lori," she told him, "was never going to be president of a Fortune 500 anything."

He thought about this for a moment, and shrugged. "Maybe not. Do you think she's serious about this wine thing?"

Comfortable now on the subject of their daughter, Cici relaxed and began to talk. She talked about the time Lori had spent at Ladybug Farm, exploring her talents and discovering her passions; she talked about their successes and their failures. As Richard ordered a second bottle of wine, she told him about Noah, and what an astonishing young man he was growing into, and about their plans and hopes for the vineyard. She talked about the rhythm of their life at Ladybug Farm, about the way the sunrise painted a pinkish yellow glow on the stone floor of the kitchen, and how the dew glistened when she went to gather eggs in the morning, and how one could hear the rain coming across the valley long before it actually reached their house. And, simply talking about it, she felt an ache of homesickness that was so intense it actually tightened her throat.

Richard told funny stories about his celebrity clients— none of which Cici was actually convinced were true—and made dry observations about life in the high-speed world of the Hollywood glitterati. And even though the tales he told were tongue-in-cheek, even though the life he described was light-years away from her own—or anything she wanted her own to be—he made her laugh. He also made her a little envious. And for two and a half hours, he took her out of her everyday worries and into a world where living was easy, and someone else picked up the check.

Over brandy Alexanders and a decadent chocolate dessert topped with amaretto ice cream and two spoons, Cici said, "You know, Richard, sometimes I forget what a nice guy you can be." She smiled at him. "Thank you for tonight. I needed it."

He lifted his glass to her and replied in kind, "You know, Cici, I really like the woman you've become. I don't know if I've told you that often enough."

She swirled a spoonful of ice cream and popped it into her mouth. "I don't think you ever told me that. Are you going to eat any of this?"

He looked at her for a moment, his eyes unreadable in the candlelight, his smile absent, almost as though he wanted to say something else. Then he picked up the other spoon. "Don't eat all the ice cream," he said.

෨ඏ

Visiting hours were over by the time they returned to the hospital, and the nurse told them Lori was asleep. They sneaked into her room anyway.

"I feel like a terrible mother," Cici whispered. "My baby is lying there with her leg in a cast and I'm two hours late. With brandy on my breath."

"I wouldn't worry about it," Richard said softly, smiling in the dark. "I somehow don't think she'll mind."

Cici tiptoed across the room, and smoothed back a strand of hair that had escaped from Lori's braid. She bent forward and kissed her sleeping daughter's cheek. When she straightened, Richard was standing beside her, very close.

"Look at that beautiful creature," he said. His voice was a half whisper, almost like prayer, and his hand dropped to Cici's shoulder, fingers massaging gently. "That wonderful girl." He looked at Cici, his eyes tender, his smile sad and far away. "You know, sweetie, whatever else we did wrong, we did this one thing right. And that makes it all worth it, doesn't it?"

Cici nodded, and returned his smile, and when he slipped his arm around her shoulder, she let herself lean into him.

They stood there beside Lori's bed, watching her sleep, for a long time.

Richard murmured, after a time, "Lori was right. You do smell good."

Cici straightened up, and stepped away. "I should go."

"Where are you staying?"

She hesitated. "The Embassy."

He smiled. "So am I." He held out his hand. "Want a ride?"

Cici found his eyes in the dimness and held them. Slowly, she smiled, too. "Okay," she said.

She slipped her hand into his, and they left.

May 21, 2008

My dearest love,

I don't know how many more letters I'll be able to write to you, and I have so much more I wanted to say. The problem is that the things I want to say can't be said in a letter. I want so much for you, and I'm so sorry I can't tell you in person.

I want your life to be filled with color.

I want you to laugh every day.

I want you to know what you want, and to learn how to earn it.

I want you to be unafraid.

I want you to remember me, but I know you won't.

I will never, ever forget you.

And I love you.

11

A Small Affair

TO: SMarcello319@mico.net
FROM: LadiLori27@locomail.com
SUBJECT: Change of Plans

Dear Sergio,

I just wanted to tell you I won't be taking the internship after all. I did something stupid and ended up with my leg in a cast, and I won't even be able to finish my last week of school, much less my final exams, so I'm out of the running. Anyway, thanks for all you've done. I'm really sorry—

Lori

TO: LadiLori27@locomail.com
FROM: SMarcello319@mico.net
SUBJECT: RE: Change of Plans

Lori, bellissima!

I am beyond consolation that you are broken! Are you in pain? Tell me what happened. Will you Skype with me? If I could fly with wings, I would be by your side before this e-mail reaches you—

Sergio

TO: SMarcello319@mico.net
FROM: LadiLori27@locomail.com
SUBJECT: RE: RE: Change of Plans

Sergio—

You're very sweet, but I can't Skype with you. Don't worry about me, I'm fine. Just disappointed. Thanks for being my friend. I guess you'd better get back to your life though, and I'll get back to mine.

Lori

TO: LadiLori27@locomail.com
FROM: SMarcello319@mico.net
SUBJECT: RE: Change of Plans

Lori, dearest heart—

What have I done? Why are you so cold to me? You are more than my friend. I can't bear the thought of not talking to you every day, even if we talk only through machine. Why are you cruel?

My heart is in pieces—

Sergio

TO: LadiLori27@locomail.com
FROM: SMarcello319@mico.net
SUBJECT: RE: Change of Plans

Lori—

Now I am anxious. I write and you don't answer. Do you know how this hurts me? Please tell me you are not dead. I cannot bear this worry.

Sergio

TO: SMarcello319@mico.net
FROM: LadiLori27@locomail.com
SUBJECT: RE: RE: Change of Plans

Dear Sergio,

Please forget about me. I'm not dead.

Lori

TO: LadiLori27@locomail.com
FROM: SMarcello319@mico.net
SUBJECT: RE: Change of Plans

Dear Lori—

Why must you be so certain of bad things? Why must you cut me from your life? I can make you smile. I can make your days go faster while you get better. I would be in the room with you if I could but if you will only let me, I will be still in your heart. You are always in mine. Do not do this unkind thing. I am now and always your friend—

Sergio

TO: LadiLori27@locomail.com
FROM: SMarcello319@mico.net
SUBJECT: RE: Change of Plans

Lori? I wait for you—

Sergio

TO: LadiLori27@locomail.com
FROM: SMarcello319@mico.net
SUBJECT: RE: Change of Plans

Still I am waiting—

S

TO: LadiLori27@locomail.com
FROM: SMarcello319@mico.net
SUBJECT: RE: Change of Plans

I will wait forever—

S

There was a light tap on Lori's door and she closed the computer screen, quickly swiping away a tear with the heel of her hand as she called, "Come in."

It was early for visitors, and she expected her mom or

dad—even though neither one of them ever knocked. At first she didn't recognize the curly-haired young man who hesitantly poked his head inside the door. "Hi," he said. "Is it okay?" He looked around uneasily. "I mean, you never know what you're going to walk in on in a hospital."

"Come in," she repeated. "No dead bodies, and I've got all my clothes on."

He smiled as he took note of her pink Hello Kitty sleepshirt and her leg, naked except for the cast, supported by a pillow atop the bedcovers. "Well, most of them, anyway."

Lori frowned a little as she tugged a corner of the blanket over her partly exposed thigh. "It's Mark—right?"

"Right. The guy who, uh . . ."

"Right," she said.

He came inside, and she noticed he was holding a manila envelope in the hand that was not in a sling. He said, "I won't stay. I know I'm probably the last person you want to see right now."

She shrugged dispiritedly.

"I just wanted to bring you this." He took two quick steps toward the bed, thrusting the envelope at her. "I spoke to Kryker," he began.

She sat up straighter, taking the envelope from him curiously. "You talked to my professor?"

"Our professor," he corrected. "Anyway, I told him what happened, and he said if you can e-mail your exam to him before his office closes at four, he'll grade it with the rest of the finals. They're essay questions," he explained, "and all the tests were different so there's no way you could cheat. Not that you would," he added quickly.

Lori opened the envelope and pulled out the papers, her eyes widening with wonder. "You did this for me?" She looked up at him. "But why? I told you, I don't blame you for the accident. It was my fault."

He shrugged. "I just know how I'd feel if I'd worked all year and then lost out right before the end of the semester."

"Oh, I . . ." For a moment she couldn't finish. "Thank you."

He smiled. That was when she noticed that he was, as her mother had observed previously, kind of cute.

"Well," he said. "I won't stay. You'd better get to work."

He turned for the door, and Lori said quickly, "Are you finished? With your exams, I mean?"

"Just about," he said. "I have one more, but it's just a matter of showing up."

"Well, maybe, if you want to, I mean, and if you don't have to study," Lori ventured, "you could come back sometime and we could talk?"

He seemed to consider that. "Are you allowed to eat pizza?"

She grinned. "Pepperoni and mushroom?"

He gave her a thumbs-up. "I'll see you this afternoon."

Lori was still grinning as she opened her laptop, closed the e-mail program, and started her exam.

❧

Cici closed the phone and returned it to Richard. "Lori says under no circumstances are we to get there before noon. Apparently her professor agreed to let her take her final from the hospital, so that's what she's doing."

"Is she well enough to do that?"

"Apparently so."

The quick worry lines that had appeared between Richard's brows smoothed, and he smiled as he tucked a strand of Cici's hair behind her ear. "Well, well," he murmured. "Whatever shall we do with the extra time?"

They were having breakfast at a sidewalk café on the downtown mall, a tree-lined, brick walkway flanked by shops, galleries, and eateries of every description. The morning sun cast dappled shadows over the iron lacework of the table and the brilliant blooming flowers that tumbled over the sides of planter boxes on either side of the street. Cici returned a smile that was hopelessly coy and picked up her to-go coffee cup. "Let's walk," she said.

He was surprisingly agreeable. He took his own coffee and twined his fingers through hers as they started down the street. "This is charming," he said. "Reminds me of Marseilles, in a way."

Cici sipped her coffee. "I've never been. But it's a little like Paris, with the shops and the flower boxes."

"We should have gone to Paris together."

She shrugged. "You were too busy going to law school. And I was too busy changing diapers."

"I've missed you."

She tried not to choke on a mixture of coffee and laughter. "Come on, Richard. All we ever did was fight."

"Not all," he reminded her. "And I miss fighting with you. No one else in my life has the balls to stand up to me like you do."

"I don't believe that. And even if I did, I'm not sure it's a compliment."

Now he laughed. "Since when did we have to worry about complimenting each other?"

She stopped to peer into the window of a not-yet-open fashion boutique. "Cute top," she said, pointing. "I'll bet Lori would like it."

"We'll come back and buy it for her when the shop opens."

When they started walking again, he draped his arm around her shoulders. It made walking a little awkward; she wasn't accustomed to matching her pace with his. But she didn't protest.

He looked around contentedly. "This is nice. A great place to retire."

She chuckled, sipping her coffee. "I can't picture you retired."

He said, "I couldn't picture you retired either. But you seem pretty happy on that horse farm of yours."

"No horses," she reminded him. "Chickens, remember? Sheep."

"I mean it, Cici. This game is for the young. You're nothing in L.A. if you're not twenty-eight years old. And what do I have to prove, anyway? I've been there, done that. And done it a hell of a lot better than any of those punks ever will."

She smiled and saluted him with her cup. "You bet you have."

Suddenly he turned to her, grasped her waist, and swept her across the walkway to a concrete bench. Before she could so much as yelp a protest, he sat her down on the bench and sat close beside her. His eyes were urgent and sincere and the hand that gripped hers was strong.

"Cici, I've been thinking," he said. "The two of us—here we are, with a grown-up daughter, all these years later, and we never really got to have the life we promised each other. But maybe it's not too late. Think about it. All those things we were going to do, the places we were going to see. We could get on a boat, we could sail the Greek Islands."

Cici said, "I've been to Greece, with Bridget and Lindsay. It was my fiftieth birthday present to myself."

He looked only momentarily disconcerted. "We could go to Antarctica, Dubai, Istanbul. Or spend a month in Fiji."

Cici laughed, albeit a bit uneasily. "Me, in Fiji."

"Or," he said, laying a hand aside her face, "we could just be quiet together. Dig in the dirt, watch the sunset, take walks on the beach. It doesn't have to be too late."

She caught his hand against her face, twining her fingers in his, and her expression softened with tenderness as she looked at him. "Richard," she said softly. "Last night was great, but . . ."

"No buts." His fingers tightened on hers, and their joined hands drifted to her knee. "I know you think this is coming out of nowhere, but it's not. I've been thinking about it for a while, about what you've done here, the life you have, and I've got to tell you, it sounds good to me. Better than good."

It became more of an effort to keep up the smile. "You'd go out of your mind within a month."

"And then when Lori . . . when I thought I might lose Lori . . ." He dropped his eyes briefly, and then looked at her again. There was nothing there except sincerity, and, she thought, more courage than she had ever known from him. "And then, seeing you again . . . Suddenly I knew what was important, Cici. The only thing that's ever been important."

She dropped her eyes to their hands so that he could not see the discomfort in her gaze. For a moment, she actually expected to see his hand as she remembered it from their youth, strong and tanned and supple, the hand that tossed a football and caressed her body to the point of madness, sporting the college ring with the sapphire stone. And she expected to see her own hand, smooth and white and delicately freckled with the sleek French manicure she always used to wear. Instead she saw raised veins and blotchy skin below his perfectly buffed nails, chapped knuckles and freckles that had turned to liver spots on hers. That made her smile a little, sadly.

"Richard," she began.

Richard said quietly, "I never stopped loving you."

Cici stared at him for a long and silent moment. And at last all she could say was, "Oh."

They were ready.

Four glasses of chilled peanut soup were lined up on the top shelf of the refrigerator. Maryland crab cakes and honey-glazed fried chicken were ready to be dropped into separate pans for frying, with the dill-caper butter softening near the stove. The mini quiches and caramelized onion tarts were baking, and the brie en croute was ready to be popped into the second oven. The Midori sauce just needed to be heated. A bowl of chopped fresh heritage tomatoes, perfectly seasoned with herbs that had been cut from the garden only that morning, was ready to be spread on crisp garlic-infused baguette slices and topped with goat cheese. And, even though it was not part of the menu, Bridget had made a double fudge cake to be served with her special caramel sauce and fresh lavender whipped cream.

The porch was decorated with four round tables covered in multicolored calico topped with Battenberg lace. All four tables displayed centerpieces of roses fresh from their garden in various containers—a silver teapot, a china bowl, a coffee urn—and set with an eclectic mix of Limoges and Haviland. White Irish linen napkins trimmed with hand tatting were rolled inside twig napkin rings, each one accented with a rose bud. Even though it was two o'clock in the afternoon, candles flickered in crystal water glasses, and the flames were reflected in the cut glass wineglasses at each place setting. Only one table had chairs around it, and on that table was a tray of four sparkling mimosas in champagne flutes.

Lindsay and Bridget looked cool and collected in light summer dresses, with their hair swept back and their makeup touched up at least twice in the past hour. Rebel was in the barn with a padlock on the door. The gate to the chicken yard, likewise, was latched and locked. The goat and the deer were in separate stalls inside the barn. And the smell of fertilizer was, for the most part, but a distant memory. They were ready.

Their guests arrived an hour and a half late in a big white Lincoln Town Car with a blue convertible roof. Catherine, in a crumpled linen pants suit that still managed to look safari stylish, was driving. Lindsay waved at her as she got out of the car, and she took off her sunglasses and lifted a hand to them regally. From the passenger seat emerged a plump, dark-haired woman in a black skirt and navy cotton blouse that they assumed was the mother of the groom, followed by Traci, scowling at her cell phone and looking disheveled and discontented. And then both back doors opened and out poured six other young women of various coloring and description, all of them stretching and groaning and all talking at once.

"Good God, Traci, could it be any closer to the end of the *earth*?"

"There's no signal on my cell phone!"

"No one is ever going to be able to find this place, you know that."

"I don't see any sheep. Do you see sheep?"

"Oh, wait, there they are. Pul-leeeze tell me we don't have to hike all the way over there!"

"Well, at least it's not as bad as Kayla's wedding, remember that? We had to walk two blocks to the beach!"

"Carrying her train!"

"Will you people shut up?" This was from Traci. "I almost had a signal!"

Lindsay and Bridget stared at the bejeaned and ponytailed crowd that was spreading across their front lawn. "They brought the whole wedding party," Lindsay said, disbelieving.

"Four people." Bridget's voice was little more than a squeak as she tried to keep the smile plastered on her face, and to keep from being overheard. "The bride, the mother of the bride, the mother of the groom, the wedding planner. There were supposed to be only four people!"

Lindsay shared with her a look of dismay. "Guess we should have taken time to read all those e-mails after all."

"I have to make more soup!"

"Forget that. Make more mimosas."

Bridget hurried into the house, and Lindsay went down the steps, plastering a welcoming smile on her face. "Hello," she said, extending her hand to the woman in black. "I'm Lindsay."

The woman did not smile, and did not take Lindsay's hand. She tilted up the oversized white-framed sunglasses just enough to get a good look at Lindsay, and she said, "Well, this could hardly be more inconvenient, could it? Giving up my entire Sunday to drive into the middle of godforsaken nowhere. I certainly hope you people are better equipped at keeping your commitments on the day of the wedding."

Lindsay's smile faded. "As I explained to Catherine," she said coolly, "we had an emergency. Our friend's daughter is in the hospital."

The dark-haired woman looked at Catherine. "Really, Catherine, what were you thinking? I can't believe all this nonsense was inspired by Michelle Obama's ridiculous little garden. I mean, it's not as though you can't have an organic wedding in the city, and no one is going to drive all the way out here no matter how trendy it is. Where are the guest cottages?"

Lindsay's eyes widened. "Guest cottages?"

Catherine looked slightly more harried than she had on the occasion of their last meeting. "Darling," she said to Lindsay, "meet Margaret Thornton, the mother of the groom. And these"—she waved in the general direction of the bevy of chattering young women who were flitting like butterflies around the car—"are the girls."

"Catherine, you know we never made any arrangements

for guest accommodations . . ." And then she stopped, looking around. "Where's the wedding planner?"

"I'm afraid she didn't work out *at all*," Catherine confided as she came forward. "Impossible to work with, and she just didn't understand our concept from the beginning. After all, we're just talking about a small affair, here. That's why, my dear"—she slipped her arm cozily through Lindsay's—"we thought it would be easier all around for you all to manage the entire project from here. Don't you agree? It will save all kinds of confusion."

"Well, I—"

Catherine suddenly pivoted and raised her arm, pointing her key fob at the car. With a small *beep* the trunk of the car lifted, and she shouted, "Girls! Bring in the dresses! And don't try to carry them all at once!"

"Dresses?" Lindsay repeated.

"Traci's had just a teensy bit of trouble making a final decision on the dress," Catherine confessed, "since we were *forced*"—the emphasis on this word was directed at Margaret—"to change the location."

"Oh, yes, it was all my fault," Margaret said. "Traci *asked* me to help her find the first venue, if you recall, since *you* were far too busy with your Save-the-Whale ball . . ."

"So, naturally"—Catherine spoke over her, loudly—"we thought the thing to do would be for her to try them on in the actual location. I'm sure the right dress will simply sing to her once she sees it against this magnificent backdrop. Now, darling, we have so much to cover and such a short time I hardly know where to begin." She turned her head and shouted, so loudly that Lindsay winced, "Traci! Bring the book!"

"Lindsay," Lindsay said, trying to tug her arm away. "My name is Lindsay."

"Yes, of course, dear. Now about the rehearsal dinner . . ."

They had reached the steps, where Bridget was standing with a tray laden with sparkling orange mimosas. "Welcome," she declared with a big, bright smile, "to Ladybug Farm."

The two mothers ascended the steps without Lindsay, removing their sunglasses, surveying the table arrangements with a critical eye. Each of them plucked a mimosa off the tray without acknowledging their hostess before moving around the porch.

"Well, now," said Catherine, smiling. "Isn't this sweet?"

"Very farmer-in-the-dell," agreed Margaret. She sipped the mimosa, made a face, and set the glass on one of the tables. "Catherine," she murmured, "we really must talk about your champagne budget."

Lindsay moved forward quickly. "I know you wanted a farmhouse theme," she said, "so I set this up to show you what we could do with the reception. I wanted to evoke an old-fashioned tearoom feeling, and of course mixing china and silver patterns is very trendy . . ."

Catherine lifted an eyebrow. "I thought we had decided on *Lawrence of Arabia*."

Lindsay bit down hard on her first reply and managed pleasantly, "That was several e-mails ago."

"Well, it is sweet," Catherine said carefully. "I only wish we were doing the bridal luncheon here."

"Bridal luncheon?" croaked Bridget in alarm. She set the tray down on one of the tables with a clatter.

"Unfortunately, we've already reserved the Fairmont," Catherine said, and Bridget sagged visibly with relief.

"Traci!" Catherine shouted. "For heaven's sake, where is the book?"

"Don't have a freakin' cow." Traci took the steps two at a time, carrying an overstuffed three-ring binder under one arm, and glaring at her telephone as she repeatedly pushed buttons. "When are you people *ever* going to get with the twenty-first century? Jeez, how can I have a wedding in a place I can't even make a telephone call?"

She dropped the heavy binder on the table beside the tray of mimosas. The table round, which was never designed to hold weight, began to tip. Bridget lunged for it, but too late. The candles, the plates, the silver, the napkins, the center-pieces, the tray of drinks, and the three-ring binder crashed to the floor.

In the aftermath, there was a moment of horrified silence. Then Catherine bent and picked up the binder, checked it for damage, and declared briskly, "Well, then. Let's look at another plan, shall we?"

❧

At seven o'clock, they left.

Calico was out; Apricot Delight and Hint of Spring green were in. Heavy hors d'oeuvres were out; a hot and cold buffet was in. Peanut soup was out, so were crab cakes, so were asparagus, catfish, and anything containing goat cheese. A mashed potato bar and Virginia ham were in.

The only thing on the entire menu of which Margaret approved was Ida Mae's fried chicken. The only thing on the menu of which Traci approved was the fruit.

The bride, after five changes, had decided upon a strapless shift of embroidered ivory silk caught at the hips with crystal studded rosettes and cascading to a half-circle demi train into which would be woven a faint ribbon design in Apricot Delight. It was imperative that the table settings and all decorations include an abundance of Apricot Delight roses, which had already been special-ordered from a florist in Richmond.

The bridal procession would approach through a set of three arches—surely they would have no trouble arranging to rent or build those—which Catherine envisioned decorated with cascading roses and fluttering satin ribbons, and would arrive at a raised podium covered in white satin—simple enough to build—and strewn with apricot rose petals. The buffet should be arranged on the lawn, and of course they would have to arrange for a tent of some sort. The porch of the house was far too casual and much too small for the table setup; but perhaps the interior of the house could be cleared of furniture and twenty or thirty tables could be set up there. The final RSVPs had come in at just under one hundred.

"You're all invited to bring a plus-one, of course," Catherine offered generously, "and mingle with the guests. Who knows how much extra business you'll pick up!"

"But if you're going to be serving at my wedding," Traci said, eyeing them critically, "you'll have to be dressed. I don't want any clashing colors." She handed them each a photocopied sheet of paper. "Here are the stores and the style numbers of some of the dresses I like. You can order them online, but you'd better do it tomorrow if you want them to get here in time. Shoes and stockings, too. No jewelry, and I'd like everyone's hair up."

Bridget took the paper hesitantly. "We're not actually in the wedding party, you know. I don't think it's customary . . ."

Catherine gave her a long-suffering smile. "Every bride deserves to have things just so for her wedding, don't you agree? And don't forget your plus-ones. We don't want the seating to turn out uneven."

Lindsay smiled thinly. "Do our plus-ones have to wear Apricot Delight, too?"

Catherine loved Noah's one-fold brochure design, with its classic charcoal sketch of the house on the front. Margaret was horrified that the nearest hotel was an hour away.

"Which brings us to the rehearsal dinner," Catherine said at last. "We'll be a party of fifteen—no, twenty, is that right, Traci? Nothing fancy—salad, entrée, and dessert—but I'm sure you'll come up with something just delightful. I expect everything will go perfectly smoothly. After all, this is just a small affair. Nothing elaborate."

And so, when they were gone, Bridget and Lindsay sat on the front porch steps with their backs to the wreckage that was left of their elegant little tasting, too stunned to even go to the porch and find their rocking chairs.

"One hundred people," Lindsay groaned. "Where are we going to put all those cars?"

"I have to make one hundred miniature gift baskets." Bridget's voice sounded heavy and thick with disbelief. "Plus twenty big ones for the wedding party."

"Cici is going to kill us."

"There are no rental places around here," Bridget said in growing horror. "Where are we going to get a tent, a hundred chairs, tables—how are we going to set all of that up by ourselves?" She caught her breath. "Oh, my God, did I just volunteer to bake a wedding cake?"

"I told you not to serve dessert. They didn't ask for dessert. They don't deserve dessert."

Bridget moaned. "Whenever anything goes wrong at a wedding, the cake is always involved. Someone drops the cake, someone sits on the cake, someone falls into the cake . . . I don't even know how to start to put together a wedding cake. It's going to be a disaster, I just know it."

"The wedding cake is the least of our problems, if you ask me. Do you have any idea what we've gotten ourselves into?"

"A rehearsal dinner," Bridget said, "for twenty people. The night before a buffet for one hundred."

"Three arbors and a podium. Cici is going to kill us."

They sat in silence, shoulders slumped, arms resting on knees, staring dully at nothing for a long time. Then Bridget said, uncertainly, "What are we going to do?"

"I guess . . ." Lindsay let the sentence drop, and for such a long time that it seemed she wouldn't say anything else. Then she looked at Bridget and sighed, "We are going to do the best we can," she said.

September 24, 2009

Dearest,

As I look back over everything I've written to you over the years I realize there's one thing I never told you, maybe because until now I didn't know how true it was. I am so proud of you. I don't know how I ever deserved anyone as strong and smart and talented and thoughtful and beautiful, inside and out, as you, and I guess the truth is that I don't. If I could have dreamed up the perfect man, down to the last detail, he wouldn't have been half as perfect as you. I want to tell you that in person. I hope you'll understand one day why I can't.

12

Homecoming

Clusters of balloons were tied to the front porch columns and bobbed gaily in the breeze. Rebel circled the car, barking madly, and from the chicken yard Rodrigo perched atop the chicken coop, flapped his wings, and screeched out a welcome. Bambi bounded across the shade-speckled lawn, cowbell clanging, as the front door opened and everyone inside hurried out.

Lori smiled for the first time in days as Lindsay and Bridget rushed down the steps to greet her. Noah followed at an easier pace, and Ida Mae brought up the rear, flapping her apron at the dog and shooing him away. There was a confusion of hugs and questions and welcomes, adjusting doors and crutches and distributing suitcases, and everyone hovering around as she carefully maneuvered her way up the small temporary ramp that Farley had built at the side of the house. She was home.

Noah carried in the boxes she'd brought from her dorm, casually congratulated her on only breaking one leg, and went back to working on the goat house. Ida Mae brought peanut butter cookies and milk to her room, and hurried back to the kitchen to attend to something that was simmering—and smelling wonderful—on the stove. Bridget, Lindsay, and Cici brought in the last of her luggage, and Bridget said, "We have you all set up in the sunroom, honey. It's only ten steps from the bathroom—I counted—and we put your bed right next to the electrical outlet so you can plug in your laptop. Farley hooked up the cable for your TV, and Ida Mae even made new curtains!"

"Fortunately," added Lindsay, with just a touch of bitterness, "I didn't need the rest of the calico."

But Lori was barely listening. She was staring, instead, at the boxes of tissue—apricot and green—and ribbon and candy and champagne glasses and small white wicker baskets, candles, CD cases, and other unidentifiable items that covered every inch of the living room and threatened to spill out into the foyer. So was Cici.

"What in the world?" Cici wondered.

"Wow," said Lori, impressed. "It looks like the shipping room of a party store."

"Oh, I meant to close the doors," Bridget apologized, as she hurried to do so. "It's the only room in the house big enough to set up for the gift baskets."

"Why are they so small?" Lori asked. "How are you going to get the herbal bath salts and the jams and the recipe cards and the scones in there?"

Bridget looked confused for a moment, and then explained, "Oh, these are just the favors for the wedding guests. The components have been arriving all week, and we're trying to get them stuffed as soon as things come in, which is why the room is such a mess. We're just waiting for the mono-grammed chocolates, now."

Lindsay said, "Come on, Lori, let's get you settled in your room. Sorry there's no other place to sit down here."

Cici was still staring at the doors Bridget had just closed. "How many of those things do we have to make, anyway?"

And Lori asked, "What about the big gift baskets? The ones you're selling?"

"Oh, honey, I haven't had time to worry about those this week! When this wedding is over, I'll get back to business as usual, and believe me it will be a pleasure. I'll never complain about having to put together five gift baskets in a week again, I can promise you that."

Lori had started to follow Lindsay to the sunroom, care-fully balancing herself on the unfamiliar crutches, but now she stopped and looked at Bridget. "Five?"

Bridget smiled and nodded. "Business really picked up after that magazine article. But right now the first priority is the wedding." She looked at Cici a little uncomfortably. "We really need to talk to you about that."

Cici eyed her suspiciously. "You mentioned on the phone that things had gotten complicated."

"Just a tiny bit," Lindsay admitted. "A few more guests than we'd counted on, and we're also hosting the rehearsal and catering the rehearsal dinner, and there's the tent ..."

"Tent?"

"Whoa, whoa, whoa." Lori held up a hand for attention, almost lost a crutch and her balance, and the three women rushed to support her. She quickly regained her composure and spoke directly to Bridget. "How long since you looked at the website?" she demanded.

"I don't know," Bridget admitted. "A week or so, I guess. I'm just not used to that stuff, honey, and hardly anyone ever visits the site anyway..."

Lori looked disbelieving. "Do you mean you haven't checked orders in over a week?"

"Well, I suppose I could do that as soon as we get you settled, if it would make you feel better."

"Maybe you'd better," Lori said in an odd, constrained tone. "Because the last time I looked, you had a few orders for gift baskets."

Bridget looked concerned. "Oh, dear. Well, I hope they don't mind waiting. How many?"

"As of yesterday afternoon," Lori said, "two hundred fifty-six."

All three women stared at her. For a long moment no one spoke. Then Lindsay smiled weakly and touched Lori's shoulder to help her to her room. "Welcome home," she said.

❧

They gathered in the sunroom-turned-temporary-bedroom because Lori refused to be excluded from the conversation and would have hobbled to the kitchen or the living room or the porch or the garden to give her opinion if they had tried to meet without her. The trip had already left her looking pale and tired, so they brought more peanut butter cookies from the kitchen, along with a pot of tea, and sat down to strategize.

"You have to fulfill the orders," Lori explained from her

position on the bed, her leg elevated on two pillows, her laptop open on her lap. "You've already taken the money. Otherwise that's fraud."

"I *hate* automatic banking," Bridget said miserably, and picked up another cookie. "Why couldn't they just send checks? That way, if I didn't want their money, I could send it back."

"No one uses checks anymore," Lindsay said. "Even I know that."

The sunroom was a long, narrow space that had once been an actual conservatory. According to Ida Mae, it had been used to house miniature citrus trees and tropical plants in the heyday of the house. The floor was hand-cut Italian tile and had a drain in the center for water runoff. One entire wall was filled with windows—the old-fashioned, double-hung kind that were elaborately trimmed with painted molding. During their first winter there, a tree branch had crashed through the roof of the room and presented a perfect opportunity for remodeling. They hadn't been able to afford completely replacing the roof with glass, as it had been originally, but they had put in four skylights, replastered, and painted the room a pale buttermilk yellow. They had furnished the room sparsely with leftover wicker, a couple of faded floral rugs they did not deem nice enough for the main house, and whatever houseplants they were currently nursing back to health.

Now, however, with Ida Mae's bright calico curtains draped back from the windows, the sunshine spilling over the bed, the potted plants inside, and the rolling green meadows, mountains, and colorful plantings outside, the room was cheery and uplifting, ultimately conducive to good health.

Or at least it would have been, if the mood of its occupants had not been so dire.

"Well, the good news is," said Lori, tapping the keyboard of her laptop, "you did put the 'allow four to six weeks for delivery' disclaimer on your order form. Or at least I did."

"Thank you, Jesus," Lindsay murmured, and when Lori glanced at her askance, she amended quickly, "I mean, thank you, Lori."

"But you've got to acknowledge receipt of the order," Lori went on, "and give them a shipping date. We can automate that if you like."

"Yes," Bridget said quickly, "automate it."

"Hold on," Cici said in alarm, "you can't promise two hundred and fifty-six baskets—"

"Two hundred seventy-three," corrected Lori, and Bridget groaned loudly.

"You don't even *have* two hundred seventy-three baskets," Cici pointed out, "much less the stuff to fill them with! How can you possibly fill all those orders *and* the wedding gift baskets?"

Bridget slumped down low in the wicker chair, closing her eyes. "I'm going to cry."

"Don't cry," Lindsay soothed absently, pouring more tea. "We'll figure this out."

"Cici's right," Bridget said. "I only have about fifty jars of jam left, and I barely have enough dried herbs left to make sachets for the wedding and don't know where I'm going to get the hand lotion and bath salts . . ."

Lori shook her head sadly. "The only thing that causes small businesses to fail more often than apathy is success."

All three women waited for her to explain, but she merely shrugged. "It's an axiom."

Cici drew a breath and turned to Bridget. "Okay," she said. "Your first priority is to fill the wedding order. They've already tasted the pinot noir jam and smelled the hand lotion."

"You can make more jam for the orders," Lindsay suggested. "And dry the herbs in the microwave."

"Microwave?" Bridget looked horrified. "How can I dry herbs in a microwave? And we don't even start to harvest grapes until October! How can I—"

"Strawberry," suggested Cici.

"You didn't actually specify the kind of jam on the website," Lori pointed out. "It just says 'Ladybug Farm vintage wine jams.'"

"Maybe," Bridget said thoughtfully, reluctantly, "a strawberry champagne jam. I've never actually made it but . . ."

"Perfect," declared Lindsay.

"Do you know how many strawberries that will take?" Bridget said, starting to sound panicky again.

"We've got tons in the freezer."

"I'm not sure you can even make jam out of frozen strawberries."

Cici had been studying the extensive notes, drawings, and color swatches left behind by Catherine. Now she looked up, her expression sober. "We have bigger problems than frozen strawberries," she announced. "You do realize that we have exactly eleven days to prepare a sit-down dinner for twenty, a wedding that includes a fifty-foot satin-lined processional with three arbors, a string quartet, a dance floor, and a buffet for one hundred people. Who's ordering the wine, by the way?"

Lindsay looked at Bridget. Bridget looked at Lindsay. Lindsay said, "I guess we are."

"Not to mention putting together all of those mini guest baskets and the big baskets for the wedding party, and, excuse me, but where are we going to get a hundred place settings and glasses?"

"And who's going to wash them afterward?" offered Lori.

Cici looked at the other two with a mixture of severity and dismay. "None of this is in the contract. Why didn't you *tell* me?"

"We figured you had enough to worry about," Lindsay said unhappily.

"Besides, we gave our word," Bridget admitted. "We've just got to figure out a way to make it work."

Lori looked up from the computer. "How much did you say you were charging for the buffet?"

Bridget answered, "Forty-five dollars a head. That includes wine."

"Plus thirty-five each for the gift baskets, and I'm guessing the rehearsal dinner is at least fifty, wine inclusive . . ." She did some calculations. "You're going to be raking in some serious cash."

Bridget sighed. "When you deduct the cost of food and wine, not so much."

Cici regarded her warily. "But you did make certain you figured the profit margin before you quoted the price, right?"

"Of course I did. But they just kept adding things and assuming things, and," she finished unhappily, "I have a feeling our profit margin is a lot smaller than it started out to be."

Cici said, "I have to go look at the contract."

And Lindsay added, standing, "We should let Lori get some rest."

"We should try to pick the rest of the strawberries, if there are any left," Bridget said. "We're going to need every last berry if I'm going to turn them into two hundred fifty-six jars of wine jam."

"We need to get Noah away from that goat house and into the cherry trees with a bucket," suggested Lindsay. "What kind of wine jam can you make from cherries?"

Lori said, without looking up from her laptop, "Leave the cookies."

Cici lingered as the other two women left the room. "You should take a nap," she said, coming over to the bed and reaching for the laptop. "There'll be plenty of time for this later."

But Lori held up a staying hand. "No, it's okay, Mom. I'm not tired, and it's nice to feel useful."

Cici smiled as she sat down on the edge of Lori's bed. "Well, there's never a lack of anything useful to do around here. And I guess you want me to leave you alone so you can e-mail your boyfriend in Italy."

Lori shrugged and tapped another key on the computer, changing screens. "He's not my boyfriend. Never was, really. And now . . ." She shrugged again.

"But you were able to take your exam," Cici pointed out. "You could still . . ."

Lori was shaking her head before she finished. "I withdrew my application," she said. And although she did not meet her mother's eyes, the heaviness in her voice betrayed her disappointment. "You heard what the doctor said. I won't be back to normal with this leg for months yet, and this was a hands-on job in a working vineyard and winery. It wouldn't be right to cheat them out of the help they were expecting, or to take the opportunity away from someone who could actually do the work."

Cici nodded thoughtfully, and then slipped her arm around Lori's shoulders and kissed her hair. "Have I told you lately how proud I am of you?"

Again Lori shrugged, but this time she returned a lopsided smile. "I'll get to Italy," she told her mother. "Eventually."

"You bet you will, sweetie. And I wouldn't be a bit surprised if your friend—your non-boyfriend—is waiting for you when you get there. You are worth waiting for, if I do say so myself. After all, I waited—"

"Nine months and eighteen days for me to be born," Lori supplied. "I know."

"Eighteen excruciating days," Cici reminded her.

"Well, Italian college boys aren't exactly known for their patience, and I'm sure he will have forgotten me long before I get there."

Cici waited. Lori clicked another key.

"He keeps writing me," she admitted, "but I don't answer."

"Over him, huh?" Cici said sympathetically.

"No," Lori interjected quickly, and with surprising fervor. "I mean . . . I don't know." She sighed again. "It just seems kind of . . . pointless. I miss him, and we were really having a lot of fun, texting back and forth. I mean it was almost like we were, you know, dating . . . Perfectly innocent, of course," she assured her mother. And then she sighed. "I guess I'll never know what it might have been. It's probably better that way."

"Then why don't you just e-mail him and tell him it's over?"

"Because," Lori said a little helplessly, "I'm just not sure it is."

Cici considered and rejected a dozen things to say, some of them pointed, some of them not, none of them particularly helpful. Finally she simply smiled, patted her daughter's hand, and advised, "Take a nap. I promise there will be plenty of opportunities for you to feel useful when you wake up."

～

Cici found Lindsay and Bridget sitting on the floor in the big parlor they called the living room, surrounded by baskets, boxes, tissue paper, and cellophane. She sat across from them, forming the third point of a triangle, and folded her jeaned legs under her. "Lori is in love with an Italian," she said.

"Good for her," Lindsay said and passed her a basket. "Fill those champagne glasses with colored candy, wrap them with cellophane, tie each one with an apricot ribbon, and put one in each basket."

Cici gave her a skeptical look. "You're the one who said I should by no means let her go to Italy."

"You're only young once," advised Bridget. She carefully cut and folded a sheet of pale green tissue paper into a triangle, and used it to line another basket.

"Also," Cici said, pouring a measure of candy into a champagne glass, "I looked at the contract and we are screwed. They have to pay for materials, but there's no limit on how much labor we signed up for—at no extra charge. How do these go in?" she asked, tying the ribbon around the cellophane.

Lindsay demonstrated how the champagne glasses fit against the side of the baskets, between the wedding-mix

CDs and the tulle-wrapped scented candles. "Save room for the monogrammed chocolates in the middle," she reminded them. "They're supposed to be delivered today."

"Catherine invited us all to the wedding," Bridget said, trying to make that sound like a good thing. "Even Lori. Plus-ones, too."

"What?"

"Dates. She meant dates."

"I know what *plus-one* means. I just don't know why she felt it necessary to invite us. I mean, we live here. We're the hostesses."

"Actually," confided Lindsay, "I think she just wanted seat fillers, in case some of her fancy friends from DC can't find their way out here. You know, like at the Academy Awards."

"Of course," added Bridget with a glance at Lindsay, "we do have to wear those outfits. Apricot Delight or Hint of Spring green only. And Nearly Nude Shimmer & Silk stockings."

Cici gave a snort of derision. "Maybe you do."

"We were bulldozed," Bridget admitted glumly, passing a tissue-lined basket to Lindsay. "We should have called you before we agreed to anything. It was stupid."

Cici released a heavy breath, and a long silence fell. "That's okay," she said unhappily. "I did something even stupider."

Lindsay slipped a CD into the case, snapped it shut, and placed it in the basket. "You mean sleeping with Richard?"

Cici stared at her. "How did you know?"

"Oh, please." Bridget cut another square of tissue. "You sleep with him every time you see him. The man is like catnip to you."

Cici shifted her gaze away, poured more candy, tied more

ribbon. Then, making a wry, resigned face, she said, "You'd think by now I'd know better."

"Well," replied Lindsay, "the good news is that neither one of you is in jail, so I guess it didn't end in violence."

"He's talking about retiring," Cici said.

"I can picture Richard in Palm Springs," Bridget said thoughtfully. "Golf carts, swimming pools . . ."

"Bikinis," added Lindsay.

"Not unless you count the ones on eighty-year-old women," Bridget said, and the two women burst into giggles.

Cici did not laugh. "Here. He's talking about retiring here."

The giggles evaporated. A kind of slow dread filled Lindsay's eyes. "You don't mean . . . *here*."

And Bridget echoed, "Here?"

Cici met their gazes grimly. "He called a real estate broker."

Bridget stopped folding paper. Lindsay stopped placing CDs in cases. A warm breeze fluttered the lace curtain at the window, a grandfather clock ticked loudly across the room; otherwise all was still. Had there been crickets, they would have been chirping. The three women looked at each other somberly for a long time.

"That," intoned Lindsay, "is not good news."

Cici nodded heavily. "You're telling me."

Into the grim silence that had fallen over the room a sudden clatter of activity spilled: Rebel's excited barking, the braying of a goat, the clang of a cowbell. Noah shouted, "Yo! Dog!" Bridget got up and went to the window. "Someone's coming," she said, surprised. And then surprise mixed with pleasure as she added, "It's Paul!"

They reached the front porch in time to see Noah dragging

a still-barking border collie away by the collar as Paul's blue Prius slid to a stop in front of the steps. Paul got out of the car, pushing his sunglasses up into his hair, and they bounded down the steps to meet him.

"Paul! What a surprise!"

"What are you doing here?"

"Where's Derrick?"

"Why didn't you call? The house is a mess!"

"You look great!"

And again, "What are you doing here?"

"I have come," declared Paul, kissing Cici's cheek, "to solve"—he kissed Lindsay's cheek—"all your problems." He kissed Bridget.

"Well, it's about time someone did," responded Cici fervently, and he laughed.

"I heard you'd had a few setbacks," he said. "Where is our little broken princess, anyway?"

"She's sleeping," replied Cici. She peered into the car, which was packed to the roof with boxes. "What is all this?"

"No, she's not!" Lori called from the porch, leaning on her crutches. "Hi, Uncle Paul. What are you doing here?"

Paul called up to her, "I came to see you, of course!" And he added to Cici as he started up the steps to greet Lori, "Be careful with those boxes. Some of the stuff in them is breakable."

Cici looked after him in astonishment, and Lindsay opened the back door of the car as Noah, having released Rebel in the sheep meadow, came jogging around the corner. Bridget surveyed the packed car. "Is all this for us?"

"I guess so." Cici pried a box from the top of the stack and handed it to Noah. "Help us unpack this, will you, Noah?"

Noah took the box and cast an appraising eye over the remainder. "Whoa, dude," he said as he started up the steps with the box. "What're you doing, moving in?"

Paul turned with an odd, rather rueful smile on his face. "As a matter of fact, I am."

❧

The boxes were sorted by content between the pantry, the office, and the living room/workroom. Two enormous suitcases were hauled to the guest room. Ida Mae brought tall glasses of iced tea laced with sprigs of mint to the porch, along with the last of the peanut butter cookies, grumbling all the while about how some folks didn't have the decency to give a person time to change the sheets before he showed up on her doorstep. Paul called after her, grinning, "I'll change my own sheets, I promise! I've been looking forward to it all the way from Maryland!"

They brought extra chairs onto the porch for Lori and Paul, along with a footstool for Lori to rest her leg. Noah relaxed on the steps with his shoulders resting against a column. All of them waited for Paul to speak.

Paul took a sip of his tea, gave the glass an appraising look, and murmured, "Interesting." He gazed around the porch.

"I'm sure you have your own ideas," he said, "but I would keep the porch decor simple for the wedding. Satin bows and rose bouquets, natural greenery, swags over the door and windows."

Noah stretched for a handful of cookies. "If ya'll are going to talk about that wedding I'm outta here. I've got things to do."

Lori said, "Not me. It took me too long to get here. Besides," she added meaningfully to Noah, "the good stuff always starts as soon as we leave."

Lindsay looked uneasy. "Noah, maybe you'd better get back to the goat house. We want to talk to Paul."

Noah started to rise, but Paul lifted a staying hand. His tone, like his expression, was weary. "No, let him stay. I'm tired of keeping secrets."

Paul's face suddenly looked older than it had when he arrived; his eyes were puffy and his skin sagged. He looked again at his glass, but did not drink. And then he looked at each of them in turn—Noah, Lori, Cici, Bridget, and Lindsay—for a moment before he spoke. "Derrick didn't want you to know, didn't want anyone to know. Some stupid, ridiculous Superman fantasy of his." He took a breath. "Last winter . . . he had a heart attack."

The chorus of gasps and soft "Oh, my God!"s was punctuated by a single flat "Crap" from Noah. Derrick had been a long-distance mentor to Noah, had encouraged his art career, had written a letter of recommendation to John Adams Academy. Even as feminine hands flew to their throats, their eyes went to Noah.

"He's okay," Paul said quickly. "At least physically. As okay as he can be, at any rate. It was a mild heart attack. They sent him home after three days on a regimen of diet, exercise, and statins—and no stress, of course."

Lindsay, Cici, and Bridget released a breath, and Lori said, "God, Uncle Paul, you scared us to death." Noah relaxed marginally, but his eyes stayed fixed on Paul. His life experience so far had taught him to be skeptical of happy endings.

"Yeah, I was pretty scared, too," Paul said. He took another sip of his tea, and grimaced. "But Derrick wanted to pretend that nothing had happened. He was back at the gallery the next day. I'm talking the very next day after he got home from the hospital. I couldn't believe it. Here I had made arrangements to take the whole week off, and he's acting as though he's just taken some time away for a brow lift or something. What *is* that? At first I thought it was vanity, but now I'm thinking Messiah complex."

"Death denial," Lori said sagely, and when everyone looked at her she explained, "We studied it in social psychology. It's a thing with Western culture, especially Americans, where you think you're going to live forever—as long as you use the right mouthwash, go to the right gym, eat the latest fad diet, stop smoking, color your hair . . . Seriously," she insisted. "It's a whole thing."

Paul tasted his tea again, held the glass out, and stared at it. "Okay," he said. "Does anyone but me think this tea tastes funny?"

Bridget reached for his glass. "Let me taste it." Bridget sipped the tea, frowned, and then looked into the glass. She plucked out the decorative green sprig and declared, "Oregano."

Paul lifted an eyebrow. "Interesting."

"We've been having some problems with Ida Mae," Lindsay confided in a half whisper as Bridget got up and tossed the contents of Paul's glass over the railing.

Bridget refilled Paul's glass from the pitcher on the table. "We understand what you've been going through," she told him sympathetically as she handed him the glass.

Paul gave a small shake of his head, even as he smiled his thanks to Bridget. "Bottom line, things haven't been exactly loaded with spalike serenity at home. He won't take time off, he won't take care of himself, he won't take his medicine half the time, and he won't listen to me. I've done everything I know to do, but I just couldn't stand by and watch him destroy himself any longer. So . . ." He smiled bleakly and lifted his glass to them. "Here I am."

"Oh, Paul," Cici said sincerely. "I'm so sorry."

Lindsay's expression was one of abject sorrow. "You've been together longer than most married people I know. I don't know how to think of you apart."

"You should have stayed," Noah said shortly, abruptly. "You don't just run out on people when they're in trouble."

Bridget said gently, "Noah, it's more complicated than that."

But Paul lifted a finger to Bridget and met Noah's eyes. "You're right. But sometimes people need some time apart to figure things out."

Noah pushed to his feet, scowling. "I've got stuff to do."

Lindsay opened her mouth to say something, but Cici stopped her with a small shake of her head.

Lori said philosophically, "Kids. They see everything in black and white." Then she turned to Paul, with only the faintest trace of anxiety. "But it's just temporary, right? I mean, you're working on things?"

Paul returned a small smile, sipped his tea, and told Bridget, "Much better."

Then he said, with forced enthusiasm, "What I'm working

on now is getting you ladies through the wedding from hell. No, no . . ." he insisted when they started to protest, "I got you into this, and I'll get you out. I knew you were in trouble," he confided, "when I heard they'd fired their fourth wedding planner. I mean, excuse me, but Angela Gabriel is only *the* premier event coordinator in the tri-state area. You have to book her years in advance, and these people obviously pulled a hundred strings to even get on the list. Then to fire her? Clearly, they're out of control. So I," he declared magnanimously, "am taking over."

They all spoke at once. "Oh, Paul, really, you don't have to—"

"You're the best friend ever! But really—"

"We'll take it!" Lori declared loudly, both hands raised over the din. And when the other three looked at her, shocked, she returned a stern gaze. "We are in no position to turn down professional help," she informed them.

After a moment, Lindsay chuckled, and even Cici smiled. "Can't argue with that," she admitted.

Bridget gave Paul a one-armed hug. "Thank you," she said. "And may God bless you and yours," she added fervently, "forever."

There was a strange, rhythmic clip-clopping sound, and they turned to see Noah leading the goat around the corner of the porch. The goat was chewing a piece of cardboard, and Noah had a strange look on his face.

"Noah!" Cici cried. "What are you doing? Get that goat off the porch!"

And Lindsay added, "How did she get out of her pen?"

Noah said with an uncomfortable shrug, "Sometimes she

chews through the latch. That's what I've been trying to tell you. She needs a house. Uh . . ." He looked from one to the other of them. "Did somebody leave a box on the back stoop?"

It took them a moment to understand the significance of the dark gooey substance that was smeared around the goat's whiskers and chest hair and the gold-edged cardboard she was slowly masticating as they watched. Bridget rose slowly, her hand over her heart.

"No," she gasped, swallowing hard. "Not the chocolates. Please say it's not the chocolates."

Lindsay's expression was grim. "UPS must have delivered them this morning while we were busy in the back of the house. The driver always leaves packages on the back stoop."

Bridget's voice sounded a little choked, even as her hand traveled to her throat. "That goat," she managed, "did not just eat a hundred individually boxed monogrammed chocolates."

"No," Noah assured her. "Not all of them."

Bridget sank back against the wall and closed her eyes.

Cici looked at Paul and managed a small smile. "Welcome home," she said.

"And," he murmured, dusting off his hands as he rose, "not a moment too soon."

January 12, 2009

Sweetheart,

I wish I could make you understand what it felt like for me to be apart from you all these years, to know you were out there in the world, making your way, making your mark, living your life—all without me. I want you to know how much I wanted to be with you and how hard I tried to find you and, in the end, why I couldn't tell you the truth. I want you to forgive me. I want you to have a good life. I want you to think of me sometimes and smile. It's selfish, I know. But that's what I want.

Because I've always, always loved you.

13

Problems of Their Own

TO: Cici@LadybugFarmLadies.net
FROM: SMarcello319@mico.net
SUBJECT: Lori

Dear Signora Gregory (Lori's mother):

I am Sergio, Lori's friend in Italy who she has told you about I am hoping. I am hoping also you will forgive me that I am e-mailing you in person from the address that is on your website, and that you will not think too badly of my English, which is better when I speak it than when I write it. Please believe that I am not, as my American friends tell me is said, stalking Lori. I am very worried. I know she is hurt with her leg & in hospital. I e-mail but she does not reply. If she is mad with me, that is OK. But I am so worried. Please tell me she is fine.

With all warmest regards,
Sergio Antonio Marcello

"Good heavens," Cici murmured. "I think *I* just might marry him."

"If you don't, I will," said Lindsay, reading over her shoulder.

"Scoot, both of you." Paul waved them away from the desk with a sheet of paper he had just taken from the printer tray. "We need a bigger office."

"You need to call Derrick," Cici said.

He placed the printout in the fax machine and tapped out a number, then took Cici's place in the desk chair as the machine began to grind. "And you," he ordered, "need to find me the telephone number of the biggest funeral home in the county."

Lindsay repeated, alarmed, "Funeral home?"

"Where else are we going to get a hundred chairs on such short notice? Not to mention tents."

Cici laughed out loud as the telephone began to ring. "You are a genius!"

Paul glanced at his watch, picked up the telephone, and declared, "Catherine, darling! You got the copy of the rehearsal dinner menu! Yes, it's true, it's me . . . don't be absurd, it's my pleasure, my pleasure entirely."

Lindsay flung her arms around his neck. "I love you!"

Paul held up his finger for silence, smiling. "No, I don't think twenty individual filets would be more appropriate for the rehearsal dinner. I think we are fortunate to have one of the most gifted chefs in Virginia catering this event, and since the groom's parents are hosting the rehearsal dinner, and since they are paying for roast turkey with fingerling potatoes, that is exactly what we should have."

Lindsay, holding both thumbs up in the air, did a little

dance. Cici sat on the floor with the wafer-sized telephone book and looked under "funeral homes."

"Now," Paul was saying, "about the monogrammed chocolates . . . I know, I know, but a little passé, don't you think? I had something a bit more unique in mind. After all, you've always been such a trendsetter." He rolled his eyes to Lindsay. "I know you don't want ordinary party favors at Traci's wedding . . . Well, as it happens, I did have an idea. Cookies. Yes! Shaped like ladybugs! Yes, exactly—just like Ladybug Farm. No, I don't think it's too late to put in an order . . ."

He covered the phone with his hand and whispered, "Can Bridget make a hundred ladybug cookies by the wedding?"

Lindsay and Cici chorused, "Yes!"

"No, not a problem," Paul was saying to Catherine, "we'll just swap out the chocolates for the cookies, and if there's any difference in price we'll bill you."

Cici and Lindsay clapped their hands over their mouths to smother shrieks of delighted laughter.

"Yes, sweetie, kisses to you, too, and the blushing bride. Umm-hmm. Bye."

"You are worth twice what we're paying you!" Lindsay declared, kissing him again.

"Easily," he agreed, absently scrolling down the e-mail screen on the computer. "Lori is in Supply, right? Tell her to order a hundred—no, better make it a hundred and fifty—three-by-five cellophane bags for the cookies, and have them overnighted. Who *is* this darling young man? And is she insane for not answering him?"

Cici scribbled a number on a Post-it note and stood. "Call Derrick," she advised sternly, and handed the note to him. "But first, call the funeral home. And"—she reached around him to click the computer mouse and exit the program— "stop reading other people's e-mails. You've got enough problems of your own."

The phone rang again and he lifted the receiver with two fingers. "Ladybug Farm," he said cheerily. "Fine foods, gifts, and mega-events."

Cici said, "I guess we'd better tell Bridget about the cookies."

"I'll tell Bridget," Lindsay said. "You get Lori on the cellophane bags."

"Oh, Jezebel," Paul sang out, and held the telephone out to Cici as she started to leave, his eyes twinkling. "One of your victims is calling."

Cici took the phone from him, puzzled, but confusion turned to dismay as she heard Richard's voice. "Who was that?" he demanded.

"Oh, hi, Richard." There was no disguising the lack of enthusiasm in her voice as she turned away from Lindsay, who was trying hard to look disinterested, and Paul, who pretended to be browsing the Internet. "That was Paul. He's helping us with the wedding, remember I told you about that? And I really can't keep this line tied up . . ."

"I know we agreed to keep our distance for a while," he said, his voice low and tender, "but I wanted to check on Lori. And I missed you."

"Lori's fine. Lori's great. I'll tell her you're on the phone."

"And I have some news."

"Really, Richard. Awfully busy, here."

"My broker found a piece of property that sounds like just what I've been looking for. I was thinking I'd come look at it next weekend. Maybe we could get together."

"Richard," Cici warned urgently, "don't you dare say a word to Lori about this."

"I won't. I told you, this is just in the speculation stage."

"Because she's dealing with a lot right now. We all are."

Paul murmured, tapping his watch, "Tick tock."

"I'll get Lori on the phone," Cici said hurriedly. "Thanks for calling, Richard. Hold on."

Lindsay stepped outside the office and called around the corner, "Lori! Your dad's on the phone!"

Cici waited until she heard a click and Lori's cheerful "Hi, Daddy!" and then she returned the phone to its cradle, feeling a little awkward in the silence that followed.

"Don't feel bad," Paul said sympathetically. "It's not like we haven't all done something we're ashamed of."

"Thanks a lot," Cici muttered. "And I certainly hope you're not thinking of giving me relationship advice."

"Relationship?" Paul's brows shot skyward. "This is worse than I thought."

Lindsay looked concerned. "Honey, you never said . . . how did you leave things with Richard?"

"That's the problem," Cici admitted unhappily. "I'm starting to think that how *I* left them, and how *he* left them are two different things."

Paul tapped a few keys on the computer. "Never mind about the cellophane bags. I just sent Lori an e-mail."

"She's in the next room!"

"And"—another click—"told Bridget about the cookies. The next sound you hear will be . . ."

But they waited, and listened, and didn't hear anything from Bridget at all.

Bridget@LadybugFarmLadies: Don't you know that we love you? And it hurts our feelings when you don't tell us these things.

Derrick@artsolo: How is he? I could wring his neck.

Bridget@LadybugFarmLadies: How do you think he is? He loves you, too.

Derrick@artsolo: This is so childish.

Bridget@LadybugFarmLadies: I couldn't agree more!

Derrick@artsolo: I meant Paul. This is just like him. Such a drama queen.

Bridget@LadybugFarmLadies: Excuse me? I don't see how you can overdramatize heart problems.

Derrick@artsolo: I don't have a heart problem! I had an episode.

Bridget@LadybugFarmLadies: That, if you'll forgive me for saying so, is the stupidest reason I've ever heard for having a fight with someone who cares about you.

Derrick@artsolo: It's more complicated than that.

Bridget@LadybugFarmLadies: I'm listening.

Lindsay poked her head into the kitchen. Every available surface was filled with clear glass jars, apricot and green ribbons, champagne glasses, tiny white silk roses, and rolls of cellophane. There were three cake layers cooling on the center island, four racks of scones cooling on the shelves that once had held recipe books, and something was scorching on the stove.

Lindsay said, "Can you make one hundred ladybug cookies before the wedding?"

Bridget replied, without looking up from her typing, "Sure."

Cici was behind her. "Where is Ida Mae?"

"I sent her to the barn to bring more jars."

"Because whatever is on the stove is burning."

"Oh, cripes!" Bridget started up from the table. "It's the lemon filling for the wedding cake!"

"I've got it." Lindsay hurried to remove the smoking pot. "You're making the cake now?"

"I've never made a wedding cake before. I have to practice." Bridget glanced distractedly at the steaming pot Lindsay transferred to the sink, then back to the keyboard.

"What is all this stuff?" Cici asked, indicating the champagne glasses, ribbons, and flowers.

"Paul brought it, for the rehearsal dinner. Each place setting will get a champagne glass decorated with flowers and ribbons and an apricot floating candle. That way we don't even need a centerpiece."

"Perfect. Do you want us to put flowers and ribbons on champagne glasses, or slice strawberries?"

"Strawberries," ordered Bridget, typing. "I'm IMing with Derrick."

"Tell him to get his sorry ass out here this minute," said Lindsay, "and make up with Paul."

"Tell him I could strangle him for not telling us he was in

trouble," Cici added. "And I'll never forgive him if he breaks Paul's heart. Or mine."

Bridget@LadybugFarmLadies: Lindsay and Cici send their love.

Derrick@artsolo: This is not my fault you know. He wants me to sell the gallery. He wants to move to the country!

Bridget looked up from the keyboard. "Paul wants to move to the country."

Lindsay slid into a chair at the table beside her. "Wow."

Cici said, "I didn't think he was serious."

Bridget@LadybugFarmLadies: So what's wrong with that? We're in the country!

Derrick@artsolo: I have to go. Customers.

Bridget logged off, closed the laptop, and went to the sink to scrape the burned lemon goo out of the pan.

"You know," Cici said, "we can't get involved in this." She removed a big yellow bowl filled with strawberries from the refrigerator. "They're grown-up people, and we have problems of our own. And I hope these are not all of the strawberries."

"It's okay. I just need them hulled and sliced. I think that will give me enough for about a gallon of jam, and I can use the ones in the freezer for the scones and the balsamic–strawberry salad dressing. As soon as Noah gets home from school I'll put him to work picking cherries for the cherry wine jam and the cherry conserve for the turkey."

Cici put an empty bowl and a knife on the table and sat down beside Lindsay. As Cici pulled off the leaves and stems, Lindsay sliced the berries into a bowl.

"It's hard," Lindsay said, "to see someone you care about making a huge mistake." She looked pointedly at Cici. "What did Richard want?"

Bridget turned to look at Cici, filling the pan with soapy water. "Richard? Was that him on the phone?"

Even as she said the word, the phone rang again. They all tensed, but it was answered midway through the second ring from the office. They relaxed.

"He wants to buy a horse farm in Virginia," Cici said.

"Whatever for?" Bridget demanded, horrified.

And Lindsay added, "Richard doesn't even know how to ride a horse, does he?"

Cici took a bite of a strawberry. "Who knows? I think he's heard Lori talk about this place so much that he's built up some kind of fantasy in his head about life as a gentleman farmer."

Bridget snorted with laughter. "A couple of days around here would cure him of that."

Lindsay raised a warning hand. "That is not an invitation."

"Don't eat the strawberries," Bridget admonished sharply as Lindsay started to pop a slice into her mouth. "I need every one of them." She set a bowl of lemons and a tall measuring cup in front of Lindsay. "Two cups of juice," she instructed.

Lindsay regarded the lemons skeptically. "Are these local?"

The phone rang again, but only once. Bridget smiled blissfully. "I *love* having Paul here."

"Which is another reason why we shouldn't interfere in things that are none of our business."

They heard the clump of crutches outside the kitchen and Cici leaned forward quickly. "Don't say anything to Lori about—you know," she said in an undertone, and tried to look casual as Lori came into the room.

"If you mean about you and Dad," Lori said, "that's like the worst-kept secret in the world. And I just want to go on record as saying that if you two get back together I'm divorcing both of you."

Cici looked chagrined, Lindsay smothered a laugh, and Lori made her way over to the refrigerator. "I posted an entry on your blog this morning," Lori said to Bridget. "I just looked up some stuff about cherry wine and cherry trees and the history of cherries in Virginia—George Washington and all that—and included lots of links. Then I put in a plug for your new line of cherry wine jams and said something about anybody who had extra cherries should send them our way."

"You," declared Bridget, clapping her hands together, "are brilliant! Sit down. What do you want, milk? I'll bring it to you. Have some pie, too."

"Speaking of pie, you had three new messages from that secret admirer of yours. He wanted to know if you had a recipe for apple-currant pie. So there's your next blog entry."

"Do you mean the one I make with the currants soaked in brandy and the shortbread crust?"

"I guess."

Cici helped Lori arrange her crutches and slide into a chair with her leg extended sideways under the table. "That seems strange to me," Cici said. "Most people would just ask for an apple pie recipe. But apple-currant?"

"See, your pie is famous."

"Maybe your secret admirer has had your pie before," suggested Lindsay.

Bridget frowned thoughtfully as she set a glass of milk and a slice of custard pie before Lori. "I can't imagine."

"Oh, and I ordered new labels for the strawberry champagne jam and the cherry wine jam," Lori said, picking up her fork. "And a gross of three-by-five cellophane bags."

"By the way," Bridget said, staring at Lindsay, "did you say a *hundred* ladybug cookies?"

"We'll help," Lindsay assured her.

Ida Mae pushed open the screen door with her shoulder, her arms sagging under the weight of a box of glass jars. "What you going to do with all them cherries?" she demanded.

Cici took the box from her. "What cherries?"

"The ones Farley's unloading out of his truck. I hope you got somebody else to help you pit them, because I sure don't have the time."

The ladies looked questioningly from one to the other. "Did anyone ask Farley to pick cherries?"

They all shook their heads.

"Well, that's just weird."

Bridget pushed open the screen door and bounded down the steps and across the back lawn, where Farley was removing white five-gallon buckets of cherries from the bed of his pickup and placing them under the shade of a maple tree. There were four so far. "Farley!" Bridget exclaimed, clapping her hands together in delight. "That's wonderful! Where did you get all those cherries?"

He took off his hat as she approached. "Picked 'em off my trees," he told her. "I was gonna take them over to my sister, but heard you needed them more."

"But how did you know?" She looked at him in confusion. "I mean, this is a lifesaver, and we *really* appreciate it, but—all that work!"

He placed the last bucket on the ground. "Not that hard." He straightened up and nodded toward the barnyard, where the frame of the goat house was almost completed, and the little goat had poked her head through the fence wires, nibbling at the grass. "You like that goat, do you? I figured she'd make a good one for you. Nice sweet milk."

Bridget said, "Wait—that goat is yours?"

"Well," he confessed, looking a little abashed, "you said you wanted one, and I didn't have no use for her. I know how you love animals and all."

"Oh." She tried to put the pieces together. "But how … Farley," she declared, delighted, "do you read my blog?" And then it all made sense, and before she could stop herself she blurted, "You like my apple-currant pie, too! Farley, are you my secret admirer?"

He glanced down at his hat in his hand, shuffled his feet, looked back up at her with frank, faded hazel eyes, and replied, "Well, yes'm, I can't deny I've been an admirer of yours for some time now, and it honors me to do some little thing for you now and then. Fact is," he added, "it would be a pure joy if you'd come out with me now and again, maybe for some barbecue or the firehouse fish fry next Saturday."

Bridget tried to speak; she was certain she did. But

absolutely no words came. She just stared at him, with her mouth open, searching for words, until the moment turned awkward.

Farley shifted his gaze away, slapped his hat back on his head, and said, "You better get them cherries in the house, before the bees get to them." He headed back to his truck.

"I, um, thank you," Bridget said. Her voice was weaker than she intended. And as he climbed into the driver's seat, she called after him, "And thank you for the nice goat!"

She carried two buckets of cherries into the kitchen when she returned, still feeling a little stunned. "Farley brought us twenty-five gallons of cherries from his trees."

"Good heavens!" Lindsay exclaimed. "That's a lot, when you're talking about cherries."

"Ida Mae is right," Lori said. "We'll be pitting them for the rest of our natural lives."

"Sounds like a perfect job for someone who needs to spend her days sitting down," Cici said. She started toward the door to bring in more cherries.

"And he asked me out," Bridget said.

Cici stopped with her hand on the door and turned to look at her. Lindsay's eyes widened. "Who did?"

"Farley." Bridget took down a colander and started transferring cherries to it.

Cici and Lindsay struggled to hide smiles, and Ida Mae took the colander from Bridget and began picking out the leaves.

Lindsay cleared her throat, trying not to giggle. "So. What did you say?"

"What could I say?" She turned to them, hands braced against the counter, her expression dismayed. "He's Farley."

Lori said defensively, "I like Farley. He's always been more than nice to me. And he's not that bad looking, if you can get around the tobacco."

The telephone rang. Paul picked it up in the next room.

"I think he's my secret admirer," Bridget confessed uncomfortably.

"No way. He doesn't have a computer," Lori pointed out.

"But his sister the real estate agent does," Cici said. "And didn't you say she reads your blog?"

Bridget said, "That would explain how he knew about the goat."

"The goat is Farley's?"

She nodded.

"Does that mean we can send him a bill for the chocolates?" Cici lost her battle with a grin.

"The man just picked twenty-five gallons of cherries and gave them to us for free," Lori chided, her frown accusatory. "You're just being mean."

Paul came around the corner. "Are those fresh cherries?" He plucked one from the colander, and Ida Mae slapped at his hand. "You ladies do in fact live in paradise. Telephone for you, Lindsay."

Lindsay groaned. "None of the North-Dere crowd, my dear," he assured her. "It's someone from Richmond."

When Paul and Cici returned from bringing in the rest of the cherries, Lindsay was sitting at the kitchen table, and neither she nor Lori were smiling. Bridget's hand rested on

Lindsay's shoulder, and even Ida Mae had stopped working, looking at the group at the table with a helpless frown.

Cici hoisted her bucket of cherries to the counter and came to them quickly. "What's wrong?" she demanded.

Paul added, concerned, "That can't have been good news."

Lindsay looked up at them, tried to smile, and failed. "No," she said wanly. "It wasn't."

14

Love Letters

They were all sitting at the kitchen table when Noah came in an hour later, the saddlebags from his motorcycle flung over one shoulder, his tie stuffed into his back pocket. Because Ida Mae refused to have idle hands in her kitchen, she had put a bowl of cherries and a cherry pitter before each person. They were making steady, though desultory progress removing the stones from the cherries. Everyone looked up when Noah came in.

"You're home early," Bridget said.

"Last day of school." He dumped his saddlebags on the counter and went to the refrigerator. "Nobody stays all day. Guess we're having cherry pie for supper, huh?"

Cici said, "Noah, come sit down for a minute."

He turned from the refrigerator, empty-handed, and regarded them all suspiciously. Paul stood up and handed Lori her crutches. "Come on, sweetie, help me out in the office, will you?"

Lori glanced at Noah, once, then avoided his eyes as she

concentrated on getting her crutches under her and following Paul. Ida Mae took Noah's saddlebags and left the room. Noah came reluctantly to the table where the three women sat with their hands folded atop its surface, and sat down. He looked from one to the other of them cautiously. "What did I do?"

Cici looked at Lindsay. Lindsay looked down at her hands. It was Bridget who said, "Noah, we've never really talked about your mother."

With her words, a shield came over his eyes. Otherwise he did not react at all.

"That's because," Cici said, "when she made the decision to let you live with us, she asked us not to. She thought it would be better if, until you were older, anyway, you didn't feel any pressure to, well, be involved with her if you didn't want to."

"I'm not saying we agreed with that decision," Bridget added. "But it's what she wanted."

Lindsay took a breath. "Noah, we had a phone call today—"

He interrupted, "I was going to tell you about it. I should've figured you'd find out anyway."

Cici asked, "Find out what?"

He glanced at Lindsay, then away. "I found her e-mail and phone number online. So after a while, I e-mailed her and said could we meet. And she said that sounded fine, so a couple of weeks ago . . ." A quick, guilty glance around the table. "That day I told you I was working late, I rode up there to the place she said."

Bridget's eyes grew big. "You rode your motorcycle all the way to Richmond?"

He shrugged and shifted his gaze away again. "I knew you'd be mad."

"But . . . why didn't you tell us you wanted to meet her?" Cici asked. "We would have helped. You didn't have to keep it such a secret."

"I didn't want to hurt your feelings, I guess," he mumbled uncomfortably. "I mean, you've been so nice to me and all, I didn't want you to think I wasn't grateful."

The three women looked at each other helplessly, but no one could find the words.

"Anyway," he said, "it was a stupid thing to do, and it doesn't matter because she never even showed up. Serves me right, I guess. I should've left well enough alone."

Cici covered Lindsay's hand with her own. Lindsay drew a breath. "Noah, the reason your mom wanted you to live with us was because she was sick, and she knew she couldn't take care of you. It wasn't because she didn't want you."

Bridget touched Noah's shoulder. "I know she would have met you that day if she could have," she said gently. "She must have been so excited when you contacted her."

Noah looked at her, confused, and then at Lindsay. "She was in the hospital that day," Lindsay said quietly, "and she has been ever since. Noah, I'm so sorry, but she passed away this morning."

There was no reaction but a slight tightening of his jaw. He sat there for a moment longer, but when Lindsay reached across the table to touch his hand he lurched to his feet, turned, and bolted from the room.

❧

The memorial service was held in a rambling white clapboard building with a big spreading oak in front and neatly tended evergreen plantings nestling against the foundation. A small brass plaque near the door read "Harbor Home." Otherwise, it looked much like any other house on the street.

Inside, rows of metal chairs had been set up, and all of them were filled with people of all descriptions—men in shirtsleeves and women in cotton dresses, boys in jeans and T-shirts, teenage girls with restless babies. At the front of the room were a bank of flowers and a picture of a pretty woman with straight brown hair and a shy smile who was far too young to die.

Noah had not spoken on the long drive to Richmond; he rested his head against the back window and watched the landscape roll by with a bleak, unseeing gaze. The women did not try to engage him in conversation. None of them knew what to say.

A woman named Sandra Wilkes identified herself as Mandy Cormier's supervisor at Harbor Home Halfway House, and spoke about the work Mandy had done there, the lives she had touched. Some of her clients stood up and told stories of what she had meant to them. Some of them wept. Cici, Bridget, and Lindsay kept stealing glances at Noah, but he remained stony faced and stoic, gazing straight ahead.

Afterward they went up to Sandra and introduced themselves. Noah mumbled, "Good to meet you," and stuffed his hands into his suit pants pockets, staring over her shoulder.

Sandra said, "Your mother meant so much to us here at Harbor Home. Just look around. There isn't a kid in here whose life wasn't changed because of her."

Noah replied, "Yeah, there is. Me." Then he said, "I'll wait in the car."

Sandra watched him sympathetically as he left. "I can't imagine how difficult this must be."

Lindsay said, "I don't think any of us can."

"She told me about her arrangement with you. I have some papers for you. A small life insurance policy, some guardianship papers . . . We'll pack up her things, unless you'd like to go through them now."

Cici said, "I don't think this is the right time."

"Oh, and these." Sandra reached into her purse and brought out a packet of envelopes bound with a rubber band. "Mandy asked me to give these to Noah. Maybe you could . . . ?"

Lindsay took the envelopes, Cici and Bridget collected the other papers, and they made arrangements to have Mandy's belongings held in storage for Noah until he was ready to go through them.

Noah was leaning against the side of the car, his jacket off, staring straight ahead. All three women went to him. Lindsay handed him the bundle of envelopes. "These are from your mother."

He looked down at the packet, but said nothing.

Lindsay glanced at the other two. "There's something I think you should know. Before we knew about your mother, I was looking into the possibility of legally adopting you. I'd like to talk to you about that sometime. If you think it's something you might be interested in."

Now he looked up at her, slowly.

"Either way," Cici said, "there's something else you need to know. You might not have been born to us, but you *are* our kid."

Bridget laid a gentle hand upon his arm. "You'd better believe it."

He dropped his eyes again. His fingers closed on the packet in his hands and he said, lowly, "I called her a liar." His voice tightened, and so did his fingers. "The last e-mail I sent her . . . I called her a liar."

His shoulders started to shake, his face began to crumple, and all three women stepped into him, surrounding him with their embrace as he sobbed.

May 25, 2010

Dear Noah,

I wish it were possible to live without regrets, to always know you're doing the right thing. The problem with choices is that you hardly ever know which is the right one until it's all over and you look back, wondering how your life would have been if you had chosen differently. When I left you with your grandmother when you were a baby, I thought I was doing the right thing for you, and for me. Then, when she died and I lost contact with you, I spent years hating myself for doing the wrong thing. But now, when I look back over everything that happened, I'm not as sure as I once was. I don't think you would have survived those years if I had tried to keep you with me. I barely survived them myself. You might not understand this now, and maybe you can never forgive me for what I've done, but please believe this: sometimes life has a poetry to it. Sometimes, against all odds, things do work out. I know you grew up in a hard way. But every step you took led you closer to home, where you belong.

I'm glad I got to see you grow up to be well and strong and happy. That was more than I ever expected, or probably deserved. I wish I'd had more time, of course I do. I wish we could have spent some of it together. But after everything else, it didn't seem fair of me to ask you to spend your teenage years watching your mother die. And that's the only reason that I've stayed away from you this past year. Because, by the time I found you, it was too late.

Over the years, when I really didn't know what had become of you or where you were, I kept you alive in my mind by writing letters to you. Of course I didn't know where to mail them, but I always believed that one day I'd give them to you in person. I'm sorry I wasn't able to do that.

I don't have much to leave you, just my words. I hope they will remind you that you were loved every day of your life—

Mom

From This Day Forward

15

On Tending Gardens and Taking Chances

The one immutable rule on Ladybug Farm was that time stopped for no one. There were eggs to be gathered and animals to be fed, rows to be weeded, ponds to be cleaned, beans and squash to be harvested, herbs to be cut, roses to be watered, flower beds to be mulched, bird feeders to be filled, compost to be turned, grass to be mowed. Sometimes a delay of even a day or two could mean the difference between a healthy plant and a dead one, an abundant harvest or no harvest at all. And sure enough, when they returned home from the memorial service, Ida Mae announced that cutworms had taken out half the tomato vines, and potato bugs had infested the potatoes. Everything came to a halt as all able-bodied hands rushed to the garden with cardboard collars for the tomato plants and insecticidal soap for the potatoes.

"You spent more time mulching and less time on that computer," Ida Mae observed dryly, knocking potato bugs off a leaf and into a tin can with a stick, "and you wouldn't have to worry about bugs."

They all knew she was probably right. But there were also one hundred ladybug cookies to be baked, decorated, and packaged, twenty large and one hundred small gift baskets to be packed and wrapped, twenty-five gallons of cherries to be made into cherry wine jam, and twenty champagne glasses to be converted to table decorations—all before the end of the week.

Noah fed and watered the animals, cleaned their pens, mowed the lawn, harvested crops, and attended to his other regular chores without interruption. But for the most part he spent his time alone, either roaming the woods or in the art studio, and the other members of the household gave him his privacy.

"The thing I feel the worst about," Lindsay said, piping black dots onto the red frosting of a ladybug cookie according to Bridget's instructions, "is that we've been so busy with our own problems we didn't even notice what was going on with him."

"That's not true." Cici was still pitting cherries. "We knew something was bothering him. We should have tried harder to find out what it was."

"Having once been an actual teenage boy myself," Paul said, glancing over the tops of the half-rim glasses he wore for close work, "believe me when I tell you that there is always something bothering them. Trying to stay on top of it every single time is crazy-making." He hot-glued another perfect cluster of miniature apricot silk roses into the center of an ivory bow and passed it to Lori, who used florist wire to secure it around the stem of a champagne glass.

"Come on, Uncle Paul. I mean, I know it was hard for you, growing up gay and all, but you went to Choate and spent summers on Cape Cod. It's a little bit different for a kid like him. Not," she added guiltily, "that I'm one to be talking, with all my whining about missing out on Italy. I never spent one day of my whole life without knowing that I had two parents who loved me. And that's why I don't think people like us can really understand what it's like for him."

Paul smiled at her. "Truer words, princess."

Bridget took another pan of cookies from the oven and set it on a wire rack to cool. "That day we came back from the hospital," she said, "and he had done all that work sprucing up the place and keeping up with everyone's chores . . . we thought it was because he was trying to get out of the trouble he was in. Now I think it might have just been his way of saying he was grateful, you know, to be here."

"He is a remarkable young man in so many ways," Cici said. "I just wish there was something we could do to make things easier for him now."

The screen door squeaked open, and there stood Noah. "You already have," he said.

They all turned guiltily, and he gave a one-shouldered shrug, and a rueful, fleeting smile. "It's okay if you talk about me. I just don't want to . . . you know, I'm more the kind of guy who likes to work things out for himself."

Lindsay straightened up from the tray of cookies. "We know," she said gently. "But if you ever want to talk, we're here for you."

"All of us," Paul added.

Lori added, "Yeah."

Noah said, "Yeah, I know. But it's nicer to know I don't have to."

Bridget smiled at him. "That's fine, too."

He looked around the room at all of them for a moment, then he said, "There's one thing I wanted to say. Then maybe . . . in a week or two, when things kind of calm down around here, maybe we'll talk, you know, about that other thing." He looked at Lindsay, an uncertain mixture of shyness, pretended nonchalance, and hope in his eyes. "That legal thing you told me about in Richmond."

Lindsay had to swallow before she could speak, but she could not restrain her smile. "Okay. That would be great."

Noah went on. "What I wanted to say was, I know ya'll are thinking I'm mad at her. My mom. But that's not it. I don't blame her, not now. I've been reading her letters. I think about her writing them to me when I was just a little baby, and she didn't even know where I was. She was kind of funny." He smiled a little, faintly. "And interesting. She sounds like somebody I might have liked to know. So that's the thing. I had a whole year, after I knew where she was and who she was, and I could have talked to her. But I wasted it. I wasted it trying to punish her, or trying to prove I didn't care, or I don't know, a lotta different things. But that's what I'm mad at. Nothing else."

He glanced around the room once again, a little more quickly, trying to hide his embarrassment, and his gaze landed on Cici. "You want me to do the cherries?"

Cici smiled, and handed him the cherry pitter. "Thanks, Noah. That would be great."

He sat down beside her, and as they all worked together in companionable ease the atmosphere around the table was a bit more thoughtful than it had been before.

≈

Trucks arrived. The UPS truck, bearing apricot and spring green frocks for Bridget and Lindsay. The postal carrier in his mud-stained red station wagon, with jar labels and cellophane bags. FedEx, with embossed place cards. UPS again, with stockings and shoes. Party Favors out of Charlottesville, with glassware, china, and cutlery. FedEx with monogrammed napkins. UPS with bolts of ivory scrim and satin ribbon. Two hearses, filled with chairs, and a Silverado carrying tents. Rebel started to lose his voice and, toward the end of the week, made only a token charge at the wheels of each vehicle before he retreated, panting hard, to the shade under the porch. The goat ran away twice and, somewhat to their dismay, returned each time. The hens stopped laying.

Paul orchestrated it all like a Broadway director on opening night. He found a hands-free telephone headset and managed to hook it up so that he could direct boxes to the kitchen, chairs to the barn, and fabric to the parlor, all while ordering table covers from a restaurant supply and measuring the rose garden for the placement of chairs, and, of course, never missing a call from Catherine or Traci. Noah was sent to town to buy every white candle he could find, and Lori spent the day wrapping them in apricot tulle. A bow-making assembly line was formed.

"We'll gather the scrim and tie it every five feet with floral wire," Paul explained to Lindsay, who was with Bridget in her room, trying on their dresses for the wedding. "Then we'll drape it around the tents to hide the name of the funeral parlor, and let it float down over the tent poles like a cabana. Bows at each corner, and no one will ever know they aren't custom wedding tents."

"Perfect," Lindsay said, scrutinizing herself in the mirror. "I hate this dress. Don't you think it makes my hair look orange?"

"You were born to do this," Bridget told Paul, adjusting the neckline of her own spring green dress. "You're the one who should go into business. I look like a cupcake."

"I have a job, thanks. This is just a fantasy." He tied the satin ribbon on the front of Bridget's dress and stepped back to observe her critically. "Lose the bow," he advised.

"What are you going to do about your column?" Lindsay asked. "You're not missing deadlines because of us, are you?"

"Are you joking? This *is* my column—for about a month. And you two in those outfits will be one entire installment. Talk about what not to wear."

"Thanks a lot." Lindsay cast a speculative look toward Bridget's spring green dress. "I should have been in green. You should have been in apricot."

"Neither one of you should be in green *or* apricot," observed Paul. "And you're both too beautiful—and smart—to let a spoiled twenty-three-year-old tell you how to dress."

"And too old," agreed Bridget unhappily.

"We're billing her for these dresses," Lindsay said. "My hips look huge."

Paul said, "I almost forgot why I came up. Company's downstairs. That fellow Dominic."

Lindsay looked quickly interested, and Paul did not fail to notice.

"He's talking to Lori," he added casually. "He asked about you, Lindsay. So for God's sake don't wear that dress downstairs."

She scowled at him. "Okay, very cute. Now get back to work before I rent out your room."

He left the room with a speculative grin on his face.

"What you have to understand about wine," Dominic was saying to Lori, "is that it's more alchemy than science, and it always has been. That's the magic of it. When you hear a vinophile use words like *precocious* and *impudent* or *dark and brooding*, or when they start going off with all sorts of flowery terms to describe the flavors, the tendency is to think they're just being pretentious. But wine is a living thing, and that's not just a metaphor. Every wine has its own character, its own personality. It takes on the taste and the texture of the very soil in which it was birthed. That's what you have to understand, Lori, if you want to make wine. The magic."

A big worktable had been set up in the grand parlor, which was crowded with cardboard boxes, cellophane-wrapped baskets, piles of white satin bows, and stacks of tablecloths. Every immovable surface was lined with tulle-wrapped candles, beribboned champagne glasses, and little net bags of birdseed that the guests would toss over the bride and groom in lieu of rice. Dominic sat at the table across from Lori, his tone earnest and his eyes alive with quiet passion, and while he spoke his fingers worked with equal passion on forming a large apricot satin bow. Lindsay, watching from the doorway, felt a smile start deep in her belly and spread, inexorably, to her lips, where it grew so big it actually hurt her face.

Lori, who was so entranced by his words that her own bow lay forgotten and unfinished on the table in front of her, saw Lindsay first. "Aunt Lindsay!" she exclaimed.

Dominic immediately leapt to his feet and turned, stumbling a little over his chair, his completed bow clutched to his chest.

Lori's face was alight with excitement as she continued, oblivious, "Did you know Dominic went to Cornell? Just like I plan to! He got his doctorate there. And his father was the vigneron at Chateau Ellyson, which was the most prestigious winery in France before the war! He said he would be my mentor."

Dominic held up the bow with a self-deprecating smile. "And I can make bows."

"So I see." Lindsay came into the room and took the bow from him, pretending to inspect it. "Very nice. Do you work on commission?"

When he smiled at her, Lindsay was glad she had changed into jeans and a T-shirt before coming down. He said, "Lori was telling me about her plans. I was telling *her* she's missing out on the true soul of wine making if she doesn't spend some time in France."

"Actually," Lindsay said, "the real history of modern wine making can be traced to ancient Greece."

He lifted an eyebrow. "As can everything else, in theory."

Cici appeared behind them. "Lori, sweetie, I know you're

busy, but I need you for a sec." Then, "Hi, Dominic. I didn't know you were here."

"I just stopped in to say hello, and got drafted." He handed the bow to Lindsay. "But I think my job here is done."

"I'll walk you out," Lindsay said, and he looked mildly surprised, and pleased, as they left.

Lori struggled to get her crutches under her. "You know, Mom, getting from one place to the other is a little bit complicated for me. Couldn't you get someone else to do whatever it is?"

"Not this time. Besides, you're supposed to get up and move around every hour. It's good for your circulation."

Cici placed a light protective hand on Lori's shoulder as she hobbled past, and Lori gave her an annoyed look when Cici gestured her toward the sunroom. "Mom, what . . ."

"Wait a minute." Cici stopped her at the doorway and reached into her back pocket for a compact.

"What is that?" Lori flinched away as her mother began dabbing the makeup over the fading yellow bruises on her cheek.

"Just a little coverage. There." She surveyed her work. "You can't even see the bruises. Hold on. Just a little lip gloss . . ."

"Mom! What's going on? Are you crazy?" She shrank back, trying to brush Cici's hand away, but Cici smoothed a peachy coat of gloss over her daughter's lips and tidied the corners before she stepped back.

"Probably," she admitted. "But there's a nice young man waiting to talk to you who has been worried sick about why he hasn't heard from you. The least you can do is thank him for his concern."

Lori stared at her, and Cici directed her attention to the laptop computer that was set up on the wicker table that served as her temporary desk. Lori hobbled over to the computer, dropped down into the chair in front of it, and gasped. "Sergio!"

"Lori, *bellissima*! It is you, at last!"

Cici saw her daughter's face light up in sheer delight as she exclaimed, "But how did you—when did you . . ."

And Cici closed the door quietly behind her as she left, smiling.

❧

"So," Lindsay said, as they walked toward Dominic's truck, "how did you get from here to Cornell, and then back again?"

"Short version? I had this grand scheme to establish the finest winery in the U.S. Remember back then, no one believed California wines had a chance, and nothing decent was being produced south of New York, so after college I started apprenticing in some of the top wineries in the region . . . which is where, of course, I fell in love, got married, and realized I had to have a real job. So I got into the graduate program at Cornell, thinking a degree would be the fastest way to a higher-paying job. I ended up teaching agriculture at Clemson for about twenty years. And after my wife died I decided to come back here. I'd always loved this part of the country, and I liked the work. I've been back eight years now."

"How long were you married?"

"Thirty-three years."

"You have children, don't you?" She thought she vaguely

remembered him mentioning a daughter, or perhaps a son, in one of their lazy front porch conversations.

"Three." He grinned. "Two of them work for wineries in California. Seems that everybody was wrong about California wines."

Lindsay smiled. "I feel like a bad neighbor. We've been acquainted for over a year, but never really got to know you."

"We keep missing out on that dinner."

"My fault."

A short, rather awkward silence fell.

Then he said, "I remember the parties Judge Blackwell and his mother used to give when I was a boy here. They'd park cars three deep all up and down the driveway, and have somebody shuttle the guests up to the house." He grinned. "I earned enough in tips to buy my own first car that way."

"So, *that*'s how they did it!" Lindsay exclaimed. "I was wondering where everyone was going to park."

"Sure." He gestured toward the flat grassy area that spread out on either side of the tree-lined drive. "Get a couple of kids to direct traffic, there's plenty of room. And I wouldn't mind taking my old job back driving the shuttle if you need the help."

She tilted her head at him. "You'd do that?"

"Sure. It's not as though I have anything else to do on Saturday."

She regarded him thoughtfully, smiling. "You really are a nice guy, aren't you?"

He shrugged. "I try to be."

They had reached his truck, and he turned to look at her

before opening the door. "Well, you let me know if you need any help."

"Actually," Lindsay said on a sudden breath, "I'm glad you're not busy Saturday because as it happens I need an escort for the wedding, and I don't suppose you'd be interested. In being my escort, I mean."

A smile started in his eyes, and traveled to his lips, where it lit up his whole face. "I thought you'd never ask." He opened the truck door. "What time?"

"Two o'clock."

"I'll be here at one," he assured her, as he started the engine.

Lindsay clapped her hands together like a girl, laughing, and did a little twirl in the driveway as he drove away.

From "Ladybug Farm Charms," a blog by Bridget Tyndale

One of the best things about living on a farm is that it's usually pretty easy to get your priorities straight. In July and August, when tomatoes are coming in from the garden by the basketful twice a day, there's nothing more important than peeling, slicing, and preserving. In March, when the little lettuces are just starting to come up and a freeze is predicted, you don't wait until your nail polish dries to start covering the rows. And when you have to choose between a Caribbean cruise and making sure there's firewood in the shed in October . . . I'm not saying that the choice is an easy one, but it is fairly obvious.

Things have been a little hectic on Ladybug Farm this

spring, with lots of changes and exciting new challenges. It's been fun, but in the middle of all the excitement it's been easy to forget what's important, and to brush aside all the things I love most about living here. But over the past few days some things have happened that have put everything back into perspective for me, and made it a little easier to focus on my priorities.

So today I'm announcing that I'll be closing this blog at the end of the month. I've loved getting to know everyone, and I really appreciate those of you who've been reading from the beginning. But everyone knows what happens to a neglected garden, and exactly the same thing happens to a neglected life. So I've decided to get back to what's important before everything is taken over by weeds.

Meanwhile, you can still keep up with the goings-on here at Ladybug Farm through our <u>website</u>, or feel free to <u>e-mail</u> me with questions.

Meanwhile, I wish you all the best, and cheers from Ladybug Farm!

Secret Admirer said:
Dear Bridget,

I'm sorry to hear you'll be closing the blog. Coming home and reading about what's happening in your world is the calmest, most pleasant part of my day. And I'll miss the recipes.

I made your apple-currant pie, but somehow it didn't taste as sweet as I remembered. Thanks anyway for your help.

Bridget smiled as she typed:

Dear Secret Admirer,

Most likely you left out a key ingredient: love.

By the way, I think you know you have an admirer here, too. I hope you'll do something about it before it's too late. As I said, it's all about priorities, and gardens aren't the only things that can die from neglect.

16

Life Is Not a Rehearsal

NORTH-DEERE/THORNTON REHEARSAL DINNER

Menu

Appetizer: Three-berry fruit cup in balsamic vinaigrette topped with Gorgonzola crumbles and toasted black walnuts, served with miniature cheese biscuits

Soup: Chilled cantaloupe soup with mint and crème fraiche

Entrée: Free-range roast turkey wrapped in applewood-smoked bacon served on a bed of fresh cherry conserve and accompanied by fingerling potatoes and baby carrots sautéed in rosemary-infused olive oil

Summer squash soufflé

Garden fresh green beans, lightly sautéed and tossed with thyme, toasted almonds, and baby onions

Dessert: Strawberry crumble topped with homemade vanilla ice cream

The event was organized with the precision of the Invasion of Normandy.

Countdown began at 5:45 a.m. Friday, when Rodrigo the rooster sounded the first call to action. By six, the troops were assembled in the kitchen, bleary-eyed and clutching coffee cups, to receive their orders. Noah and Cici: Construction and Assembly. Ida Mae and Bridget: Kitchen and Amenities. Lindsay: Design and Decoration. Lori: Hospitality and Incidentals. Everyone: Housekeeping and Aesthetics.

By ten, the windows were washed, the baseboards scrubbed, the furniture oiled, the carpets vacuumed, the floors washed, waxed, and buffed; the curtains washed and rehung, the draperies steamed, the linens freshened; the porch pressure-washed; and every bathroom polished until it gleamed.

At ten fifteen, florists' trucks began to arrive. The bridal bouquet, the bridesmaids' bouquets, the groomsmens' boutonnieres, the mothers' corsages, and the loose flowers that Bridget intended to use to decorate the cake were all stored in the supplemental refrigerator in the cellar. Giant potted ferns were placed strategically around the porch and on either side of the garden arbor. Silk dogwoods defined the reception area and screened the barnyard. Lindsay set up a workstation in the cellar, where it was cooler, to start trimming, arranging, and storing the dozens upon dozens of Apricot Delight roses that piled up in columns of boxes around her.

The tents were erected on the back lawn, the scrim was secured, and the folding tables rented from the party supply company were set up beneath them. One hundred folding chairs were snapped into place along a precise fan-shaped path that Paul had outlined in the rose garden—and not a single rose, flower bed, or tree branch was disturbed. Noah assembled the twenty-five decorative table rounds that Cici had purchased at the dollar store, and arranged them around the dance floor. Tomorrow they would be covered with ivory satin and decorated with tulle-wrapped candles and apricot roses. The wedding arbor—a lacy affair built of bender board and balsa wood that Lindsay had spotted in the florist's shop and purchased on the spot for a hundred dollars—was decorated with silk ivy, white roses, and satin ribbon. Anchored in place in the center of the rose garden, it framed the mountains and the vineyard in the background, and the fountain and the reflecting pool in the foreground. The three supplemental arbors that Catherine had insisted upon were suitably decorated with tulle, ribbons, and silk ivy. Roses were deadheaded, petals were swept off the rock paths and the grass. Satin ribbons were wrapped around one hundred funeral chairs. An altar table—which was actually a butcher block repurposed from Cici's workshop—was set up for the unity candles. Cici had to admit—as she stepped back with her arm around Noah's shoulders to admire their work—that it was magnificent.

The six cake layers that had been deemed perfect enough to make the final cut were removed from the freezer, filled with lemon custard, carefully wrapped in the fondant that Bridget had been working on all week, and—with breath suspended—arranged with cake separators on a wheeled cart, and then stored carefully in a corner of the butler's pantry with dire warnings from Bridget regarding what would happen to anyone who dared even breathe in its direction. The bride was bringing the cake topper to the rehearsal dinner, and it would be decorated just before serving with fresh flowers and fruit, in keeping with the "simply organic" theme.

The turkey was removed from its brine, garlic and herbs were inserted under its skin, and it was wrapped in applewood bacon and put in the oven to roast. Bridget left Ida Mae with the recipe for the cheese biscuits and the dressing for the three-berry appetizer while she prepared the strawberry crumble and mixed the ice cream for the rehearsal dinner, and put two hams in the second oven for the wedding reception. They were working together like a well-oiled machine, and Bridget reminded herself to apologize to Ida Mae, when all this was over, for whatever unflattering things she had thought about her over the past several weeks.

Lori reported that the entire bridal party and several of the guests had already checked into the Holiday Inn, the gift baskets had been delivered to the appropriate rooms, and Catherine was on her way with the wedding dress. Lindsay snapped a freshly ironed white tablecloth over the giant dining room table, lined the center with magnolia leaves, and set the table. She used the plain white china Paul had brought, a mixture of their own three silver patterns, and sparkling glassware from the butler's pantry. Lori inserted a tiny apricot rosebud into each napkin ring and Lindsay arranged the floating candle champagne glasses in front of each place setting.

At four thirty Paul did a final walk-through, adjusted a table setting here, a languid rose petal there, and declared,

"All right, troops, hit the showers." He checked his watch and smiled approvingly. "And right on schedule."

❧

Things remained on schedule for another twenty-two minutes, at which point Ida Mae called up the stairs, "Somebody's here!"

Cici dashed out of her bedroom in a terry robe, her hair half-dry and clipped up in sections on her head, barefoot and un-made-up. "That's impossible!" she cried in dismay. "It takes an hour to get here from the Holiday Inn! Catherine couldn't have made it already."

Noah called, "Hey, no fair! I was supposed to park the cars!"

"It ain't her," Ida Mae called back. "It's some man!"

"My hair is wet!" Lindsay checked in.

"I'll be dressed in five minutes," Bridget called, panic in her voice. "Paul is in the shower."

"Crap!" Cici muttered. She raced back to her room, flung off the robe, and began to tug on the silk slacks and floaty white shirt that were tonight's hostess uniform. "Is there anything worse than an early guest?"

The next thing she heard, almost as though in answer to that question, was Lori's astonished exclamation from the front hall: "Daddy! What are you doing here?"

Cici, holding the blow-dryer like a weapon and staring at her own grimly horrified reflection in the mirror, said simply, "I'll kill him."

"Richard, you have to leave," she declared, buttoning her cuff and tugging the clips from her hair as she hurried down the stairs. "I don't care what your excuse is, you can't be here."

"Nice to see you, too, sweetie." He was standing at the bottom of the stairs with Lori, grinning up at her, and he kissed Cici's cheek as she skidded to a breathless stop in front of him. "Gorgeous old place," he added, gazing around appreciatively. "Lori's description didn't do it justice."

"Lori, finish getting dressed," Cici demanded.

Lori, who was wearing a clean pair of khaki shorts and a T-shirt that left three inches of her waist exposed, explained, "I'm on kitchen duty, Mom. I don't have to dress up."

Cici stared at her. "Whose idea was *that*?" Then, focusing, she whipped her head back to Richard. "Richard, I told you we're having an event here this weekend. I don't have time—"

"I told him about the rehearsal dinner," Lori said. "Did you know half your hair is wet?"

"What are you *doing* here?"

He rested a gentling hand on her arm, smiling his easy confident smile. "I told you I was flying out this weekend to look at property. I thought I'd surprise my girls."

Lori's face lit up. "Are you buying a place here, Dad?"

Cici gave him a look that could have shattered glass. And he was completely oblivious. "Ooops," he said, "guess the cat's out of the bag." He grinned and gave Lori's shoulders a one-armed hug. "And the word is *bought*, sweetie. I *bought* a place about ten miles away."

Before Cici could recover her breath, Lindsay said from the landing in a carefully controlled tone, "Cici? Am I hallucinating?"

The next few minutes were a melee of voices, questions, explanations, and introductions as one by one the residents of Ladybug Farm came to discover that the guest who had arrived was not among those who were expected. "As I was trying to explain," Cici said at last, raising her voice to be heard, "we're having a party tonight, so Richard, you have to go. *Now.*"

"Mom, he's come all this way!"

"I could help," Richard volunteered. "I don't mind."

"So he could," Paul declared, adjusting the knot in his apricot silk tie as he came down the stairs, jacket over his arm. "The only person I know who's more charming than I am is your ex, sweetie, and we need a bartender." He extended his hand to Richard as he reached the bottom of the stairs. "Nice to see you, Richard." He glanced over Richard's polo shirt and khakis and decided, "You'll need a jacket. Noah, take him upstairs and pick out one of mine, then give him a quick tour of the house. Bar supplies are set up on the side porch."

Richard winked at Cici as Noah led the way upstairs. "Looks like I'm hired."

Cici stared after him in helpless dismay, and Paul looked her over critically. "You might consider a little lipstick and blush," he suggested. "And the hair is a bit trendy for this crowd, I think."

Bridget looked at her uncertainly. "Did I hear correctly? Did he say he had bought a place?"

"Ten miles away?" questioned Lindsay, and even Paul lifted an eyebrow.

"Look at it this way, Mom," Lori offered helpfully. "At least you have a plus-one for the wedding tomorrow."

Cici clutched the wet side of her hair with one hand and clapped the other over her un-made-up face. "My life," she muttered, "is over."

"Focus, ladies," Paul commanded. He made a little shooing gesture to Cici. "Hair, makeup, go." He tapped his watch. "Tick tock."

"Bartender!" Cici glared at him as she started up the stars. "I'll get you for this, and that's a promise."

But it was a promise she did not have time to keep, since before she reached the top of the stairs Catherine's car was pulling up, horn honking imperiously. Before Lindsay and Bridget could even get the bridal gown out of the car and up the stairs to Lori's room—which would be the bride's staging room for the wedding—the bride herself arrived with three of her bridesmaids, demanding to see the garden setup. By the time Cici finished drying her hair and applying her makeup, strangers were wandering through the downstairs rooms of her house with drinks in their hands, gazing around like tourists in a museum, and more were meandering around the porch and spilling onto the lawn. Paul was in earnest conversation with Catherine, and Richard could be heard to say heartily, "Welcome to our home," as he poured a glass of red wine for a bald man in a linen suit.

"My home," Cici corrected sharply, and then tried to soften the words with a smile. "Welcome to Ladybug Farm. I'm Cici Burke, one of your hostesses this evening." She passed a sideways glance to Richard. "He's just helping out."

While she conducted a rather pointless conversation with the man, who turned out to be the bride's uncle and the officiant of the ceremony, she heard Richard say to one of the bridesmaids, "Now you look like someone who'd be interested in the bride's special, an apricot-tini. Believe me," he confided, "the color is the best part." The girl burst into giggles, melting into his charm as effortlessly as any other twenty-three-year-old whose path he had ever crossed.

"Just like old times, huh, Ci?" he said, coming around the bar to stand beside her when they both found themselves momentarily alone. He handed her a martini glass with something apricot-colored in it. "You and me, good times, good food, good people."

"No," she said firmly. "No, it's not just like old times." She took a sip of the drink and grimaced a little. Apricots and martinis clearly were never meant to be mixed. "Our old times were beer and pizza and chicken pox."

He smiled and caressed her back briefly. "Which is why we deserve to treat ourselves now." Then, with a deep breath of the clear fresh air, "God, this place is beautiful. Just look at those trees. What are they, anyway? Just like a movie set."

She stared up at him in blank incomprehension for a moment. "Richard, what are you doing here?"

"Living the dream, baby," he replied, smiling at someone across the way. "Living the dream."

"Richard, for heaven's sake, what were you thinking? You bought property? In Virginia?"

He looked extremely pleased with himself. "Not just property, Ci, but eighty-seven acres of the most beautiful horse country you've ever seen. Fenced and cross-fenced, with a fifteen-stall barn already standing. I can't wait to show it to you. It's exactly what I was looking for. Exactly."

"Eighty-seven acres?" Her voice was bordering on shrill as her incredulity rose. "Are you crazy? Why would you do such a thing?"

He chuckled. "At today's prices, I'd be crazy to pass it by.

It's a great investment, less than half an hour away from my little girl, everything I've always pictured when I thought about where I wanted to retire."

"You are not retiring here," Cici stated flatly. "You're not."

"Listen." He took her arm, turning her a little away from the crowd that was milling around at the bottom of the steps, and he bent his head close to hers, lowering his voice earnestly. "I know how we left things, and that's fine with me, really. I know this probably seems impulsive but I've been thinking about it for years, and now everything is coming together. The timing is perfect. Don't look at this like I'm trying to pressure you. Think of it as a chance for us to take our time, enjoy each other, settle into the feeling of being a family again . . ."

With every word he spoke her eyes grew wider, and by the time he finished she was shaking her head adamantly. "No." She downed the remainder of the martini in a single swallow. "No. Let me be clear about this, Richard—no." She started to walk away, then spun back to him with a wide sweep of her arm. "This," she declared, indicating all that surrounded them, "is my dream, not yours, don't you see that? And now all of sudden you come swooping down like—like some kind of conquering hero and decide you want what I have, and it feels like you're trying to steal my dream. That's what it feels like!" The flash of hurt in his eyes stabbed at her, and she drew a breath, trying to gentle her tone. "I'm sorry, Richard, I really am, for whatever insane midlife crisis made you think this could work out. But we're not a family. We're barely even friends. You don't belong here, and I . . ."

It was at that moment that a Mustang convertible came

screeching up the driveway, top down and belching the *thrum, thrum, thrum* of woofers from the back speakers. It stopped with a spray of gravel in front of the house, dislodging a bevy of drunken young men, one of whom, wearing a mis-buttoned Hawaiian print shirt and baggy shorts and a silver paper crown, appeared to be the groom. He staggered and grinned with a goofy two thumbs-up as he clambered over the closed doors of the car.

"I have work to do," she said, and walked away.

❧

It was the arrival of the groom, everyone agreed, that signaled the downward turn of the event. Before he had even stumbled completely out of the car, Traci burst out of the house and started to scream at him. "Jason, where have you been? You're late! I told you we were starting at five and I told you not to be late! Where's the cake topper? Did you bring the cake topper? Don't you dare stand there with all your drunk friends and tell me that you didn't do the one thing I asked you to do!"

At which point Jason, who had been struggling to look suitably chastened, suddenly burst into laughter, and was supported by his groomsmen with a rousing chorus of "Here Comes the Groom." Traci dissolved into tears and ran into the house, followed by her mother and all six bridesmaids.

Margaret, Jason's mother, arrived in a print silk suit and three-inch spiked heels, which sank immediately into the soft ground of the lawn when she tried to cross it. She did, however, bring the missing cake topper, and insisted upon inspecting the dining room setup to make certain her instructions for the evening had been carried out. So while Lindsay tried to comfort the hysterical bride and Paul took charge of the groom, Cici was left to escort Margaret on her tour of inspection.

"Really, Mrs. Thornton," she insisted, "why don't you just have a glass of wine and enjoy your evening? Leave everything to us."

To which she merely snorted, surveyed the dining room arrangement, and demanded, "*Where* are the place cards? I sent silver-framed place cards and a seating chart. What did you people do, pawn them?"

Cici, whose temper had already been tested to the breaking point, drew a sharp breath for a reply. But, fortunately for her, before she could release it, Bridget, looking like an executive chef in a black straight skirt and high-collared white shirt, came through the swinging door with a bright smile and a box of silver-framed place cards in her hands.

The mother of the groom was mollified, the bride, having been informed of the arrival of the cake topper, was persuaded to leave her room, and Paul somehow managed to get everyone to the garden for the rehearsal. Margaret did not like the location that had been set aside for the string quartet, so four chairs, a potted fern, and two silk dogwoods were moved from the center of the fan-shaped rows of seats to the front, near the podium. Catherine thought there should be a microphone for the officiant, and wondered how much trouble it would be to round one up before tomorrow.

Nonetheless, Paul, with his clipboard and precisely orchestrated schedule of events, managed to keep everyone on task until Margaret started complaining about the heat, and why no one had thought to erect a shade canopy to keep the guests out of the sun, and whose idea was it to have an outdoor wedding anyway? Then the videographer realized that—speaking of sun—at two o'clock in the afternoon, he would be shooting directly into it, and Cici pointed out that if they moved the wedding arch they would lose not only the frame of the mountain and sheep meadow background that Traci had insisted upon, but the entire line of the bridal procession.

It was at this point that one of the groomsmen started baaing to the tune of "Here Comes the Bride." Traci was in the middle of screeching at her mother that this was all her fault, that *she* was the one who wanted a sheep-farm wedding and that *she* should have known where the sun was—and when she heard the baaing, she went suddenly stiff. She turned, eyes blazing and cheeks flaming, and marched over to the offender—who by this time had smothered both his singing and his giggles and was trying to look innocent—and told him flatly he was out of the wedding.

As it turned out, the sheep imitator was not just a groomsman but the best man, and also the groom's brother. Jason informed Traci that if his brother was out of the wedding, so was he, to which Traci retorted that that suited her fine, at which point Margaret turned on Catherine and demanded that she control her daughter, and after that, it was pretty much a free-for-all.

"After all this work," Cici muttered to Paul, "she is marrying that jerk if it's the last thing she does on this earth."

"And I am not moving a single chair," warned Paul darkly.

Cici waded into the melee, shouting for attention. "Ladies!

Gentlemen! This is a wedding! We should be cooperating, not fighting!" She looked for help to the officiant, who, well into his third apricot-tini, merely smiled beneficently. "What if," she suggested to Traci, "the videographer shot from behind the podium, which means he would be away from the sun? And you'll be doing the wedding photographs in the morning, so you'll still have your shot of the mountains and sheep, just like you wanted, with no sun in the way."

The videographer agreed that he could shoot from behind the screen where the musicians were stationed, which would make him as unobtrusive as possible, and Traci reluctantly conceded accord.

They lined up again, boys on one side and girls on the other, all of them glaring across the lawn at each other, looking more like the Jets and the Sharks from *West Side Story* than the friends and family of a happy couple about to be united forever in the sacrament of marriage. The groom was persuaded to take his place at the head of the aisle, joking with his best man and sipping from a bottle of beer, as Traci, in jeans, a T-shirt, and a shoulder-length tulle veil, made her way down the aisle on the arm of her father, whom Cici could not have picked out of the crowd until that moment.

All proceeded smoothly until the officiant rehearsed the vows, beginning with "Do you take this woman?" And the groom, grinning, nudged his best man and replied, "Let me think about it."

Traci turned to him, snatched the beer bottle from his hand, and poured it over his head.

In the stunned silence that followed, Cici muttered, "I'll kill her. I'll kill her with my bare hands."

Paul laid a soothing hand upon her arm. "Don't be ridiculous, darling. You have a child. Let me do it," he said grimly, and strode forth to place himself between the warring bride and groom.

"Dinner," he announced loudly, hands upraised, "is served."

❧

As the official wedding planner, friend of the bride, and unabashed celebrity, Paul's place for the evening was at the table, serving as host. Lindsay and Cici were the designated servers, and Richard, with his customary élan and unflappable self-assurance, had appointed himself *homme de maison*, telling jokes as he poured the wine and seated the ladies. Cici found reason to be grateful, for once in her life, that Richard had never met a woman he didn't like.

Bridget ran her kitchen with an efficiency the top chefs in the world would admire. The menu was taped on the wall above the stove and the recipes for each dish were encased in clear plastic holders and propped up in sequence around the prep station. Ida Mae was on sauces and sautés; Bridget finished and plated each dish; Lori was stationed at the "pass"— currently the kitchen table—to garnish and polish each plate before it was placed on the serving tray to leave the kitchen. Noah was responsible for loading the two dishwashers as the courses were cleared, and for keeping the workstations clean and free of clutter as food was plated. The kitchen was hot and steamy, redolent with the flavors of garlic, butter, herbs, and roasting meats, and—for the time being anyway— running like a well-oiled machine.

Lindsay burst through the swinging door. Her hair was

starting to escape its neat bun and catch in curls in the sweat on her face, and her eyes had a slightly wild look to them. "Okay," she said. "The groom just announced that he's ordered a foosball table for the honeymoon suite. We need to get the first course out there now."

Bridget thrust two fruit-filled martini glasses into her hands. "Get these to Lori and help her sprinkle gorgonzola and toasted walnuts on top. Lori!" she exclaimed as she watched Lori dip a spoon into one of the glasses she had just garnished and take a bite. "What are you doing?"

"No good chef lets a dish leave her kitchen without tasting it," Lori said.

Lindsay delivered two glasses of fruit to the table and went back for two more. "Where did you hear that?"

"Food Channel."

"Hey," Noah complained, "sounds to me like you got the best job. When do we get to eat, anyway?"

"Well?" Bridget demanded, handing off two more glasses. "How is it?"

Lori shrugged, and that was all it took for Bridget to snatch up her own spoon and taste the fruit. She whirled on Ida Mae. "This is syrup!" she cried. "You dressed the fruit in syrup!"

Ida Mae scowled at her. "So? You always make your fruit salad with a sugar sauce, just like I do."

"Not this time! This time it's a vinaigrette! Didn't you read the recipe?"

"Do you want my help or not?"

But Bridget was already dumping the contents of the glasses into a colander. "Quick," she commanded Lindsay, thrusting the fruit at her, "rinse this off while I make the dressing."

The swinging door swooshed as Lindsay rushed to the sink with a colander full of fruit, and Cici demanded, "What's the holdup? If these people get any drunker we're going to have a riot!"

"Wrong dressing," Lori informed her. And she grinned. "Hey, Mom, it's kind of nice to have Dad around again, isn't it?"

"I love you beyond all measure," Cici replied distractedly, and rushed to the refrigerator. Noah helped himself to the fruit that clung to the bottom of the colander when Lindsay dumped it into a bowl.

Bridget was frantically chopping garlic when Cici whirled with a bottle of store-bought vinaigrette in her hand and dumped the contents over the berries Lindsay had just transferred to a big bowl. "Problem solved," she declared to Bridget's horrified look. "Now for heaven's sake *hurry up*."

Bridget, with no time to argue, took the cheese biscuits out of the oven as Cici let the door swing closed behind her. "Two on each serving plate," she told Lori, "with a sprig of rosemary." And then, with only a moment's hesitation, she picked up one of the biscuits and tasted it. Almost immediately she started to cough and choke, fanning her mouth with her hand.

Ida Mae gave her a quelling look, and Lindsay rushed over with a glass of water.

"Cayenne!" gasped Bridget. "It was supposed to be roasted red pepper puree, but it's cayenne!" She turned an accusing gaze on Ida Mae, who was oblivious. "Could she be trying to sabotage me?" she whispered to Lindsay.

Lori took a small taste of the biscuit. "I kind of like it," she said. Then she took a quick sip of water. "Maybe one per plate, though."

Bridget ran to the pantry and was back in an instant with a jar of strawberry champagne jam. "Quick," she commanded, tugging Lindsay into the chair beside Lori. "Spread jam on each of the biscuits, it will cut the heat. Lori, back to staging. Gorgonzola, walnuts, move, move!"

The ten-minute delay in serving the first course was far more excruciating to those in the kitchen than it was to those in the dining room—with the possible exception of Cici, who returned after serving the fruit cup to report in a dull, stunned tone, "Richard is telling the story about Harrison Ford and the chimpanzee. Is there any way under heaven we could serve dessert and coffee now?"

"I like that story," Lori protested.

To judge from the burst of laughter that came from the dining room, so did everyone else.

The good humor lasted through the soup course, when Lindsay reported that the best man—the groom's brother—had just presented the groom with two tickets to a baseball game in Richmond tomorrow night as a wedding present. The bride objected that she did not intend to spend her wedding night at a baseball game, to which the groom replied that was just fine because he was taking his brother. High fives and laughter all around, and Lindsay was extremely concerned about the fate of the glassware within the bride's reach.

Bridget discovered that the cherry conserve was, in fact, cherry sauce, but managed to rescue it with mustard, horse-radish, chopped spring onions, and a prayer. Similarly, the green beans lacked thyme and the almonds hadn't been roasted, but—Lori declared—they tasted fine.

"Believe me," Cici assured her as she left with her tray loaded down with entrées, "the last thing anyone in there is interested in is food."

Lindsay noticed Bridget's heartbroken look as she picked up her own tray. "But they loved the cheese biscuits," she assured her. "And thought the fruit cup was wild!"

Noah, leaning against the counter as he helped himself to a plate of sliced turkey and potatoes, added, "What they don't eat, I will."

Bridget rallied herself for a smile and gave Noah a quick kiss on the head in passing as she went to place the straw-berry crumble in the oven.

Cici returned with her empty tray and sank down at the table beside Lori. "They're discussing politics," she said. "The groom thinks we should invade China."

"What for?" Lori wanted to know.

"Spite."

Lindsay came in and deposited her empty tray on the counter with a loud clatter. "The father of the bride," she reported furiously, "just pinched my butt."

"Ya'll need to try this," Noah said, going for more turkey. "It's great."

Bridget sat down at the table beside Lori and Cici. "This marriage," she declared unhappily, "doesn't exactly sound as though it was made in heaven."

"He's a Neanderthal," Lindsay said, kicking off her shoes as she dropped into the chair opposite Bridget, "and she's an idiot. You tell me."

"We worked so hard for this." Bridget's gaze, as she turned it toward the closed door to the dining room, was more than a little resentful. "I can't believe it's all going to waste."

"Don't think of it like that," Cici said, trying to comfort her. "Think of it as . . . a dress rehearsal for the next time."

Bridget looked glum. "Like I would ever do this again."

"Come on, Aunt Bridget," Lori said, "I might get married one day, you know. And I wouldn't let anyone cater the wedding but you."

"You," Cici informed her, pointing sternly, "are going to elope. Promise me."

Ida Mae slapped plates down in front of each of them. "Better eat fast," she advised sourly.

Cici picked up her fork and added casually, "Speaking of which, you never told me—how is Sergio?"

Lori smiled at her mother. "That was the sweetest thing ever, Mom. Thank you. Sergio thanks you, too. And we'll keep in touch. I really like him. But . . ." She examined her plate thoughtfully before cutting into her turkey. "Sergio is a fantasy, you know. And since I've been home I've come to realize that even that kind of fantasy has a hard time competing with my real life." She grinned and waved her fork to indicate the room beyond. "Besides," she added, "I invited Mark to the wedding tomorrow."

"Mark?" Lindsay asked.

"He's the boy who ran her down," Cici explained with an approving smile toward her daughter.

Lindsay raised her palm for a high five. "You go, girl."

Lori slapped Lindsay's hand, and Bridget tasted her turkey. "This is delicious," she said, looking surprised.

"Told you," Noah said.

Bridget took another bite. "Those people are Philistines."

Richard pushed open the door. "So, this is where the help comes to eat," he said. Lori, with her mouth full, pointed happily to the chair across from her, and he took it. Cici avoided his eyes. "If there's coffee," he said, "I'd serve it if I were you. The bride's mother just called the groom's mother pretentious and tasteless, and the bride refused to drink to the toast her future brother-in-law just made."

Cici swallowed quickly and wiped her lips with her napkin, getting to her feet. "Make out your bill," she instructed Bridget.

"But we haven't even cleared the table!"

"We're clearing it now." She caught Lindsay's arm. "Serving dessert. And no one is leaving this house until the bill is paid."

"So," Richard observed, pulling Cici's unfinished plate in front of him and taking up her fork, "this is what you girls do for fun?"

❧

The table was cleared, the dishwashers were running, and the bill was paid—surprisingly, without comment. The last bit of drama had come when Traci had refused to get into the car with the groom, or with her mother, or with the bridesmaids who had delivered her. "I can't even look at your ugly face right now," she told her betrothed. And she expanded her

vitriol to include everyone who was gathered in the spill of
porch lights upon the gravel drive in front of the house where
Noah had lined up their cars. "I can't look at any of you! You're
ruining my wedding! My one day, and you're ruining it!"

"Ah, come on, honey," the groom offered weakly, perhaps
beginning to realize he had gone too far. "We'll go back to the
hotel, have a few drinks . . ."

"And if you," she declared, pointing a furious finger at him,
"have one more drink I'm not marrying you. You're going to
be all hungover for the wedding pictures!"

"Well, maybe there just won't be any wedding pictures!"
he told her.

"Maybe there won't! Maybe there won't even—"

And that was when Bridget stepped forward, touched Traci's arm gently, and said, "You know, it's really bad luck for the
groom to see the bride before the ceremony anyway, so why
doesn't Traci just stay here tonight?"

Of course Traci's mother objected to that, and the maid of
honor complained that it would mean they would all have to
get up early to have their hair and makeup done, and Traci,
apparently pleased with the amount of inconvenience she
was causing everyone, declared that she was, in fact, spending the night at Ladybug Farm—and this despite the fact
that Lindsay and Cici practically tied their eyebrows in knots
trying to signal Bridget to retract the invitation. Finally the
groom drove off with a spray of gravel and the bride screaming after him, "You'd better be here at eleven thirty in the
morning for pictures if you know what's good for you!" and
Traci stomped up the stairs to her room.

Now, however, it was blissfully quiet. Richard sat with Lori on the porch, where a surprisingly brisk breeze had blown up to cut the humidity. Paul and Noah finished putting away the bar supplies and carrying the cases of wine for the reception up from the cellar. Noah set up another ten decorative tables on the porch. It was just after ten o'clock when Cici, Bridget, and Lindsay joined the others on the porch.

"Richard," Cici said wearily, "what are you still doing here?"

"He's staying over, Mom," Lori declared cheerfully.

"We don't have any extra rooms," Cici told her flatly.

"I'll sleep on the sofa." Richard smiled.

"Fine." Neither Cici's tone or expression changed. "You're in my chair."

He politely stood up and offered her the rocking chair.

"Whose chair am I in?" Paul wanted to know.

"Mine." Lindsay sat on his knee and leaned back. "What a night."

"I made seventy-five dollars in tips," Noah said, practically chortling as he counted it. "And that was just for thirteen cars! Wait till tomorrow."

Bridget sat down thoughtfully in one of the folding chairs that had been set up for tomorrow's guests. A gust of wind blew her hair across her face and she absently pushed it back. "I think I've figured it out," she said.

"Thank God," muttered Cici, with no idea what she was talking about.

"No, I mean about Ida Mae." She leaned forward earnestly and lowered her voice. "I think the problem is—she can't read."

"How can that be?"

"That's not possible!"

And then Lindsay said, looking interested, "No, a lot of illiterate adults spend their lives hiding the fact that they can't read. They get quite good at it."

"It would explain everything," Bridget went on, her voice growing excited. "All her problems began when we started the business, and everything was written down—recipes, instructions, shipping labels. And then tonight—the mistakes she made were on recipes she didn't know, don't you see? She had to read them!"

"Are you talking about that old lady in the kitchen?"

The voice belonged to Traci, who was standing inside the screen door, head down, futilely pushing buttons on her phone. "She can't see. I asked her to help me pin on my veil this afternoon and she couldn't even find the bobby pin. My granny was like that before she had her cataract surgery. Are you people *ever* going to get telephone service?"

Lindsay, Cici, and Bridget looked at each other in dawning amazement. "Cataracts," Cici said.

"Of course," Bridget agreed with a slow shake of her head. "Of *course*."

"I'm going to make an appointment with the ophthalmologist first thing Monday," Lindsay said.

Bridget turned in her chair to beam at Traci. "I guess it took a stranger to see what we were all too close to her to notice."

Traci pushed open the door and came outside. "There's no television in my room."

"Oh, that's right," Lori said, a little apologetically. "They moved it downstairs to mine."

Traci gave her a somewhat incredulous look. "What do you people *do* at night?"

"This, mostly," Lindsay said, relaxing back against Paul's shoulder.

"We do have telephone service, by the way," Cici pointed out. "It's called a landline."

Traci looked at her for a moment as though she had just said, "Telegraph." Then, "I need to call my maid of honor and tell her to bring my overnight bag out here."

"Oh, honey, don't make her turn around and drive all the way out here tonight," Bridget protested.

"I'll loan you a nightshirt," Lori volunteered.

"It's her job," Traci replied, folding her arms as she leaned against one of the columns and fixed her gaze on the darkened lawn. "She's the bridesmaid and I'm the bride."

Another stiff gust of wind made a flapping sound against the plastic of one of the tents and Cici said, "We might get a little storm."

Paul asked worriedly, "Noah, you *did* stake down the tents, right? Maybe we should have waited until morning to put up the scrim."

Traci turned on him accusingly. "It had better not rain on my wedding day!"

And although everyone on the porch, it seemed, drew a breath to reply, only Bridget actually spoke. "Honey, are you sure you want to go through with this?"

Cici stared at Bridget in disbelief. So did Lindsay, so did Paul, and even Lori. But in the end all they could do was wait for Traci's reply. It was brief and sharp. "Why shouldn't I? I deserve this. It's my day."

"What I mean is..." The wind rattled the wind chimes loudly and everyone's attention was momentarily diverted. Bridget repeated, "What I mean is, you're about to make a lifetime commitment. Do you love Jason?"

Traci shrugged, but did not turn around to look at Bridget. "Whatever that is."

Paul winced. "The last person who said that ended up at the center of one of the most famous divorces of the twentieth century."

Traci's expression was puzzled.

"Prince Charles?" he prompted.

"Prince who?"

"He married Princess Diana," added Lori helpfully, and Cici reached across to pat her daughter's knee proudly.

"But before the wedding," Lindsay said, "he did this famous interview where a reporter asked if he was in love with her, and the prince replied, 'whatever that means.'"

"I think we all knew that was the beginning of the end," Paul said sadly.

"Did he ever figure it out?" Traci wanted to know. "What love means?"

That had them all momentarily perplexed. "I don't think anyone can tell you that," Bridget ventured after a moment. "Not entirely. It means so many different things."

"Like being willing to put someone else's dreams ahead of your own," Paul said quietly. "Even when you don't think those dreams are the best thing for him."

Lindsay looked at him sympathetically. "Or," she added, with a small reminiscent smile, "like trying to keep someone's voice alive in the only way you know how, years after she's gone."

Cici caught Noah's gaze and held it gently. "Or like letting go of someone you love so that he can have a better life."

Noah's brows drew together briefly, and then eased. He smiled a little, uncertainly at first, and then with more confidence. "Yeah," he said.

Lori glanced across at her mother with a lopsided grin. "Or like arranging a video date for your invalid daughter even though you'd rather chew your own arm off than have her fall in love with an Italian."

Cici looked surprised, and then she returned the grin and caressed her daughter's cheek.

"Or," Bridget said softly, "giving someone a goat."

They all turned to look at her, and then Noah suddenly sprang to his feet. "Man!" he exclaimed. "I forgot to let the animals out of the barn!"

"Listen." Richard had been so quiet in the shadows of the steps that they had almost forgotten he was there. He stood slowly. "What is that sound?"

Lindsay heard it first—a distant rushing, roaring sound. "Rain," she said. "You can hear it coming down the mountain before it gets here."

Cici stood, too, peering out into the yard at the pale underside of tree leaves, stripped upward by the wind. Noah started past her toward the steps, and just then a gust of wind caught one of the decorative tables and sent it tumbling across the porch. Traci squealed. The roaring sound grew closer, and Cici said, "I don't think that's just the rain."

She grabbed Noah's arm as the wind suddenly tunneled across the porch, sending the wind chimes straight out at a ninety degree angle, overturning more tables, tearing a ribbon off the porch and sailing it into the night. "Forget the animals!" she cried.

There was a cracking sound from a nearby tree and Lindsay leapt to her feet. So did Bridget.

"Inside!" Cici had to scream now to be heard over the roaring of the wind. "Everybody inside! *Hurry*!"

17

Here Comes the Bride

The thundering wind, the explosive *crack* and crash of trees, the slam of debris caroming off the side of the house, and the somehow even more alarming tinkle of broken glass lasted less than five minutes. The roar of rain and hail lasted considerably longer. The residents of Ladybug Farm huddled together in the cellar, where Ida Mae, wearing flannel pajamas, a barn jacket, and hiking boots, distributed emergency flashlights about two minutes before the power went out. Traci, terrified, covered her head with her arms and sobbed. Lori buried her face in her father's chest. Cici held Lindsay's hand. Lindsay held Noah's. Bridget held Paul's.

When the roaring of the rain faded to a steady drumming, and finally to a patter and then at last to nothing more than a steady *drip-drip* from the eaves, they cautiously made their way back up the stairs to the light of their combined flashlights. Lindsay ran to close a window that had been left open in their haste to escape the storm. The breeze was playing with a sodden flap of lace curtain, a lamp had been broken, and there was enough water on the floor to splash when she walked, but she noticed no other damage inside.

They opened the door and moved slowly out onto the porch. Paul had to pick up a rocking chair, which was partially blocking the front door. Tables and chairs were overturned and piled against the far railing. A tree limb rested against the front railing. The floor itself was not visible for the covering of green leaves, two or three inches deep in places.

"Good God," Richard said softly. He set Lori, whom he had carried up the stairs, on her feet.

"Holy cow," echoed Noah.

They directed their flashlight beams over the yard. A half moon chose that moment to appear from behind a tattered scrap of cloud, illuminating a lawn that looked as though it had been seeded with crystal, a glittering white carpet as far as the eye could see.

"Snow!" gasped Traci. "In June!"

"Hail," Cici corrected, a little overwhelmed by the sight herself.

Lindsay's flashlight beam slowly climbed up the trunk of the giant poplar nearest the house. "Good heavens," she said. "Is that a chair in that tree?"

Bridget cried suddenly, "The cake!" and ran toward the pantry.

"It must have been a tornado," Paul theorized, with a kind of dreadful wonder in his voice.

Traci's voice started to tear up again. "We could have died!"

"Well, we didn't," Cici said briskly. She had to set her teeth to keep them from chattering, but she wasn't sure whether that was because of the cool layer of air that rushed up from the hail-covered ground, or the leftover terror. "But we do have a lot of cleaning up to do. So let's get to work."

"I'll check the animals," said Noah, dashing off.

"I'll start the coffee," Ida Mae said.

Lindsay disappeared into the house and returned a moment later with a broom, which she thrust into Traci's hands. "You can start," she told her, "by sweeping the porch."

❧

They gathered in the kitchen an hour later for coffee. The hail was melted, the floors had been mopped, the glass swept up, and reconnaissance, as much as could be done in the dark, was complete. An oil lamp on the kitchen table provided a pale yellow light that did not come close to reaching the corners of the big room.

"At least the cake is safe," Bridget reported glumly.

"And we have gas for cooking and hot water," Lindsay offered helpfully.

"And the dishes were done before the power went out," said Cici, who hated doing dishes by hand almost more than she hated cleaning the chicken coop.

"The animals are all okay," Noah said. "Good thing they were locked in the barn. Except," he added, "the goat ran away when I opened the door. Do you want me to go look for her?"

"No!" shouted all three women at once. Bridget patted his hand gratefully. "Maybe in the morning."

"We lost two cases of wine," Paul reported heavily, sinking into a chair. "And all the tents. Half the chairs are mangled. I can't even find the tables."

"There are tree branches down all over the driveway," Richard said. "Some of them as big as a car. There's no way traffic can make it to the house tomorrow."

"All my pretty candles," Lori mourned. "Covered in mud or blown away completely. And my bows!"

"I shouldn't have been in such a hurry to get ahead of the game," Paul said. "We should have waited until the morning to start the decorating and setup."

"Don't be ridiculous." Lindsay tried to comfort him. "There's no way we could have gotten all that done in one day."

Traci sat huddled at the table with her hands wrapped around her coffee cup. "We could have died," she repeated brokenly.

Bridget reached across the table and patted her hand helplessly.

There was a muffled, distant, mechanical bleating coming from outside, which they managed to ignore for a time. Then Bridget said, frowning, "What is that? A storm siren?"

"There aren't any storm sirens out here," Cici pointed out.

"It sounds like a car horn," Lindsay said. She got up and opened the back door, the others following. The sound was much clearer now, and it was definitely a car horn. When it stopped, a faint, small voice echoed through the night: "Traci! *Traci!*"

Traci gasped. "Jason!"

She pushed past them and scrambled around the porch. Lindsay thrust a flashlight into her hands just before she bounded down the steps. "Jason!" she cried. "Jason, I'm here! I'm here!"

They watched her run down the debris-littered driveway,

flashlight beam bobbing to meet her true love. "Just like in a movie," Bridget observed contentedly, folding her arms across her chest in satisfaction.

Jason was soaked and covered in mud and scratches, and Traci couldn't hold onto his arm tightly enough. "He came through the storm to make sure I was okay!" she told them, beaming at him. "He did that! He came through the storm!"

They got him dried off and somewhat cleaned up, and fed him hot coffee and strawberry crumble as he told how, upon arriving at the hotel, he had heard about the coming storm on the radio, and had driven through hail and sleet and falling trees to get back here and save the woman he loved from whatever fate had befallen her. While the older members of his captive audience took his tale with a grain of salt, Traci was enraptured with her newly anointed Prince Charming.

Proving the axiom that men and small children will always rise to the level of your expectations, the groom-to-be swept Traci into his arms at the bottom of the stairs and demanded, "Which room are we in?"

Traci, with eyes sparkling so brightly electric lighting was hardly needed, looked over his shoulder to catch Bridget's eye. "Now," she said, "I know what it means."

She turned her flashlight to light the way upstairs.

Lori sighed. "That is *so* romantic."

"They're going to have sex on our nice clean sheets," Lindsay said, grudgingly. "I just know it."

Bridget looked worried. "If it's bad luck for the groom to see the bride before the wedding, just imagine what kind of luck it is if he has sex with her."

Cici stared at her. "We just endured the worst rehearsal

dinner in the history of rehearsal dinners. Our house was almost blown away by a tornado. We have people arriving for a wedding in less than twelve hours, and there is a fallen forest on our driveway. How much worse can our luck get?"

"The goat could eat the wedding cake," Bridget suggested morosely.

"The goat ran away!"

"The lovebirds could burn down the house with scented candles," Lindsay said.

Lori rolled her eyes. "You guys," she said, "are really old. I'm going to bed."

"Me, too," Lindsay said, and Bridget agreed, "There's not much more we can do until we have enough daylight to assess the damage."

Paul said thoughtfully, "If no one is using the phone, I think I should make a call."

"It's after midnight," Cici pointed out.

"That's okay. I happen to know the person I'm calling is still up." And he smiled. "Besides, as the girl said—we could have died. I don't think this phone call can wait any longer."

Cici and Richard stood alone at the bottom of the stairs in a foyer lit only by the two flashlights in their hands and the battery-operated lantern on the table a dozen feet away. Cici looked at him.

"Richard," she said, with some difficulty. "Tonight—when you swept Lori up in your arms and carried her down to the cellar, without even hesitating or asking a single question, just like some kind of, I don't know, hero or something..."

He smiled at her in the pale yellow light, and she smiled

back, uncertainly. "And then, walking down the driveway in the dark to check the damage after the storm ... I just wanted to say I'm sorry I yelled at you earlier. And I'm glad you stayed."

He curved his hand around the back of her neck, and kissed her cheek. "How about bringing me a pillow," he said, "and showing me the sofa?"

♻

Rodrigo sounded the alarm at five thirty. By six, Noah had fired up the chainsaw, and at seven fifteen, Farley's blue tractor puttered around the side of the house, climbing over broken tree limbs and navigating around ditches. Bridget, who was taking an egg casserole out of the oven, ran out to meet him with the casserole still clutched between her oven-mitted hands.

Farley tipped his hat to her as he climbed off the still running tractor. "Thought I'd see if you had any storm damage over this way," he said. "I'll go push some of them big limbs out of your driveway and over the bank, if you like, or I can help the boy cut up some stove wood."

"Yes," said Bridget breathlessly. "That would be wonderful. And then later ... if you're not doing anything, that is ... I was wondering if you might consider being my escort to the wedding we're having here this afternoon?"

Bridget held her breath as he returned her gaze for a long and thoughtful moment. Then he said, "Why, Miss Bridget, I don't mind if I do."

She beamed at him. "Wonderful! But first come inside and

have some breakfast. And," she added as he drew up beside her, "do you mind if I ask—is Farley your first name or your last?"

❧

They managed to rescue most of the chairs, although there was nothing to be done about the tents or the buffet tables they had once protected. Cici and Paul dragged sheets of plywood out of the workshop, arranged them atop sawhorses, and covered them with linen tablecloths. They robbed the bedrooms of full-length mirrors and set them in the middle of the tables, surrounded by green leaves—which were available from the yard in abundance—and apricot roses.

The rose garden itself was stripped to bare, naked rose twigs, and the beautifully decorated arbors were smashed beyond recognition. Lindsay's eyes filled with tears when she saw it. "We can't let Traci see this," she declared, forcefully recovering herself. "The photographer will be here in two hours." She whirled on Cici. "Do we have any beanpoles left?"

"I'm way ahead of you!" Cici called over her shoulder, running toward the barn.

They built a wedding canopy out of eight-foot-tall beanpoles, tulle, and beribboned rose bouquets. Paul swept all of the fallen rose petals into a colorful path for the processional. The fallen silk dogwoods were hosed off, fluffed up, and set in the sun to dry. Lindsay put Lori to work with twist ties, silk ivy, and apricot roses, trying to recreate the look of the real rosebushes that had fallen.

"I don't believe this," Cici said. "You're tying florist roses and silk ivy onto real rosebushes."

"It's a wedding," Lindsay assured her hurriedly, thrusting an armful of freshly washed candles into her hands. "It's all about the fantasy."

They lined the processional path with the pillar candles, now stripped of their soiled tulle and arranged in holders of every size and description—from plant stands to lazy Susans—that they had gathered from the house. Every holder was decorated with apricot roses, accented with a variety of green leaves gathered from the yard and tied together with draping ivory satin ribbon. The look was charming, eclectic, and hopelessly romantic.

Paul stood back with arms crossed on his chest, one finger resting aside his nose, to survey their work. "Well, dip me in chocolate and fry me in butter," he murmured. "I think we pulled it off. The place looks like a freakin' fairyland."

The girls, sweaty and lank-haired, with fingers thorn-pricked and bleeding, stared at him for a moment, and then burst into laughter. They laughed for almost thirty seconds, leaning on each other, catching Lori when she almost over-balanced on her crutches, and then they each hurried on to their next task.

Chain saws buzzed all morning. The tractor roared. Bridget flew through the house, hiding lanterns and flash-lights, freshening bathrooms, dusting and polishing. In the kitchen, Ida Mae cut the cheese biscuits—which Bridget had made herself—into perfect little circles and placed them in the oven to bake, sliced the ham, and battered the chicken breast strips. Two five-gallon clam steamers filled with sliced potatoes simmered away on the back burners, and the pressure cooker, filled with a combination of the season's first blackberries, onions, apple vinegar, and hot peppers, hissed and groaned as it labored to turn the concoction into Bridget's signature sweet-sour dipping sauce. Heritage tomatoes were marinating in olive oil and herbs. Four dozen baby beef Wellingtons were wrapped in pastry, arranged on cookie sheets, and stored in the refrigerator—which no one dared open for fear of allowing whatever precious cool air remained to escape—waiting to be baked. Ida Mae gathered three dozen eggs and began whipping them into quiche filling.

The bridesmaids arrived with the hairdresser, the makeup person, and so much paraphernalia that their dresses had to be stored in the hallway. Jason, now banished from the kingdom of the women, wandered around looking lost until Paul put him to work making bows. To the young man's credit, he didn't object and actually did a passable job. It turned out that sober—and away from the influence of his buddies—he was really quite nice.

"Ice!" Paul demanded as he burst into the kitchen. "What are we going to do about ice?"

"Send someone to town for it," Bridget said, taking a tray of cheese biscuits out of the oven. "We have a cooler in the cellar."

"It's going to take more than one. I should go myself. We need at least another case of champagne. There's a liquor store in this county, right?"

Cici admitted reluctantly, "Well, about that . . ."

Lindsay suggested, "Maybe we can call the hotel and have Catherine stop on her way out and pick up what you need."

Traci suddenly burst into the kitchen, wearing a short silk robe and a full-length bridal veil. "Listen," she said, "I know there's no electricity or anything, but the photographer is going to be here in twenty minutes and we really need to plug in the curling iron ..."

It was at that moment that the pressure cooker exploded. The pressure valve sailed across the room, dented a copper teapot on a display shelf, and knocked over a serving tray. Blackberry sauce spattered the ceiling and everything else within a six-foot radius. Ida Mae dived to protect the cheese biscuits with her arms. Cici and Lindsay covered their heads. Traci screamed and ducked, but not in time to avoid a shower of blackberries over her hair, her robe, and her veil.

For a moment no one moved. Bridget, crouched beside the stove, caught Cici's eye and mouthed, *Bad luck.*

Then Paul plucked a blackberry from the tip of his nose, examined it for a moment, tasted it, and decided, "Needs more salt."

Bridget tried to rinse out the veil, but there really wasn't much to be salvaged. Traci watched, looking shelled-shocked, as Bridget spread it over the line outside to dry, saying something about the sun bleaching out the dark spots. "I tried to tell you, sweetie," Paul said, "a hat, not a veil."

It was at that point that Lindsay rushed upstairs, tossed her closet, and came back down with a white linen portrait hat. While Cici and Bridget tried to wash the blackberry stains out of Traci's hair without completely ruining her style, and while the stylist bemoaned the lack of a blow-dryer and the bridesmaids hovered around with eyelash curlers and bobby pins, Lindsay draped the hat in white tulle, wrapped the brim with ribbon and roses, and, to everyone's amazement and delight, Traci actually smiled when she put it on.

The mothers arrived, and Cici assured them that the front lawn would be cleared of chicken feathers before the ceremony. She then looked around in amazement, because, until that moment, she hadn't even noticed that last night's storm had somehow swept up so many feathers from the chicken yard and deposited them on the front lawn that it looked as though someone had opened a feather pillow.

The groomsmen arrived, and they actually remembered to bring the groom's tuxedo. Noah got a rake and tried to sweep up some of the chicken feathers. Cici made what repairs she could to the flower beds. Lindsay stapled bows and banners and swags and drapes on every possible surface, then began to trim down the smallest of the fallen leafy branches, supplement them with apricot roses, and arrange them in baskets that she hung from the porch rafters with ribbons. Catherine noticed and declared the touch "Utterly charming!" as though she had approved the plan from the beginning—which she no doubt thought she had.

The chain saw stopped buzzing, and Farley's tractor puttered back down the road toward his house. Cici brushed some of the dirt off her hands as she came up the steps, and Lindsay, standing on a chair, made a final tuck in the satin banner over the doorway and stapled it. "Okay," Cici said, "I guess we might as well get cleaned up, and then see what we can do to help Bridget in the kitchen."

Lindsay stepped off the chair and pushed it aside. She glanced around. "There's not much more we can do," she admitted.

"Not without an army." They heard a car turn into the driveway. "That's got to be the photographer."

But it wasn't. As the car drew closer their looks of curiosity turned to astonishment, then to joy. Lindsay called through the screen door, "Paul!"

The car stopped in front of the steps and the two women grinned at each other as the driver got out.

"Derrick!" Cici called happily. "What are you doing here?"

"Friend of the bride." He reached into his jacket pocket and withdrew a cream-colored invitation, smiling his greeting. The screen door squeaked open, and the smile softened to something else as his eyes went over their shoulders. "Besides," he added, "I heard a friend of mine needed some help."

"Well, that depends." Paul spoke in measured tones, a glue gun in one hand and a cluster of silk flowers in the other. "How are you with a glue gun?"

"Passable."

Derrick came up the steps, the two embraced, and just then the lights inside the house flickered on.

❧

The bride, wearing a strapless gown and a portrait hat, walked the rose-strewn path to the silken sounds of a chamber quartet playing the wedding march, escorted by her father—looking stiff and hungover but otherwise pleased—and preceded by six bridesmaids in apricot silk. The groom and his attendants were handsome and composed in gray cutaways. When the groom kissed the bride, Cici, Bridget, and Lindsay all reached for tissues—partly because of the tenderness of the moment, but mostly because it was over.

The storm had cooled and cleaned the air to a pleasant

seventy degrees, and left behind a perfect summer blue sky decorated with fluffy, lavender-bottomed cumulus clouds that played out a slow-moving shadow show across the mountains and the lawn. The guests talked a lot about the storm that had swept through the night before, but if they noticed any of the alterations it had made to their surroundings, they said nothing. Many of them admired the ingenuity of the rose garden, and declared how clever it was to strip off the original blossoms and replace them with roses in the bride's own color scheme.

Once the lawn was covered with laughing, drinking guests in party wear, the damage to flower beds, trees, and wedding decorations was difficult to spot. If there weren't enough tables for everyone to sit down, that only encouraged people to mingle, and no one cared that the buffet was not under a tent once they tasted Bridget's food.

Lori's date, Mark, was entertaining and attentive, helping her with her crutches, bringing her food and drink, and being extremely polite to her parents. When Bridget asked Lori to sit behind one of the buffet stations for a few moments, Mark took off his jacket and worked as her assistant. For the first couple of hours all of them worked—carrying food out from the kitchen, making certain there were plenty of napkins and silverware and that the serving dishes were never empty. Derrick rolled up his sleeves and helped Richard open bottles and fill glasses, while Paul, clipboard in hand, kept everything neat, tidy, and on schedule. Noah, who had already made a small fortune parking cars, barely complained at all about bussing the tables and loading the dishwasher and carrying boxes of clean glasses out of the kitchen and dirty glasses in. Farley, who looked surprisingly handsome in his blue suit, struck up a conversation with the mother of the groom, who declared him to be one of the most fascinating and amusing people she had ever met, and kept everyone happy by keeping her happy. Dominic mingled effortlessly with the crowd, but always kept an eye on Lindsay, and whenever there was a table to be unfolded or a chair to be moved or a heavy tray to be lifted he was there, taking care of it.

When the bride and groom had their first dance and the DJ cranked up the music, Dominic caught Lindsay's hand and pulled her, laughingly protesting, onto the dance floor. Cici grabbed a glass of wine and sank down at a table in the shade across from Paul and Derrick. She had just taken her first sip when Richard dropped his hands on her shoulders.

"Come on," he said, drawing her to her feet. "They're playing our song."

She groaned. "I'm tired. Besides, we don't have a song."

He said, "We do now."

She listened, and smiled, and let him lead her to the dance floor to the music of "Through the Years."

"Lori said you built the dance floor," he said as they fell into an easy, natural rhythm.

"It wasn't hard."

"She's been showing me all the things you've done to this place."

Cici tilted her head up to look at him. "You didn't know I could use power tools?"

"All in all," he admitted, "I think that's something I was better off not knowing. There's a lot I don't know about you, I guess."

She leaned her head against his shoulder. "We've been apart a long time."

They danced in silence for a while. His fingers absently stroked her hair. He said, "You were right, you know."

"I usually am."

He smiled. "It's been great being back on the East Coast, seeing trees that are taller than a palm, spending time with Lori, and you . . . but this isn't the life for me. I don't belong here."

She almost missed her step, and when she looked up at him she was surprised by the stab of disappointment she felt. "But—what about the dream? What about retirement? You made so many plans!"

He chuckled. "Hell, sweetie, if this is what you call retirement, I'm going back to L.A. where I can get some rest. You people work too hard for me."

She said, "It's not like we have tornados and weddings every day."

The look he gave her was both amused and regretful. "If it wasn't a tornado, it would be something else. But it's not that. It's just . . . there's no room for me here. You don't need me anymore. If you ever did."

She rested her head against his shoulder again, and was quiet for a time. Then she asked, "What was this fascination you had with a horse farm, anyway? You don't even like horses."

For a moment he seemed surprised, and then he chuckled. "You don't remember, do you? When we were first married, that's all we talked about. Moving to the country, buying a horse farm. That was the big dream."

Cici looked at him for a long time, sadly. "No," she said finally. "I don't remember."

The music faded into a hip-hop number, and they left the dance floor. Richard's arm was around her waist, and she leaned into him. "I'm sorry it didn't work out for you, but I'm not sorry you came. I think it's been good for us."

His fingers squeezed her waist. "Maybe we can try relating to each other on a more adult level a little more often now."

She pretended to consider that as they reached the table where Paul and Derrick sat, looking completely relaxed and as comfortable as though they had never been apart. They were sipping wine and pointing out to each other the idiosyncrasies of various members of the wedding party. "That would be different," she agreed. "We could give it a try."

"Now," he said, holding her chair for her, "all I have to do is figure out what to do with eighty-seven acres of prime Virginia horse country, fenced and cross-fenced."

Paul stopped talking in the middle of a sentence. Derrick looked at Paul. Paul looked at Derrick. They both looked at Richard.

Derrick said, "I don't suppose you would entertain an offer?"

❧

Paul, Derrick, Richard, and Dominic moved through the crowd, filling glasses with champagne. The bride and groom were finishing up their last dance before the toast and the cake-cutting, and they couldn't take their eyes off each other. The groom's mother was dancing with Farley. He kept glancing worriedly at Bridget, but she waved him on gaily.

Cici, Bridget, and Lindsay stood together behind the serving station near the cake, saucers and cutlery at the ready, cautiously relaxing as the day began to draw to a close.

"Well." Bridget released a cautious sigh of relief. "I can't believe it, but it looks as though we pulled it off."

"Thanks to you." Cici slipped her arm around Bridget's waist in a brief hug. "The buffet was spectacular."

Bridget glanced anxiously at the cake, which was beautifully decorated with cascades of sugared fruit and Apricot Delight roses. "They haven't cut the cake yet."

"The cake is fine," Lindsay assured her.

"Dominic seemed to have fun," Cici commented, teasing her a little. "You two looked cute together."

"He is fun," Lindsay agreed. It was impossible to tell whether the slight flush on her cheeks was from sun, champagne, or pleasure. "Funny how I never noticed before." She looked at Bridget. "And how about Farley? He really cleaned up nice, didn't he?"

Bridget smiled, her eyes seeking, and finding Farley. She waved again. "What a surprise. I suppose there are all sorts of things we don't notice about people if we never look for them."

Cici's smile was a little sad as she watched Richard, laughing and charming the bride's grandparents as he filled their glasses. "Yeah."

There was a disturbance in the crowd, squeals and laughter, toward the edge of the yard. The DJ lowered the music and said, "Ladies and Gentleman, fill your glasses for the toast to the bride and groom. Fill your glasses!"

The laughter seemed to take on more of the tone of shouts,

and the squeals sounded more like screams. Heads turned. Cici, Lindsay, and Bridget stood on tiptoe. "What in the world . . ."

They all saw it at once, an outrageous tumbling, streaking, galloping whirl of a creature wrapped in white gauze tearing through the crowd like a mad ghost on steroids.

"Is that—?"

"Rebel!" cried Bridget, her hand flying to her throat. "And he found the veil that was drying on the line!"

"How did he get—"

"Sorry!" Noah called from across the lawn. "I opened the barn to give him some water and he saw something and broke out! Don't worry—I'll catch him!"

Rebel rolled head over heels, tangled in the lacy veil, bumped into a plump woman in satin shoes who squeaked, jumped back, and doused him with champagne. He stumbled to his feet, charged a few riotous paces, tripped over the veil, and rolled again. Noah dived for him and caught part of the veil, but the dog squirted through his fingers like toothpaste out of a tube.

The DJ, oblivious, announced, "Ladies and Gentleman, the father of the bride!"

Lindsay scrambled around the serving table. "I'll head him off!"

Bridget ran after her. "I'll go this way!"

And Cici said, "Oh, my God." Because she had seen what Rebel was chasing. And it was heading straight for the cake.

The microphone squeaked feedback. The father of the bride cleared his throat. The nanny goat, bleating in panic, broke through the crowd at a trot. Cici cried, "No!" and charged around the serving table to place herself between the goat and the cake.

The goat charged her. She leapt forward, flinging her arms around the goat's neck. The goat screamed and shook her head violently, connecting with Cici's cheekbone with a resounding *crack*. She fell backward on the ground, seeing stars. The goat ran off.

But the cake was saved.

❧

Three and a half hours later the bride, the groom, and the guests had departed. The goat was in the barnyard. Rebel, dragging a scrap of tangled veil from his hind foot, had collapsed beneath the shade tree, panting. The dishes had been packed away, the leftover food was in the freezer, and Ida Mae was taking a nap. Cici, Bridget, and Lindsay sat on the debris-littered porch and tried to process the day.

"You know," Bridget observed after a time, "all things considered, it really was a lot of fun."

Cici tried to lift her head to look at her, winced in pain, and settled back again. "You did not just say that to me."

"Well, I mean, except for the storm."

"Tornado," corrected Lindsay.

"That hasn't been confirmed yet," Bridget objected.

"And the dog," Cici said without opening her eyes.

"And the groom's mother."

"And the groom."

"And the explosion."

"And the goat."

"Like I said," Bridget said uncomfortably. "All things considered."

No one spoke for a measure of time. No one had the energy.

"You know what the problem was, don't you?" Bridget said after a moment.

"Personally," replied Lindsay, a rather tired smile twitching at her lips, "I blame Michelle Obama."

Bridget smothered a giggle, and even Cici, without opening her eyes, managed a lopsided smile.

"Okay," Cici said. "Tell me what the problem was."

"Sex."

Cici opened her eyes, and lifted her head to look at her two best friends. The three women thought about that for a while. Then Cici gave a slow, reflective nod of her head. "Do you know, Bridget," she said, "this time I think you've got it exactly right."

Lindsay agreed regretfully, "Sad but true."

"But it was a beautiful ceremony," Bridget said.

Cici glanced at one of the half-empty champagne glasses on the small table beside her chair. She had no idea to whom it belonged. She picked it up dubiously, sniffed the contents, gave the rim a cursory examination for lip marks, and drank it down.

"Yeah," she said, and smiled just a little. "It was."

Bridget sighed. "I'd like to think that, after all this effort, those kids will have a good marriage. But I don't know."

"Well," Lindsay said, "the groom did agree not to spend his wedding night at a baseball game with his brother. That's a step in the right direction." The screen door squeaked open, held by Mark, and Lori clumped out on her crutches, accompanied by Noah. She had changed from her formal wedding clothes to a floral cotton skirt and T-shirt, although she was still beautifully made up, her hair cascading from a clip in curls around her shoulders. Mark had removed his tie and jacket, and Noah, in apparent solidarity, still wore his suit pants and dress shirt—although he had changed into running shoes.

"Hey, Mom," Lori announced. "Noah's taking us out for pizza. Do you want us to bring you some?"

Noah shrugged at the questioning look from the older women. "I lost a bet," he admitted, deadpan. "I said you couldn't catch that goat."

"Very funny." Cici deliberately removed the frozen peas to show off her black eye, and Lori winced.

"Been there, done that, Mom," she said sympathetically. "Two words: pancake makeup."

Mark said, "It was a great party, Ms. Burke. I hope you feel better."

"Thank you, Mark," Cici replied. "Please drive carefully."

"Don't worry." He grinned. "I'm *much* better behind the wheel of a car."

She couldn't help smiling a little as she watched the attentiveness with which he helped Lori negotiate the steps. When they reached the car Lindsay commented, "Now that's a nice young man, to take Noah along on their first date."

"I like him," Bridget agreed.

"Me, too," Cici said. "Although . . ." Her tone grew speculative. "Sergio has a lot going for him, too."

Lindsay slanted a grin at Bridget. "Say, Bridget, Farley can really dance, can't he? If we hadn't invited him, I don't think the groom's mother would have had any fun at all."

"You know something?" Bridget said, sounding only a little surprised. "I had a really good time. I'd forgotten how much I missed being treated like a lady—having someone hold my chair and bring me drinks and ask me to dance. And even keeping that horrid woman occupied—it all made me feel important. Taken care of."

"Yeah," agreed Lindsay and Cici simultaneously. Their voices were wistful.

And when the other two women looked at her questioningly, Cici shrugged. "The one thing Richard knows is how to treat a lady. And it was nice, having a date at a party."

Lindsay nodded. "I think that's one of the things we forgot when we were trying to list what men are good for. There's really nothing like them when it comes to dancing at a wedding."

Cici and Bridget laughed tiredly.

Then Lindsay added thoughtfully, "But you know, as much as I do like Dominic, at this age dating takes on a whole new meaning, doesn't it? You're past the looking-around stage, and you have to ask yourself really quickly where the relationship is going."

"And?" Cici prompted.

Lindsay shrugged. "Easy decision. I like my life, and I like myself in it. I've worked too hard to get to who and where I am now to want to change anything. It's like Lori said—romantic fantasy has a hard time competing with my real life."

Bridget nodded. "Relationships are really all about meeting

each other's needs, and when you don't need anything..."
She let the sentence complete itself.

Cici nodded reflectively. "So true. But it's kind of sad for the
guys we leave behind, isn't it?"

"I don't know." Lindsay grinned. "That doesn't mean we
can't still have fun."

Cici chuckled, even though it made her face hurt, and so
did Bridget.

"Speaking of which," Bridget said, "is that Dominic walking back from the orchard?"

"You know him." There was a pleasantly affectionate tone
to Lindsay's voice. "He can't stay away from the vines."

"Do me a favor, will you?" Cici said. "Make sure he has lots
of fun. I don't know what we would have done with the vineyard if it hadn't been for him, and we've still got a long way
to go."

Lindsay threw a paper napkin at her. "Very funny."

"All right, ladies." Paul and Derrick came through the
door, loaded down with Paul's luggage. "Are you sure you
don't want us to stay and help with the cleanup tomorrow?
Because we don't mind."

Lindsay and Bridget leapt to their feet, dispensing hugs.
"Are you kidding? Like you haven't done enough!"

"You saved our lives," Cici told Paul. She was last in line
for kisses, which were delivered cautiously, mindful of her
bruises. "You know you deserve the money so much more
than we do."

"But you need it more than I do," Paul assured them. "It
was a labor of love."

"Although," Derrick reminded him, "now that we're about

to be property owners, you might want to think about being a bit less generous."

Paul grinned at him.

"We love you guys," Lindsay said.

Derrick touched his fingers to his lips, and then to each of their foreheads. "My heart," he said.

Bridget said, "And thanks, by the way, for being my secret admirer."

Lindsay, Cici, and Paul looked surprised, and Derrick lifted an eyebrow. "How did you know?"

"Oh, please." Bridget gave a dismissing wave of her hand. "You didn't fool me for a minute."

Their eyes locked in a smile for a moment, and then there was a repeated flurry of good-byes and well-wishes and promises to e-mail as soon as they got home.

Last to leave was Richard. With his leather travel bag slung over his shoulder, he stopped on the porch to address Lindsay and Bridget gravely. "Ladies," he said, "you are . . . indescribable."

As one, they returned broad grins. "Aren't we, though?" said Lindsay.

Richard bent to kiss Cici's unbruised cheek. "Sweetheart, it's been real."

She smiled at him. "I think I'm going to miss fighting with you."

He winked at her. "What do you want to bet I can do something to tick you off before I get to the airport?"

They stood on the porch and waved as he got into his rental car and drove off. And then they were alone.

Rebel finally freed himself of the remnants of the veil and

trotted off. A breeze caught the loose end of one of the pillar ribbons and flapped it forlornly. The silence echoed.

Bridget looked around at the tattered remnants of gaiety— the spilled drinks, crumpled napkins, wilting flowers. She said, "You know that empty feeling you get after everyone goes home and you're all alone?"

The other two nodded somberly. "The letdown," Lindsay said.

"The adrenaline crash," added Cici.

Bridget smiled. "I don't feel that."

Lindsay stretched out her legs and wiggled her toes, looking content. "That's because we're not alone."

"And we don't need a single thing," Bridget said.

"Well, a nap would be nice."

Cici picked up the frozen peas and plastered them to her eye again. "You know, it really wasn't such a disaster, when you think about it. For our first attempt."

Bridget nodded her satisfaction. "We'll get better, with practice."

"And I was thinking," Cici mused, "after all that work building the dance floor, it would be a shame to tear it all up after one use. If I put a roof over it, and maybe enclosed it with lattice, we'd virtually have an outdoor party room. And it would really set off the garden."

"Sounds like a lot of work," said Bridget.

"And a lot of money," added Lindsay.

"Not so much. Noah can help. And Farley."

"Dominic," said Lindsay warmly, standing. Cici opened her good eye to see him coming up the steps, his jacket slung over one shoulder, his eyes squinted against the low rays of the sun. "How did everything look?"

"Can we get you a cup of coffee?" offered Bridget. "Or a glass of wine?"

"No thanks," said Dominic. "I've got animals of my own to feed, and I need to get back home."

As he reached them they could see that his expression, and his demeanor, were somber. Cici removed the pack of peas from her eye and sat up straighter. Bridget stopped rocking, and Lindsay looked at him curiously.

"I wanted to thank you for asking me to the wedding," he said. "You ladies throw a heck of a party, and I really enjoyed myself. I can't tell you how much I hate for it to end like this, or that I'm the one who has to tell you."

Now alarm began to creep into each of their faces. "Tell us what?" Cici demanded, and Lindsay echoed, "What's wrong?"

"Hail," he said, simply. His voice was heavy. "It's not good for any crop, but grapes, this time of year . . ." He shook his head slowly. "The older vines have been stripped bare, and the new ones . . . well, there's not much we can do but pull them up and start over."

Both Bridget and Cici stood then, staring at him in disbelief. Bridget's hand went to her heart. Cici asked, "Not all of them? Surely we didn't lose everything!"

He said gravely, "I'm sorry. We can protect against an early frost or a late freeze, and we can treat most diseases and pests, but a hailstorm can wipe out a farmer faster than just about anything else. I wish there was something I could do."

Lindsay forced a weak smile. "We know you do, Dominic."

And Bridget added, "You worked harder on the vineyard than any of us."

Cici gazed in the direction of the vineyard with a bleak, stunned expression on her face. "Unbelievable."

Dominic dropped his hand lightly onto Lindsay's arm. "I'm really sorry," he repeated. "I'll call you in the morning, okay? We'll figure something out."

Lindsay pushed back her shoulders, forced another smile, and squeezed his fingers. "Thanks, Dominic," she said. "Really."

No one spoke for a long time after they watched him drive away. Then Bridget said uneasily, "We should probably check the vegetable garden, and the berry bushes. And the fruit trees, to see if there's anything left. We were so desperate to get the wedding back on track we didn't even think about our crops."

Cici said, "It's too late to save anything. And I can wait until tomorrow to see the damage."

"What are we going to do?" Bridget asked.

Cici just shook her head.

And suddenly Lindsay grinned. "Did you hear what he called us?"

Both of them looked at her as though she had lost her mind.

"Farmers!" She answered her own question proudly. "He called us farmers."

"That's right," Bridget said, looking impressed. "He did."

"And this from a man who knows a thing or two about farmers," Cici had to admit, and even her own shoulders straightened a little as she said it.

"And I guess we know what farmers do when they hit a setback," Lindsay said. "They start over."

Bridget grinned. "Which is a subject *we* know a thing or two about."

Cici reached into the pocket of her pantsuit, unfolded the check, and regarded it longingly for a moment. Then she smiled. "Easy come, easy go."

Lindsay found half a bottle of wine, and three almost-clean glasses, and poured.

"To Ladybug Farm," she proclaimed, lifting her glass.

"To starting over," said Bridget.

"To us," said Cici. They touched their glasses, drank, and returned to their rocking chairs, content for the moment to simply watch the sun set.